KARMA

With a Vengeance

KARMA

With a Vengeance

A novel by

TASH HAWTHORNE

WAHIDA CLARK PRESENTS PUBLISHING

Wahida Clark Presents Publishing, LLC
134 Evergreen Place
Suite 305
East Orange, New Jersey 07018
973-678-9982
www.wclarkpublishing.com

Karma: With A Vengeance
ISBN 13-digit 978-0-9818545-0-2
ISBN 10-digit 0-9818545-0-8
Library of Congress Catalog Number 2009929484
1.Urban, Contemporary, Women, African-American, Cuban-American – Fiction

Cover design and layout by Oddball Dsgn
Book design by Oddball Dsgn
Contributing Editors: N. Thelot, K. Caldwell and R. Hamilton

Printed in United States

DEDICATION

This book is dedicated to my late great-grandmother, Sarah T. Quinlan, better known as "Mimi" to those of us who knew her best. I came to you as a little girl and told you I dreamed of being a star when I grew up. We were going to walk down the red carpet one day and I was going to be able to finally thank you in front of millions of people for being my biggest fan and the driving force behind my success. It was going to be the best acceptance speech in Academy Award history.

You left this place in peace after fighting and suffering for so long. Before I left for school, I kissed you goodbye while you slept. When I came back home a week later, I kissed you again. Only then, your slumber was eternal. Out of the few regrets I have in this life, the greatest one of all was leaving you. I'm sure you already know that I haven't forgiven myself for it and probably never will. But I pray that you and God have.

I love you and miss you, Mimi...more than words could ever express. I hope I've made you and Poppy proud!

- Tash

Chapter 1

I ndigo sat on the edge of the plush leather couch tying the shoelaces on her sneakers. She couldn't believe she was actually awake and alert at this time of morning. Had her body not been trained to do so on its own, she would have still been asleep beneath the thickness and warmth of the sheet, blanket, and comforter lain across the pullout. Even after a long night of heavy drinking and hard dancing with her boyfriend and cousin, Indigo was, indeed, wide awake and ready to seize the day. She took a quick glance at the time on her watch. It read: 5:25. She ran her hand over her mouth before she jumped up and straightened out her dishevelled sweats. The word "POLICE" was printed in bold black letters on the back of her hooded sweatshirt.

For as long as Indigo could remember, she'd always wanted to be a police officer. And why wouldn't she? Her father, now retired, was one of Newark, New Jersey's finest. He served over forty years as an officer, twenty-five of them as a captain. Indigo definitely had some serious shoes to fill. Her parents, particularly her father, weren't exactly ecstatic when she told them she wished to pursue a career in law enforcement after graduating from high school. Her mother, Marguerite, prayed and called upon every saint there was to convince her only child to pursue another career; something more safe and promising. And her father, Victor, gave her a royal verbal thrashing in English and Spanish. Victor felt there was no place for a woman on the police force. Not because he was a chauvinist, but because he was well-aware of the mistreatment female officers received from their peers and those in the streets. Many would surely try her because of her beauty and petite stature. Oh no, Victor wasn't going to hear of it by any means.

Indigo figured her parents' disapproval was caused by their West Indian ancestry and strong islander beliefs that girls were to be nurses, teachers, secretaries, and mothers. It was the sons of the Caribbean who were to take such positions as doctors, police officers, firemen, and soldiers. Unfortunately, Victor and Marguerite had a little girl, not a little boy. With her mother being from St. Kitts and her father's people coming from Cuba, Indigo felt she didn't have a chance, let alone a prayer, of following in her father's footsteps. But with a lot of crying, begging, and persuading, she finally got her point across to her parents and they eventually gave her their blessings. Now, here she was nine years later, one of the city's best and worst kept secrets.

The average person would never guess Indigo Alonso-James was a cop. She could easily be mistaken for a model or someone whose job requirement was to be beautiful and maintain that position, but never a police officer. She stood at five-foot-seven and a half inches, weighed in at one-hundred and ten pounds, and was absolutely striking. Her small chest and backside accentuated her tiny frame. A ballet dancer for most of her life, Indigo's form turned into something fierce once she reached womanhood.

Indigo was well-aware of the beauty she possessed and used it to her full advantage. By no means was she vain, but she wasn't hesitant to put another female in her place when jealousy and envy reared their ugly heads. Oftentimes, these exchanges occurred at the lounges Indigo frequented. She always found herself in the middle of a lover's quarrel-with her being the primary cause of it. What she did with these men, who acted as if they were single for the moment, was innocent. There was no harm in flirting, was there? She didn't do much to get their attention. All she did was look in the guy's direction, smile, and turn away once the connection between them was made. What the gentleman did in response to her afterwards was all on him.

Indigo wore little make-up. Her natural beauty spoke for itself. She only enhanced it with lip-gloss or mascara to stretch her long lashes more when hitting her favorite hot spots throughout the Tri-State Area. Any other time, her face was bare of any beauty products. Her smooth caramel complexion was complimented by dark brown almond shaped eyes, a thin nose, and long black hair that fell to the middle of her back. Her small lips stretched a mile wide, allowing all to see the tiny gap between her top front teeth when she smiled. And if there was anything Indigo loved to do, it was smile. She appreciated the gap between her teeth. It wasn't one a person could "walk through," so she showed no shame when something funny tickled her. But standing in the middle of her only cousin's living room at 5:25 in the morning was far from being humorous. Indigo was tired and it showed. She pulled a hair-tie off her wrist and pulled back her hair, styling it into a loose ponytail. She then rubbed her eyes and sighed as she made her way down the hall to her cousin's closed bedroom door. She knocked lightly.

Indigo entered the dark room cautiously. She noticed the spotting of light in the room peeking through the blinds from the street-lights outside. Indigo spotted the shadow of a heavily covered body in the center of the queen-sized bed. She walked over to the queen-sized wooden structure with quiet steps shaking her head and smiling. She placed her hands on her small hips and watched her cousin's body lay motionless.

"Karma," Indigo whispered as she stood over her cousin, waiting for a reply. There was no response.

"Karma," she repeated in a louder tone, causing her cousin to stir a little and turn over.

"Hmm?" Karma asked sleepily.

"Come on. Get up," Indigo stressed.

"Mm-mm," Karma expressed lazily.

Indigo plopped down on the bed beside her cousin. She looked around the spotless room mentally questioning herself. How and why she always drowned herself in alcohol every other Friday night at the local lounges was beyond her. Maybe stress from the job was the cause. Maybe it was the constant anxiety and worrying about her drug-dealing boyfriend being out in the streets every night. Whatever the reason, it always landed her on the pull out couch at her cousin's condo. She didn't mind partying hard. That was one of the things Indigo did best. It was tending to her hang-overs the next day that she wasn't too keen about.

Indigo snapped back into reality and shook her cousin.

"Get up. It's five-thirty. You told me to come and wake you up." Indigo was losing her patience. Karma was not a morning person. She never was. Trying to wake her up was like trying to wake the dead. Indigo was definitely losing her cool.

"Just let me…sleep…" Karma managed to say before drifting back off to sleep.

Indigo slapped Karma hard on the behind.

"Karma!" Indigo yelled.

Defeated, Karma threw the covers off herself in frustration.

"I'm up. Okay? Damn," she said through a long yawn.

Indigo stared at her cousin in disbelief and held her eyes there until Karma's reached hers.

"What?" Karma asked.

Indigo shook her head from side-to-side.

"Nothing. I'm on my way to the deli. Do you want me to get you tea and a bagel or a Taylor ham, egg, and cheese sandwich with orange juice for breakfast?" Indigo asked sincerely.

"A Taylor ham, egg, and cheese sandwich with the O.J., please," Karma replied as she wiped her heavy eyes.

"Okay."

"You sleep alright?" Karma asked with a sly grin.

"Yeah, thanks for offering me your bed," Indigo spat sarcastically.

"You coulda slept in here with me if you didn't snore so loud," Karma responded with a chuckle.

"What? I don't snore!" Indigo replied.

"Yes, you do," Karma said with a smirk.

Indigo rolled her eyes.

"Whatever. At least I don't talk in my sleep."

"What?" Karma asked in confusion.

"You heard me," Indigo said with attitude as she rose off the bed. "You tell all your business in your sleep."

"Shut up, Indigo," Karma said as she waved her cousin away with her hand.

"You do!" Indigo stressed as she smiled and laughed at the thought.

Without warning, Karma pulled the pillow from beneath her head and threw it at her cousin. Indigo, too fast for her, dodged it by a few inches.

"Too slow," she teased as she moved towards the door. "And who's Michael? You were saying his name last night."

Karma picked up another pillow and hurled it toward her cousin. Indigo attempted to side step it, but failed. It hit her dead in the face.

"Get out!" Karma screamed in embarrassment.

"And change those bed sheets. I know you came on yourself last night," Indigo teased as she opened the door.

"Get outta here! I hate you!" Karma yelled.

"I love you, too," Indigo replied with that wide smile of hers. She exited the room, closing the door behind her. Karma sighed and settled herself back underneath her covers. But as soon as she got comfortable, the door reopened. Indigo poked her head back into the room and smirked.

"And get up!" she screamed at the top of her lungs.

Before Indigo knew it, Karma, unexpectedly, jumped out of the bed and chased after her into the hallway. The girls screamed and wrestled each other like they had so many times before in their youth...once upon a time. Once upon a time...a time when they were little girls looking at the world through the eyes of their mothers. But today, today was different. Indigo and Karma were grown women. Neither one had children of their own; agreeing as little girls, that this world was no place to bring a child into. It was a shame to have believed such a thing so early in life. But it was true and it was a necessary belief to have for each one's own survival.

Indigo and Karma knew better. Newark, New Jersey was one big cemetery. One wasn't walking amongst the living. She, in fact, was walking amongst the dead.

Chapter 2

The sun beamed in through the kitchen's window blinds. The silhouette of a leafed tree danced on a distant wall in the quaint room. Karma and Indigo sat at a small, round table set against the wall eating their breakfast and engaged in entertaining conversation. Indigo changed out of her sweats into a pair of fitted jeans, a black fitted long sleeved turtleneck, and comfortable black laced boots. A tasteful silver belt rested around her petite waist. She turned the ponytail loose for the day and allowed her thick, long mane to rest at the middle of her back. She studied her cousin's equally jaw-dropping beauty from across the table.

If she were to feel threatened by any other female in the world, it would have unquestionably been her cousin Karma. But luckily for her, Karma had other things on her mind besides competing with her. Beauty, fashion, and all the superficial things that came with them were unimportant factors in Karma's life. As long as she was clean, healthy, and her overall appearance was up-to-par daily, Karma was good to go. It was the principles behind family, loyalty, and trust that drove her. Her main concern was keeping her loved ones whole; especially her mother.

Indigo respected and accepted the differences between herself and Karma. While she was one to think before she spoke, Karma said the first thing that came to mind and made no apologies afterwards. Karma's sharp tongue was a force to be reckoned with and if you were one to fall victim to it, may God have mercy on your soul. Indigo's mild temper complimented her cousin's quick, hot disposition. Karma was indeed rough around the edges, while Indigo was consistently smooth. Indigo enjoyed being seen and heard, while Karma found solace in sitting back in the cut and observing everyone and everything around her. The girls were like night and day, but they loved each other so and acted more like sisters than cousins. Indigo would have it no other way. She would give her life for Karma and Karma would do the same for her in a heartbeat.

Karma Alonso-Walker sat across from her cousin donning fitted jeans, a fitted cream-colored sleeveless turtleneck, and a pair of high-heeled boots on her feet to match. She, the daughter of Soleil and Lorenzo Walker, deserved every verbal and non-verbal compliment that came her way. Karma, the color of bronze, stood at five-foot-eight and was one-hundred and twenty pounds of shear muscle. A sprinter all through high school, Karma acquired a thick frame like that of her African and Cuban-born mothers before her. She was petite in the waist, full in the chest and hips, and was continuing to measure into her pristine shell. Thick arched eyebrows accentuated her doe blue eyes. The nurse who held her as a newborn baby girl twenty-seven years ago told her mother that her eyes shared the same hue as the Caribbean Sea. And what a sight they had been on that warm spring day in 1980. Her keen nose complimented her full lips. Her lips quaintly housed perfectly straight, white teeth that were set along a sharp, square jawline. Her hair was dirty blonde and once hung as low as Indigo's in her early years. But in 2007, her mane was cut short and styled with gel, allowing it to appear as miniature golden flames.

Indigo just shook her head in awe as she watched her first-cousin take a sip of her orange juice.

Karma gently placed the miniature juice carton down on the tabletop before asking her next question.

"You goin' in today?"

Indigo sighed.

"Not until tonight. And don't worry; I'm going to make sure I stop by the party while I'm on patrol. I also plan on going into the restaurant and helping today."

"It's about damn time," Karma replied with furrowed eyebrows.

"Uh-uh. Excuse you," Indigo spat with the roll of her neck.

"No, excuse you," Karma smiled and mimicked her cousin's neck motion. "You *need* to go in and help. Give me a fuckin' break for once."

"You do know I'm just going in to do the register, right?" Indigo stressed.

Karma shook her head in disbelief.

"You're triflin' as hell."

The girls shared a warm laugh.

"That's okay. I'll be trifling. And besides, you're the manager. I don't do managerial, nor do I clean or serve rude behind people. So please don't expect me to do any of the above. It's going to be too early in the morning for all of that," Indigo stated adamantly before taking a bite out of her second bagel.

Karma shrugged her shoulders.

"Fine by me. You don't have to serve anyone today. You can protect 'em from chokin' on a muffin or somethin'," Karma teased as she laughed at her corny joke.

"Ha, ha. You're not funny," Indigo replied with a pout. "I'm a good cop."

"You are," Karma shook her head in agreement.

"I'm serious, Karma," Indigo stressed.

"Me, too," Karma agreed again. "You're a very good cop…one of the best. There's no denyin' that. And I'm very proud of you, *mami*. There's no denyin' that either."

Hearing Karma tell her how proud she was of her almost brought tears to Indigo's eyes. Karma was the only one who understood how important being a police officer was to her. In fact,

Karma was the only one who understood her as a whole and she held on to her cousin's pride and acceptance like her life depended on it.

"So, what'cha got planned for my aunt this morning?" Indigo continued.

It was Karma's mother's fifty-second birthday and she'd spent the last six months planning a big birthday bash in her honor at the family's restaurant. She managed to fly in friends and family from all over to celebrate her mother's day this evening.

Karma looked down at her watch.

"Well, it's six-thirty now, so she shouldn't be up until a quarter to eight since she's got today off. I'm thinkin' about puttin' her gifts on the tray with the food, but-"

"No, don't put both of them on there, just the tickets. Keep the jewelry on you until she gets dressed and everything," Indigo said excitedly.

"Okay. Yeah, that sounds good." Karma smiled and nodded.

"You're not going to do it," Indigo uttered with squinted eyes.

Karma laughed at the little faith her beloved cousin had in her. "Yes, I am."

"Alright, you better." Indigo chuckled to herself. "I can't believe you got my poor aunt thinking you're just taking her to a spa today."

"That's right," Karma said proudly.

"Ooo. I can't wait until I hear about it at the party tonight."

"Yeah, *the party*," Karma said in a low, sarcastic tone. "The party she wasn't supposed to know about. And she still wouldn't, had Uncle Vic not opened his big mouth."

"*Mirar*, don't talk about my father like that, okay?" Indigo threatened playfully. "He can't help it if he doesn't know how to keep a secret. The whole family knows he can't keep anything to himself." Indigo took another bite out of her bagel.

"It's Uncle Miguel's fault anyway. He had no business telling him in the first place."

Karma laughed at the stated fact.

"You are absolutely right."

"I'm excited, though!" Indigo beamed as she wiped her mouth with a napkin.

"Me, too!"

A loud silence suddenly fell. A dark cloud had abruptly formed above their heads. Indigo didn't want to ask Karma the next question, for she already knew what her response was going to be. Her cousin's mood would change in such a significant way when this man's name was brought up in conversation, it was almost frightening. Just the thought of him troubled her heart.

Indigo hesitated for a moment.

"Is Jimmy going to be there?"

As she expected, Karma's facial expression changed in the blink of an eye. A scowl formed and her eyes averted to the floor. She sighed and slowly shook her head from side-to-side as if trying to remove him from her mind, body, and soul all at once.

Indigo waited patiently for an answer.

"I don't know. Probably," Karma replied in a whisper. She held her suddenly throbbing head in her hand. "We don't need his bullshit tonight."

"You can say that again," Indigo mumbled.

Karma sighed heavily.

"I just want her to have one good birthday, you know? One good night."

"I know, K," Indigo spoke softly as she reached across the table and clasped her hands with her cousin's.

"Just one," Karma reiterated in a weary tone.

"Listen, if he starts any mess before I get there tonight, *any mess*…you know what to do. Call me and I'll be there," Indigo stated seriously.

"Okay."

"My aunt is going to have the time of her life tonight. And she's going to have you to thank."

Indigo squeezed Karma's hand and waited for her to make eye contact. Karma slowly lifted her eyes and met her cousin's genuine gaze. There was so much love and hope there. Indigo could always find the positive in any situation life had to offer. Karma absolutely loved that about her cousin. The last six years of her life had been so tumultuous, filled with so much heartache and pain. Karma eventually gave up on believing there were better days to come. She wasn't living. *This* wasn't living. Her state of being was that of a 21st-century slave and her master was Jimmy. Karma was merely existing, a shell of a person, a walking time bomb waiting to explode at any given moment. She lay awake many a night in fear of that man. Fear of what he might do next; not to her, but to the one whom she loved the most. Had he not come into their life and turned their world upside down four years ago, she would still have some inkling of hope for their future. But the future was yet to be determined.

Chapter 3

Karma's mother grew up in a household full of hate. Her grandmother, Ava Alonso-Cruz, hated her mother for being born. She was an accident. That's what Ava told her daughter all of her life. Way before she was even thought about, her grandmother was content with being the only woman in her home surrounded by three men. She was the sunshine of her grandfather's life and epitomized God's image of a perfect woman in the eyes of her two uncles. She was a woman without fault. A proud Cuban woman to the core; no questions asked. But it wasn't until the birth of her mother, Soleil Marisol that Karma's grandmother was sought as a woman and just that...nothing more, nothing less.

Karma never understood how a woman could hate her own daughter, especially when she looked so much like the man she devoted her life to. As a young woman, Ava was tall with skin the color of vanilla and a figure the shape of an hourglass. Her chest was high and heavy with full breasts. Her bottom was round and ripe like an apple. Her dirty blonde hair fell below her shoulders and her gray eyes sparkled like two silver dollars when the sun hit them.

Her lips were full, but no one could ever outline them because they were always thinned by the constant smile she wore. Her voice was husky and when she laughed, the laughter bellowed from deep down within her soul. Karma knew her grandmother's laughter very well. She heard it as an eerie echo that forced its way through her mother's desperate cries every time her father left to fight in a war.

Her grandfather, Victor Alonso, Sr., was just as beautiful as her grandmother before hate and contempt consumed his soul. He was a tall man as well with broad shoulders and big, masculine hands. His wavy black hair was untamed. No matter how much palmade he put on it to lay those wild waves down, they remained unrelenting. His gingerbread brown skin was flawless. Only a pencil-thin mustache donning his upper lip and a set of deeply embedded dimples on each cheek left creases of imperfection behind. His sons, Victor, Jr. and Miguel, would grow to be spitting images of him. One would share his mother's eyes and the other would posses his father's silence. Karma's grandfather was a quiet man who only spoke when something needed to be said. He was the quiet and her grandmother was the storm.

Karma's mother grew up in a household full of hate. It sat among other split-level homes in the Allegheny Mountains of Clifton Forge, Virginia. It was the place where her mother found security in her daddy, humility in her brothers, ugliness in her mother, and shame in herself.

After giving birth to her daughter, Ava took one look at her and hated her from that very moment. Karma, 'til this day, really didn't know what her grandmother expected to see. Maybe she didn't expect to see so much of her husband looking back at her. Whatever the case, she knew she didn't expect her grandfather to cry when he laid his eyes on her mother. He hadn't shed a tear when her uncles were born. Those baby boys were men-children. They were to be born and bred with hearts of steel. But this baby girl, whose eyes burned like a summer sunset, cheeks indented with dimples, locks the color of coal, skin the color of brown sugar, and lips full and pink, had come into their lives unexpectedly. And from his reaction to her mother's birth, alone, her grandmother saw the beginning of the end.

Her mother's favorite seat in her childhood home had been daddy's lap. Her grandfather would come home from working on the railroad, sit down in his favorite rocking chair, spark up his favorite pipe, and call to his favorite girl. Karma's mother would come running from her bedroom and hop into his lap. He'd pick her up, hold her high in the air, then bring her down and shower her with thousands of kisses. He'd pull out a small trinket or piece of candy from the pocket of his jumpsuit and place it in her little hand. Always grateful, her mother would take it from him, rest her head on his broad chest and study the treasure while she hummed an old Cuban tune. She'd place her thumb in her mouth as her father placed his pipe in his and they'd lose themselves in each other. Karma's grandmother would look on from the kitchen and curse them under her breath while turning away and settling back at the stove to cook dinner.

Karma's father used to tell her that Ava was so cruel to her mother because she possessed so much more than just outer beauty. She was beautiful inside as well and anyone, had it been a stranger or a neighbor, who crossed her path wouldn't hesitate to tell her so. People always complimented her grandmother for having such a beautiful and polite little girl. She would smile and thank them kindly, then, as the patrons proceeded on their way, she'd look down at her mother and roll her eyes. Instead of being given cookies and milk before her bedtime, like any other toddler, Ava would give Soleil a piece of her mind.

"I hate 'chu. I hate everything about 'chu. I hate everything 'chu stand for. Innocence. Beauty. I should have killed 'chu when I had the chance, but 'chour damn father never left me alone long enough to follow through with my plans. Don't think I didn't try. Hmm, one good thing I will say about 'chu. 'Chu aren't too smart. 'Chu never will be. 'Chu got 'chour papi and hermanos around here chasin' after 'chu like 'chour a new piece of ass. Throwin' that little thing around the way 'chu do is just going to get 'chu in trouble when 'chu grow to be a woman. And I hope 'chu get everything 'chu deserve. I gave

KARMA

birth to a whore. I've known it since the moment I laid my eyes on 'chu. 'Chu too goddamn pretty. 'Chu remind me of my own good-for-nothing mother. Same eyes. Same hair. Same face. And 'chu got the nerve to have her legs too. 'Chu going to bring shame on me for having them like she did. They going to stretch a mile wide to welcome every negrito between them, 'cause that's all 'chu'll ever be good for, if that. Mi madre wasn't shit…so 'chu will never be shit. I guess I got lucky."

Her words were as heavy as the smoke of a Cuban cigar. With them spoken and lingering above Soleil's head, Ava would laugh. This laugh would carry around the room and bounce off the walls. Karma's poor mother would watch the woman who gave her life rise from her bed, turn away, and leave with a smile of satisfaction etched across her face. At three-years-old, Soliel didn't know what a whore was let alone half of the other things her mother bestowed upon her that night. But she did know and understand that tone in the scorned woman's voice. It was haunting. It was sober. It was honest. It was self-hatred in its rarest form.

Karma's grandmother expressed her disliking of her mother the same way, at the same time, every night until she was eighteen years old. The only thing she didn't do was lay a hand on her. She never had to. Her words had beaten the poor child senseless. Ava Alonso-Cruz's spitfire of a tongue had the greatest influence on her daughter's life. And for years to come, she would suffer from it.

For fifteen years, her mother never dreamed because she feared the night. For fifteen years, her mother stuttered and was teased by other children for it. Only Karma, her uncles, and father knew her mother stopped speaking altogether until she entered high school. For fifteen years, her mother was told she would be nothing more than a whore. For fifteen years, her mother believed it until she met Lorenzo Walker, Karma's father. Apart from her new love, Jimmy, Lorenzo had been the only man she ever gave herself to.

Ava Alonso-Cruz's self-hatred reconstructed the skeleton of Karma's mother's childhood home in Clifton Forge, Virginia. Her grandmother hated her mother for being born. Her grandfather hated her grandmother for hating her mother. Her uncles hated each other for not siding with the same parent. And her mother hated herself for disrupting a family that knew only love before her existence.

They say with every death, there is a birth. And it must be true, because Ava died on the very same day Karma was born. Her uncles believe a battered and broken heart was what killed her. If so, then knowing that a restless spirit haunts the living withstands the test of time. For the third generation of Alonso-Cruz women, Ava's rage was passed on to her daughter's own. Karma and her mother both knew she possessed it, but her hatred was far more tamed. And, unlike her grandmother's, hers was just.

As Karma drove to her mother's house on that cold September morning, she wondered what the love of her life was doing at that very moment. *What was she feeling? How was she feeling?* It was her fifty second birthday and she was going to spend half, if not all of it, with the man her daughter undoubtedly despised.

Karma pulled into the driveway of her mother's Tudor home on Newark's tree-lined Highland Avenue. She pressed down hard on the brake before hitting the back of the navy blue Oldsmobile parked before her. Karma sucked her teeth loudly in contempt. She knew exactly who the car belonged to and wasn't at all happy to see it sitting in her self-proclaimed parking spot. She backed out of the driveway and parked in front of the house.

The Tudor's defining characteristics were half-timbering on bay windows, upper floors, and facades that were dominated by steeply pitched cross gables. The patterned stonewalls, rounded doorway, multi-paned casement windows, and large stone chimney were wonderful sights to see. Karma stepped out of her 2003 Acura 3.2 CL into the crisp autumn morning air. The brown leather pea coat she'd put on over her outfit matched perfectly. She slung her large pocketbook on her shoulder and closed the car door behind her. She beeped the alarm with the remote control, and then placed the keys into her purse as she made her way up the steps to the house.

As Karma stepped inside the dimly lit foyer, she began to have second thoughts about wanting to surprise her mother so early in the morning. After seeing Jimmy's pimpmobile in the driveway, she wasn't in the mood to act like everything was alright when it really wasn't. Karma shrugged off the negative thoughts and placed her house keys in the bowl on the endtable set against the wall to the left of her. She heard muffled voices from the second floor, but she paid them no mind. She proceeded to remove her boots at the door and managed to take off one boot before hearing a loud thud and a masculine moan escape from above. The abrupt harmony of noises caused her to stop and question herself again. Karma decided to step out of the other boot with caution before heading to the kitchen down the hall. As she began to take a couple of steps away from the door, the noises started again. The moaning and thudding from the bed above found a steady rhythm. The cacophony of sounds was loud and consistent. Karma cringed and shook her head in disgust. Hearing her mother and her repulsive boyfriend go at it like animals was the last thing she wanted to be subjected to. And the worst thing about standing below the sexcapade was having to listen to Jimmy, the only audible one.

Karma took a slow, deep breath in, then released it. She continued to walk forward, but tripped over two large construction boots that were lying in the middle of the floor. She cursed under her breath, picked the boots up in frustration, and threw them violently up the stairway. They hit a wall to her satisfaction. She hoped the thump of the boots would bring the sounds of unadulterated passion to a halt, but it didn't. She cursed under her breath again and turned her focus back to her task at hand. She proceeded down the hall to the kitchen. As Karma stepped into her place of solace, she closed the swinging door behind her.

Karma stood at the stove, frying ham in one pan and cooking pancakes in another. The toast that was in the toaster had not yet sprung. A portable radio set on the counter played an old R&B tune softly in the background. Karma walked over to a cabinet, opened it, and retrieved a stack of expensive china plates. As she began to separate them, she heard the sound of heavy footsteps walking towards the kitchen. Karma's face tightened as she acknowledged who the distinct steps belonged to. The door swung open and a tall, full-figured man with a slight potbelly entered the room. He and Karma locked eyes. He smiled mischievously at her while she rolled her eyes and focused back on the food. His dark skin shimmered in the kitchen's bright track lighting. His tight slanted eyes, broad nose, and full lips gave away his Geechee roots. Jimmy Hayes, dressed in a gray one-piece jumpsuit and construction boots, crossed behind Karma and retrieved a cup out of one of the cupboards.

"Well, look who's here. I knew I smelled ham cookin'," Jimmy said as he took a small piece of cooked ham off a cooling plate on the island. He placed it in his mouth and smiled.

Karma watched him chew and swallow the meat in one breath. She turned her head and closed her eyes to keep herself from telling him off.

"Damn, that's some good ham," he continued. "How you doin' this mornin', Karma?" Jimmy travelled over to the refrigerator and retrieved a carton of orange juice.

"You stink," Karma said impassively.

Jimmy turned to face the young woman before him and ran his tongue across his teeth as he outlined her statuesque body with his eyes.

"What do I smell like?" he asked as he took a swig of his juice.

Karma raised an eyebrow and smirked.

"You know what you smell like," she said as she turned the stovetop off with the vicious snap of her wrist.

"Your momma smells the same way too, you know," Jimmy replied as he repositioned his hardened manhood under his jumpsuit.

Luckily, Karma missed the indirect sexual advance. Had she seen the act, there was no telling what would have happened.

"I didn't need to know that," Karma said curtly as she proceeded to dish her mother's plate.

"Well, she does," Jimmy smiled proudly.

Karma sighed heavily.

"Jimmy, what the hell did you come down here for?" she asked impatiently.

"I just came down to get a glass of juice before I go to work. I'm a little dehydrated," he stated before taking a big gulp of the orange liquid. "Your momma wore a muthafucka out up there. A nigga's potassium intake is important. He's gotta keep his strength up for certain thangs, if you know what I mean." Jimmy smiled at Karma pompously. He knew if there was one way to disrespect his woman's daughter, it was by throwing his explicit sexual exploits with her mother in her face.

Karma bit her bottom lip to keep herself from stooping to his level. She was well-aware of what Jimmy was doing and she didn't appreciate it one bit.

"No, I don't know," she responded slowly.

Jimmy had Karma right where he wanted her. He went in for the kill.

"You're right. I'm sorry. I know you ain't had none since-"

Karma lost her cool just as Jimmy wanted. The butter knife in her hand suddenly stopped buttering the toasted bread.

"Don't worry about when I last got some or not. That's none of your fuckin' business," Karma spat.

Jimmy sipped his juice calmly.

"Alright, Karma. I think you better calm down," he warned.

"No, nigga, I think *you* better calm down. I'm not my mother, alright? You not gonna come up in here and talk to me any kinda way." Karma's patience was wearing thin. How dare this man come into her childhood home and speak to her as if she was a child. As if he had authority over her. As if he was her father. She wasn't having it.

The half-empty glass of juice slowly crept down from Jimmy's lips. He gently placed it down onto the counter.

"Who the fuck you think you talkin' to?" he asked in a measured tone.

"*You*, muthafucka," Karma responded without hesitation.

Before she knew it, Jimmy was walking swiftly around the table to meet her face-to-face. Expecting him to make an attempt to do major damage to her face or some other part of her body, Karma picked the hot, grease-filled pan up from the stovetop and held it tightly. Jimmy stopped short when he saw it dangling loosely from her hand. Acknowledging her fearlessness of him, he backed away and laughed nervously at her graveness.

"You sure ain't your mother," he mumbled as he rubbed his mustache.

"Yeah, you better trust and believe dat shit," Karma proclaimed, keeping her piercing blue eyes on Jimmy as he drank the last of his juice. "She better be in one piece when I go up there too, Jimmy. 'Cause if she's not, you and I are gonna have a problem."

"Is that a threat?" Jimmy asked with raised eyebrows.

"No, it's a promise," Karma stated earnestly as she placed the frying pan back down on the stove.

Jimmy ran his hand over his meticulously trimmed, short high top and smiled nervously.

"Look, baby doll-" he began.

"Don't call me dat," Karma advised him, completely cutting off everything he wanted to say after that. "Baby Doll" was a nickname her father had given her as a little girl and he was the only one who was allowed to call her by it.

"Okay, hey…look…whateva. There's no need for you to worry your pretty little head over nothin', alright? She's fine. I took *real* good care of her this mornin'," he replied smugly.

"That's not what I'm talkin' about and you know it." Karma could feel her blood boiling. If looks could kill, Jimmy's sweat drenched black body would have been shredded into little itty-bitty bloody pieces already.

"Oh…that," he laughed arrogantly. "Well, I can't say there was any need for all of that today. It's her birthday, you know? That was my present to her…along with the, uh, Princess-cut diamond ring she got on her finger up there. Make sure you check it out when you go up to see her," he said proudly as he knocked on the island top twice. "See you at the party tonight." Jimmy flashed another crooked smile before leaving.

Karma placed her hands on her muscled hips and began to pace the floor. She fought back the tears that were forming in her eyes. Her worst nightmare had come true. Jimmy was there to stay. He'd just made the most definitive step any unwanted man could make in solidifying his position in a woman-child's life. And with knowing that, Karma still had to go upstairs and face the woman whose life was her own and the reason why she woke up each day.

Chapter 4

Karma walked into the brightly lit, spacious room with the tray of food in hand. The room encapsulated matching wooden furniture with their cherry-wood finishing accommodated by the burgundy colored walls and dark wall-to-wall carpeting. The queen-sized poster low profile bed was centered in the room with a nightstand beside it. A single lamp and two childhood photographs of Karma were settled atop it. A dresser with a landscape mirror set on top of it was located along a wall next to the bed. It was filled with toiletries, jewelry, and other trinkets. A five-drawer chest was positioned at the foot of the bed while the armoire rested along a distant wall.

A full-figured, mocha-colored woman dressed in a cotton floral bathrobe tucked her shoulder length black hair behind her ear before she continued to strip her bed of its sheets. Soleil Walker-Alonso had aged well. One could only tell she'd had a child by her slight weight gain. Karma smiled at the sight of her oblivious mother and quietly walked up behind her.

"Don't you think you've done enough bendin' over for today?"

Karma asked jokingly.

Soleil stopped what she was doing, dropped her head, and laughed whole-heartedly at her daughter's crudely humorous remark.

"Karma." Soleil turned around with the worn, soiled sheets in her arms, smiling and shaking her head. "You gotta fresh mouth, you know that?"

Karma raised her eyebrows and grinned.

"I wonder where I got it from."

Soleil rolled her honey brown eyes and smiled. She leaned in and kissed her only child on the lips.

"Morning, baby."

"Mornin', Ma. Happy Birthday," Karma said joyfully as she held the heavy tray of food up in her mother's face.

"Thank you, angel." Soleil looked down at the tray in query. "Is all of that for me?"

"Yup."

"You're too much, little girl," Soleil blushed as she walked away and into her personal bathroom. She placed the sheets in a wooden hamper as Karma made herself comfortable on the edge of the bare bed. "You told me we were just going to the spa today!" Soleil expressed in a moment of confusion.

"Come on, Ma! Did you really think I was gonna tell you I was makin' you breakfast in bed this mornin'?! Where would the fun have been in dat?!" Karma teased.

Soleil sucked her teeth and travelled back into the room. She walked over to the bed and sat down beside Karma.

"I swear, you're just like your father," Soleil said knowingly as she retrieved the plate of food from Karma and placed it on her lap.

"Thank you," Karma replied. She watched her mother cut into her pancakes and ham. Soleil's approval of any and everything that she did was very important to her. Not that it took much to make her happy. Still, Karma felt like the little girl she was so long ago in her mother's eyes and often acted like it when in her company. This day was no different. The only thing that took Karma by surprise was the glow of her mother's skin. Soleil had taken on an angel-like appearance. It was as if she was sitting before her daughter as a seraph in disguise.

Although, Soleil wasn't one to brag about her own beauty, she had every right to. Then, again, she didn't think she possessed such a thing. Her heavy, raven black hair that rested at her shoulders, ginger colored skin, full lips, almond shaped honey brown eyes, and broad, white smile brought many men and women, if one could believe it, to their knees. Soleil was absolutely stunning. From her sharp jaw line to her high cheekbones, her face was chiselled and symmetrically precise like it had been carved out of stone by one of the ancient Greeks. And as an extra token, each cheek was imprinted by deep-seeded dimples. Even with the slight weight gain that crept up on her during her forties, the extra pounds suited Soleil and had not affected her face at all. Everyone saw Soleil's beauty, but her. Her mother told her as a little girl that she would suffer for being so pretty and she did. Suffering was what Soleil knew all too well and she didn't want Karma to fall victim to it like she had. It was unfortunate her only child bore that same pain nonetheless.

Soleil took a bite out of her food and smiled.

"Mmm, this is delicious, baby. Thank you."

"You're welcome, Ma."

Soleil reached for the napkin beneath her plate. As she grabbed it, she noticed a long white envelope enclosed in it. She looked over at Karma in distrust.

"What's this?" she asked, holding the envelope in her hand.

Karma shrugged her shoulders.

"I don't know. Open it," she lied with a straight face.

Soleil cut her eyes at her daughter before turning her attention to the envelope.

She slid her index finger between the sealed flap and ripped it open. She pulled out a brochure with two tickets stapled to it. Soleil's eyes widened as a smile crept across her flawless face.

"A cruise?! I'm going on a cruise?" she screamed excitedly.

"Yup! It's for seven days and six nights. And look, Ma..." Karma pointed to the brochure. "...you get to go to six different islands: Puerto Rico, St. Thomas, Dominica, St. Lucia, Barbados, and Antigua."

"Oh, baby." Overwhelmed with joy, Soleil placed the tray of food down beside her and hugged Karma tightly. She felt she was undeserving of such a gift, but felt blessed, nonetheless, to have such a thoughtful child. She had every right to thank God for her daughter. As the two pulled away from each other, Karma wiped her mother's fallen tears from her cheeks.

"I really need this cruise," Soleil was able to muster between sniffles.

"I know you do, Ma. That's why I got it for you. You need a vacation."

Soleil placed her hand gently on her daughter's cheek, leaned in, and kissed her on the lips once more.

"I think you have somethin' else on that tray," Karma hinted.

"What? There's more?" Soleil asked in disbelief.

"Last time I checked, there was somethin' else on the other side of your plate."

Soleil snapped her head back towards the tray and proceeded to probe it. She noticed another napkin folded over something. She picked the covered item up and removed the napkin from around it. A long velvet box came into view. Soleil opened it slowly and lost her breath for a moment when she set her eyes on a pair of diamond earrings set beside a matching diamond tennis bracelet.

"Oh, Karma. Baby, I can't-" Soleil looked back and forth from the gifts to Karma.

Before Soleil could further her thought, Karma cut her off.

"Yes, you can, Ma. And if you don't, I'm gonna cry and then I'm gonna call Daddy and tell 'im you hurt my feelings by not acceptin' my gifts."

Soleil looked over at Karma and watched her form her lips into a pout. Soleil knew the pouting routine all too well. She was unable to deny Karma of anything as a little girl once she pouted. And, in that moment, she had been set up for the kill…again.

"That's not fair, Karma. Your father has nothing to do with this."

"So? I'll put 'im in it. You know I will. And you know he'll take my side," Karma informed her mother.

Soleil just chuckled to herself. Karma had her father wrapped her finger and they were all well-aware of it. She was just as much as a "Daddy's Girl" as she was a "Mama's Girl." All Karma had to do was cry to bring Lorenzo to shame and the rest was history.

"Humph. He always takes your side," Soleil finally admitted.

"That's right. So do you really feel like bein' ganged up on today?" Karma asked.

"No, I don't," Soleil answered with a half smile.

"Well, then, you better take my gifts."

"Karma-"

Karma put her hand up before her mother and shook her head.

"Ma, I've watched you give so much of yourself to other people for years… since I was a little girl. And never once have you ever asked for anything in return. You give and you give and you give, but you never take. And today is the day that I think you should. Please, Ma? If not for yourself, then, for me?"

Soleil studied Karma's desperate blue eyes. There was that infamous look she used to give her as a child. *How could she say no to those eyes?* She never could before, so why start now? Soleil finally submitted to her daughter's wishes.

"I never could say no to you," she replied before sucking her teeth in dismay.

Karma opened her arms widely and pulled her mother close for another hug of appreciation.

"Thank you, Maaa. I love youuu," Karma sang.

"Mm-Hmm. I love you, too. My baby. You're too much," Soleil responded.

Karma pulled away and smiled victoriously.

"Can you wear 'em tonight?"

"Of course I'll wear them tonight. I gotta show them off, especially to your aunt Maggie," Soleil grinned wickedly. Her sister-in-law was sure to be envious of the "bling" she was going to be sporting tonight. Oh, how she loved to get under Marguerite's skin and vice versa. The rivalry was nothing serious. The two just enjoyed competing with one another. Birthday and Christmas gifts were what the duo fought over mostly and were quite a pair to watch in action.

Karma laughed at the thought of her aunt's face once her mother showed her what she'd gotten for her big day. But her laughter came to a swift halt once she realized Jimmy had also given her a piece of important jewelry this morning.

"What about your ring? You gonna show that off too?" Karma asked tersely as she locked eyes with her mother. Soleil averted her eyes first. She didn't know Karma knew about the ring. She wasn't going to mention it to her until she handled her unfinished business with Jimmy. Soleil closed the jewelry box, picked the tickets up, and placed them all back on the tray.

"Where is it? You're not wearin' it," Karma continued. She was trying to read her mother, but Soleil was hell-bent on keeping a straight face. She was the mother here, not Karma. She had to take control of this situation before it got way out of hand. Karma was waiting for her to give her a reason to blow up and she wasn't in the mood for it this morning. After all, it was her birthday.

"That's because I don't need to wear it. It's wrong for a woman to wear the ring of a man she doesn't plan to marry, especially when that woman is still married to her daughter's father," she replied calmly.

Karma stared at her mother in shock.

"But you accepted it."

"No, I didn't. He just placed it on my finger and went on about his business. He didn't give me a chance to say anything," she explained.

"So does this mean you're breakin' up with him too?" Karma asked with hopeful eyes.

Soleil hesitated before she spoke once again.

"No. It just means that I'm not marrying him."

Karma slapped her thighs in abhorrence.

"Unbelievable." Karma angrily rose from the bed, leaned over her mother and removed her birthday gifts from the tray. She set them on Soleil's bare pillow and went on to retrieve the tray before storming towards the door.

"What, Karma?! What?!" Soleil asked in a high-pitched voice.

Karma spun around and faced her mother with a pain-ridden glare. There wasn't a trace of the bright ocean blue hue that her eyes held there seconds ago. The color of her eyes had taken on a life of their own. They were now set as dark steel- gray stones. She had her grandmother's eyes and Karma kept the departed woman's rocks fixed on her mother. The scowl was all too familiar to Soleil. She had no other choice but to look away. She couldn't bear the sight of her mother's troubled spirit invade her only child. But Karma remained. She wanted that look of despair to reach the core of her mother's soul. She needed Soleil to see her pain and know the cause of it. Karma didn't turn away. She *wouldn't* turn away.

"You already know what! You're not gonna marry 'im, but you're gonna stay wit' 'im anyway?! You might as well marry his sorry black ass! It wouldn't make no fuckin' difference anyway!" she yelled back.

Soleil jumped up from the bed and stormed over to her irate daughter. Karma had every right to be angry, but cursing her was overstepping the boundaries.

"You better watch your mouth. I don't know who the hell you think you're talking to, but you better recognize this face and quick," Soleil warned.

Karma bowed her head in humble submission. She figured that was the smartest thing to do before she said something else she would later regret.

"*Mireme cuando hablo con usted,*" Soleil instructed through clenched teeth. She only spoke her native tongue when her patience was tried and she had finally reached her wits end.

Karma slowly lifted her stoned face back to her mother. Even though the woman was four inches shorter than her, the greatness of her presence had so much more height than her own. Any other day, it would intimidate her, but it didn't in this dark hour. Karma's rage was far greater than her mother's stature.

"Now, I understand you dislike Jimmy. You've got every good reason to. But, like it or not, he's not going anywhere. He's been here for the past four years and he'll be here for another four if I want him to be. You can thank your father for that," Soleil spat as she thought about the six long years she'd been legally separated from her husband. She and Lorenzo agreed upon separating after Karma graduated from college. Up until that time, the couple lived together in the same house, shared the same bed, and united as one in the late hours like any other normal married couple. The only reason they decided to stay together while Karma was still in school was because they both knew a separation during such a critical time in her life would have affected her and her studies immensely.

There was no doubt Soleil still loved and missed her estranged husband, but as deeply as she yearned for him, she couldn't accept the fact of or being treated as second best to the United States Army. Had Lorenzo put her and their daughter first, Soleil wouldn't have had so much of a problem. But he hadn't. The Army was Lorenzo's life. Taking care of his country was far more important than taking care of home and Soleil had become fed up with it. Yes, she'd met him as a young soldier, but Lorenzo was old now and it was time for him to retire like he said he would years ago. Then again, what did Soleil care? She was with Jimmy and Lorenzo was with Debbie, his girlfriend for the month. However, if Lorenzo called her up and told her he was retiring today, she would drop Jimmy like a bad habit. It was just a shame she hadn't even received a birthday card, let alone, a phone call from him this morning.

Soleil regained her train of thought.

"There are plenty of couples who've been together for years and have strived without the inconvenience of marriage, Karma. I don't see why Jimmy and I have to be any different," she said unemotionally.

Karma stood astounded. She knew her mother had it bad for this fool, but her behavior and the answers she was giving her were way beyond unacceptable.

"You gotta be kiddin' me, right? Do you hear yourself? I mean, do you really hear yourself right now? We're not talkin' about some random nigga off the street, Ma. We're talkin' about your boyfriend here. Jimmy is not gonna accept no for an answer. You know that. You know how we feel about 'im. Goddamnit!" Karma screamed as she flung the tray of food across the room. "I can't do this shit anymore! I can't just stand back and watch you lose yourself behind this nigga! He's no fuckin' good! Why are you doin' this to yourself?!"

Karma wanted to shake some sense into Soleil, but it wouldn't have swayed her. *Who had her mother become? When did she settle for less? How could she allow this man to have so much control over her?* Soleil was standing before her daughter as someone, even she, didn't recognize anymore. Karma's heavy chest heaved up and down. She searched her mother's empty eyes for an answer. There wasn't one. Soleil's spirit was worn and Karma knew she was the cause of it just as much as Jimmy was. Too bad she hadn't caught herself from going off a few seconds ago.

Soleil shook her head and sighed. She ran her hand over her mouth and looked into her daughter's distressed face. She stood there thinking about how she was going to use her next set of chosen words. Karma was in a fragile state.

"I don't know what to tell you, *mi amor*. All I can think to say is that I love him…and it's just not that easy to walk away."

Karma shook her head in disgust.

"Well, if that's what you call love…then I don't want it. I don't wanna know it. I don't wanna fall into it," she replied in an almost inaudible tone, looking over at the thrown food and broken chinaware on the carpet and wall. "I'm goin' downstairs to get somethin' to clean up this mess. Our appointment's at nine, so you better go take your shower and do whatever else you need to do." Karma turned her back and walked out of the room shaking her head.

Soleil remained in the middle of her room holding her throat. She hadn't seen such pain in Karma's eyes since that Easter day Lorenzo's one nightstand walked into their church with a child she claimed to be his. Or the day she pulled Karma close, told her she had ovarian cancer, then sent her away to California to run for Olympic gold in the same breath. The affair, illegitimate child she later found not to be her husband's and bout with cancer all happened ten years ago. And by the grace of God; Soleil survived all three crises. She was a survivor-a woman who had overcome the odds.

Time heals all wounds. Isn't that the saying? Well, how come no one told Soleil they left nasty scars behind? She stood in silence thinking about Karma's last remark about love. Her child was obviously aware of its true meaning and she was also aware of the wrongness in Jimmy's interpretation of it. Soleil thought about whom and what was more important to her. She knew she didn't want to become one of those women who were so blinded by "love" that she put her man before her child. That was a definite no-no. But she would surely have to ask herself this morning, *Have I?* after seeing Karma's reaction to her professed "love" and loyalty to Jimmy.

Chapter 5

Easter Sunday. 1997. A congregation of one hundred parishioners gathered at St. Rocco's Roman Catholic Church. The array of pastel colors and hues of brown faces decorated the subtly designed place of worship. Soleil decided to don a light lavender pantsuit with a matching church hat cocked down to one side of her face, while Lorenzo sat sharply in a black Hugo Boss suit and matching satin lavender tie. The couple settled down among the crowd in the center pews. Soleil greeted an attractive dark-skinned woman with a hug as she settled herself down beside her. The woman's hair was cut into a sharp bob, highlighted with tints of red. Marguerite "Maggie" Alonso, wearing a mint green skirt suit, wiped the lipstick mark she left on her best friend's cheek with her thumb. She locked her left arm with Soleil's right as Lorenzo leaned over and kissed her on the cheek. The women then turned their attention towards the choir and smiled at the sight of their children.

"Now, tell I de truth, Soleil," Maggie whispered into her sister-in-law's ear. "If Karma wasn't your child, wouldn't you just stand back and say to yourself, 'Dat sure is a beautiful child.' Her not yours, now. Remember dat."

Soleil looked over at her beaming friend who was waiting eagerly for her answer. Maggie nudged her in the arm and questioned her with her eyes.

"Go on and admit it. You're in de house of de Lord now, so me advise you not to sit up here and lie."

Soleil shook with laughter. She looked back towards the choir pit smiling and nodded slowly.

"Yes, even if she wasn't mine, I'd still say she was a beautiful child."

Karma was sitting next to Indigo, their hands interlocked with each other. She whispered encouraging words into her nervous cousin's ear before taking a stand at the podium.

"Good morning!" Indigo shouted.

"Good morning!" the congregation responded weakly.

Indigo shook her head in playful disgust. She repositioned the microphone at the stand.

"Oh, I know you all can do better than that! Good morning!" she placed her hand behind her ear to receive the response loud and clear.

"Good morning!" the congregation managed to shout back with more enthusiasm.

"Now, that's what I like to hear! Amen. Before we begin this morning's service, I'd like for you all to stand and grab the hand of your neighbor," she kindly requested.

The congregation stood at their feet and grabbed the hand of their neighbor.

"Let us bow our heads. Heavenly Father, we come to you this Easter Sunday morning in humble submission. Lord, we celebrate this day as *Your* day. You rose from Your tomb after being whipped, beaten, spat on, and crucified all because You loved us. You didn't have to give Your life for ours, but You did. And today we stand here in Your house of worship to thank You for all of Your merciful blessings. None of us are perfect Lord. We're not what we used to be and we're surely not where we want to be. But what I do know, as I look out into this congregation today, is that we are all here to praise Your Holy name. In Jesus' name we pray...," Indigo spoke humbly.

"Amen," the congregation replied in unison. A storm of applause erupted afterwards.

"Amen. Please remain standing as our sister, Ms. Karma Alonso-Walker, leads us in our morning musical selection. If you know the song, please sing along. And please sing along if you know the song," she joked.

The congregation joined together in laughter. Karma and a young man stepped before the youth choir. He grabbed the microphone as Karma nodded her head to the pianist. The pianist counted off and proceeded to lead the band in their rendition of Thomas A. Whitfield's arrangement of "Walk In The Light." The members of the congregation and choir swayed, sung, and hummed to the chosen musical selection. Karma directed the choir in choreographed hand and body movements. Soleil, Lorenzo, and Maggie smiled with pride and cried in joy.

As the church continued to rock, a tall, broad-shouldered man in a gray suit stepped before the choir and watched them in amazement. Father Salvatore Pacella turned to the congregation and smiled. He outstretched his arms to the sky and shook his head in disbelief.

"Amen," he said to himself as he rocked from side-to-side.

As the song ended, Father Pacella gathered his thoughts. He continued to stand back and watch the youth in awe as Karma gave the gesture to end the selection. The congregation commended the young people with a roar of hollering and applause. The choir and band bowed in recognition. Father Pacella gestured for Karma to approach him. As she met him, he received her with a big hug and kiss. Karma, taken aback by his gesture, blushed.

"Amen!" he yelled as he held on to Karma tightly.

"Amen!" the congregation yelled back at him.

"You all may be seated."

The congregation settled down.

"I just...I just want us all to take a look at these young people up here today. I look at them and I know there is still hope for our children. All is not lost for this generation," he explained as he wiped the sweat from his brow.

The congregation applauded his truth.

"This young lady right here is only seventeen-years-old. In all my years, I have never seen anyone conduct a choir the way you have today, Karma."

Karma smiled bashfully as she bowed her head in modesty.

"Where's mom and dad?"

"Right there," she whispered, pointing in their direction.

"You've done very well," he reassured them.

"Thank you," the two proud parents beamed.

"She's something special," he stressed.

Salvatore kissed Karma on the cheek again and she graciously accepted it before walking back to her seat beside Indigo.

"I thought it was necessary for us to have the youth choir sing this morning, because they are our future. They are going to lead us one day. Every time you turn around, it seems like there's nothing but bad news arising. There's hardly any good news being spread these days. I thought it was appropriate that we have our young people spread some good news through song this morning. And they did just that. Walk in the light," he thought out loud.

"Take your time, Father!" the church responded.

"That young lady right there…" he pointed at Karma. "…is the only daughter of Sergeant and Mrs. Lorenzo Walker."

The congregation spoke out and smiled at the deserving titles earned by Soleil and Lorenzo.

"*Two* great minds in the home. Mom is a restaurateur of Caribbean cuisine and real estate entrepreneur. Dad, a sergeant and special operations analyst in the United States Army. Amen. She goes to the same high school my nephew, Giovanni, attends and makes straight A's."

"Amen," the congregation replied in unison.

"And is on her way to becoming the next Florence Griffith-Joyner. No, I didn't say Marion Jones. I said Florence Griffith-Joyner. Why, because Flo Jo still holds the world records for the 100 and 200 meter sprints. Hallelujah! And our little Karma will be training for a spot on the United States Women's Track and Field team for the next Summer Olympics in Sydney, Australia. God is good."

"Yes, he is," the congregation chanted.

"Let us keep the Walker family in our prayers, especially Karma who is in the early stages of her journey of running all the way on the other side of the world this time three years from now. And Sister Soleil, who, as her mother, will be letting her daughter go for the first time in her life. We all know that it is never easy for a parent to let their child go off on their own, but the time has certainly come."

"Amen."

"If you don't know what today is, please ask the person sitting next to you. And if you do know, tell your neighbor, Today...," he instructed.

"Today...," the congregation followed.

"...is the day our Lord and Savior, Jesus Christ...," he went on.

"...is the day our Lord and Savior, Jesus Christ...," they repeated.

"...rose from the dead!" he exclaimed.

"...rose from the dead," the parishioners reiterated.

"Now, you know, I can take this subject matter anywhere I want to this morning, but I'm not going to. I'm going to take it here instead. The Lord rose from His tomb and it was Mary Magdalene who saw Him first. And what did she do after she laid her eyes on the Son of God? She ran to spread the good news," he smiled.

"Amen!" a woman yelped from the crowd.

"That's what today is about...spreading the good news. See, I know that some of you were ready to bite my head off when I started to talk about the Walker's daughter. Oh Lord, Father's talkin' about somebody's child again," he mocked as the church laughed. "I have kids. He never says anything about my kids. Juan hasn't been arrested in six months. That's good news. You're right! It is good news! But you have to tell me! I can't spread your good news if you don't tell me! How do you all really think I know so much about our little Karma's life?" he asked with raised eyebrows and wide questioning eyes.

"How?!" A couple of parishioners voiced.

"Her mother told me," he exposed as if it were a secret.

The house laughed and applauded his honesty.

"If you see me on the street, stop me. If you have a computer, e-mail me. If you have a phone, call me. I'll spread your good news. In fact, I want to take this time out to hear your good news. If you want to spread your good news, there are two microphones, one in each aisle. Step up to the mic and say your piece. We are open and willing to listen and receive you," he informed any moved members before taking his seat in the pulpit.

A young woman walking with her grandmother, dressed in her Sunday best, approached the microphone. The aged woman pressed her cane firmly into the carpet so she could stand and speak on a firm foundation.

"Good mornin' Father, congregation, my Lord. I lost my glasses this mornin' and if anyone who has a handicapper with their eyes, you know thangs appear differently. Thangs ain't as clear as they are when you have your glasses on. Well, I sat down on my bed and I asked my Lord, "Why has thou forsaken me?" I'm tryin' to go to church this mornin', but I won't be able to go 'cause I cannot see...nothin'. And the Lord said, 'I want you to see thangs for what they really are...illusions of grandeur.' You see, sometimes we become dependent on people and thangs and we forget how to survive on our own. Well, once I figured that out, I found my glasses in my pocketbook. Amen," she said, closing her piece abruptly.

"Wonderful. Sister Emma, everyone," the Father said, tickled with laughter.

The church laughed and applauded as the young woman escorted Sister Emma back to their pew.

A husky young man with freshly twisted locks stepped before the other microphone and repositioned it before he spoke.

"Good morning, everyone. I just want to say that I'm thankful for just being here today. My girl just had my son yesterday. I ain't been livin' right and it's mostly because I didn't know what my reason for livin' was, nah mean? But now I know," he confirmed and stepped back, grinning sheepishly.

"Amen!" everyone replied as Father Pacella rocked contentedly.

A woman dressed in a tight crimson red and white skirt suit approached the adjacent microphone with a little girl in tow. Her tasteless outfit quickly became a topic of discussion amongst many of the female members. The suit was terribly snug around her midsection. Her full chest overlapped the cotton spaghetti strapped top she had on beneath the jacket. Her make-up application was excessive and her copper-dyed hair was matted as she stood motionless. Brenda Haughton wrapped her arms around her daughter as she locked eyes with Lorenzo and smiled.

"I'm here today, because this is where God told me to be."

"Amen," the crowd spoke out.

"I brought my daughter here with me, because I wanted her to know who my God truly is."

The house responded again.

"She's all that I have in this world, but I needed her to know that I am not all that *she* has in this world. You see, she has a sister she's never met. A father she's never known. I think family is important and there's nothing like the bond between siblings or the love a father has for his daughter. I'm tired of lying to my child. She should know her other family. Karma is engaged in so many wonderful things and my daughter should be a part of her sister's world and everything in it as well."

The congregation gasped as Brenda nodded and smiled victoriously before walking out of the church with her daughter. The parishioners spoke among themselves, many shaking their heads in disbelief and embarrassment for Soleil. As they turned back around to face the couple, the women waited to see Soleil's reaction. She showed them nothing. She refused to. Instead, she inhaled and slowly exhaled before turning back around.

Lorenzo managed to keep his posture erect and his eyes closed tightly. Afraid of what Soleil might say or do next, he braced himself for the worse. Soleil slowly turned back to the front and cut her eyes at him from the side. Never shifting her eyes away from him, her lips tightened as Maggie squeezed her hand as a sign for her to maintain her composure. Maggie proceeded to whisper words of encouragement in her best friend's ear as Soleil fought to keep her attention on her husband. With much coaching, it gradually broke. Maggie reminded her that Karma was looking at her and she needed to appear unmoved for her daughter's sake. Soleil took her girlfriend's words into consideration and focused in on Karma. Her baby girl was crying. Soleil locked eyes with her daughter. With her fingertips, she lifted her chin as a gesture to Karma to dry her tears and hold her head high. Karma shook her head up and down in recognition and sniffled back her tears.

The Walker family entered their home in silence. Karma swiftly walked to her room, slamming her bedroom door behind her as Lorenzo removed his suit jacket and placed it on the back of one of the stools at the island. He sat down loosening his tie, then ran his hands over his distraught face. Soleil watched her husband closely as she slowly removed her hat from her head and placed it down on the island top. She then removed the hairpin from her chignon, allowing her long mane to fall. Uncertain of where to begin, she gathered her thoughts before she spoke.

"I see you don't know how to keep your bitch under control."

"Soleil, please."

"No, Lorenzo, *you please*!"

"Just calm down, honey."

"Don't tell me to calm down!"

"Look, baby, you can't afford to get yourself all worked up. Let's just discuss this in a civilized manner."

"Don't patronize me, Lorenzo." Soleil knew what Lorenzo meant by saying that, but she wasn't worried about her hibernated condition right now.

"I'm not patronizin' you, Soleil. I-"

"How did she know what church we went to?" she cut him off in mid-sentence.

"I don't know," he said, shaking his throbbing head.

"You don't know?" she asked, leaning into him.

"No. *I don't know,*" he responded sternly.

"I don't believe you. After all this time, she just pops up unannounced at our church and you know nothing about it?! Do you think I'm stupid?! And how dare she come into *my* house of worship and call *my* child out!" Soleil began to pace the floor.

"Karma's my child too, Soleil." Lorenzo followed his wife's unpredictable movement with his eyes. Anxiety grew along his face.

"Was she yours when you were fucking that bitch in your car? No, I didn't think so. The thought must have slipped your mind. Fuck you! That's my child! You have your daughter!" Lorenzo's calm nature was setting Soleil off. He was far from handling the situation with nonchalance, but his natural laid-back demeanor was making her look like a raging lunatic.

"Watch what you say, alright?" he warned her. "Now, I understand that you're upset-"

"What could you possibly understand, Lorenzo? You couldn't fathom how I'm feeling right now! The woman who fucked my husband and claims to have had his child disrespected me in the place where I go to find peace of mind and the strength I need to forgive you for sticking your dick in something like that! You know, I looked at that child today and I...I saw you. I forgot what hatred felt like; it's been so long. But I remember now." Soleil shook her head in confirmation.

"I can't take back what I've done!" Lorenzo's nostrils flared.

"Fuck you!" she spat.

Lorenzo jumped off the stool abruptly, causing it to fall violently back onto the hard-woodened floor.

"No, fuck this! You're goin' to listen to what the fuck I got to say, goddamnit! I never meant to hurt you! I never meant to hurt Karma!"

"And I never meant to stay, b-b-but I did!"

Soleil heard how that word came out of her mouth. Lorenzo did as well. This was the "worked up" he had been trying to avoid. But it was too late now. Soleil was far too deep in her rage to turn back or away from her emotions and the speech impediment that punished her throughout her childhood and adolescent years.

"You didn't have to s-s-sleep with her, b-b-but you did! You didn't stop yourself! Y-y-you didn't stop her! What I had w-w-wasn't good enough for you?! Is that wh-wh-what it was?! N-n-not only d-d-did you put your life on the l-l-line when you fucked that bitch, but you p-p-put mine right on the line with it! You didn't know what sh-sh-she had! She could have infected you w-w-with HIV, Lorenzo! You could have b-b-brought that shit h-h-home to me! You were thinking with the w-w-wrong head and it could have killed us b-b-both."

It seemed like it had taken Soleil forever just to say what Lorenzo already knew. The couple had this same argument nine years ago after Lorenzo returned home from doing a stint in Panama and confessing his infidelity to his wife.

Soleil was out of breath. Not only was she fighting her husband, but she was fighting this malfunction in her brain that was fighting back just as hard to break her thoughts like it was breaking her words.

Defeated, Lorenzo asked, "What do you want me to say?"

"I d-d-don't want you to s-s-say anything. I don't care about w-w-what you have to s-s-say." She breathed in deeply before continuing. This method usually worked when she needed to recompose herself and cease the stuttering.

"You w-w-whisper in my ear at night and I hear nothing *but* sweet *nothings*." The technique worked. Relieved by the functioning stratcgy, she stepped back and pressed her back against the counter next to the island. She held herself and shook her head in frustration as Lorenzo looked on.

"I slipped one time. One time, baby, and I've shown you in every way possible how sorry I am for breakin' your heart. Three weeks of apologies. I love you. Can't you see that? I love you." Lorenzo walked towards Soleil and reached for her, but she pulled away from him and walked around the island.

"I've given myself to you more than I probably should have over these last couple of weeks. I've beaten myself up for giving into you time and time again. *Berating* myself for not resisting you.

That...," she pointed to his crotch. "...between your legs is what bonds us. That and this ring are what consecrates this marriage and you broke that when you gave that bitch what belonged to me. When we lay together, the thought of you and her is never too far back in my mind. As much as it pains me, I always wonder if you kissed her the same way you kiss me. If you touched her the same way you touch me. Did you take your time entering her like you take your time entering me? What did your eyes say to hers when they finally met? I know it happened nine years ago, but it feels like you just told me only nine minutes ago."

Lorenzo closed his eyes and shook his head. He had nothing to come back with. Brenda meant nothing to him—then or now. It had been a mistake. She had taken advantage of him at his most vulnerable, and then trapped him with this child who may or may not be his.

"I'm not going to put myself through this anymore, Lorenzo. She's put herself back in the picture and...there's only room for one of us."

Lorenzo looked over at his wife and shook his head at the next remark she had not yet uttered.

"Don't say what I think you're goin' to say."

He knew what was coming, but he didn't want to hear it. He didn't want to believe she was going to say it.

"I'd appreciate it if you would get your things and find yourself somewhere else to stay tonight."

Soleil walked back around the island and retrieved her hat and hairpin. She proceeded to walk out of the kitchen until Lorenzo strode over and grabbed her by her arms.

"Soleil, baby, don't do this. Don't do this! I love you."

"It's not enough."

"Honest to God, baby, I didn't know. Don't leave me now. I need you."

Lorenzo's desperate grip became tighter and Soleil struggled to free herself from him.

"It doesn't matter. It's over."

"You don't mean that. It's not over."

Soleil began to fight back tears. She never wanted her marriage to end like this. She never wanted her marriage to end at all. She always had in her mind that she and Lorenzo would grow old together…'til death do they part. But it was not to be. Not after this. She couldn't even look him in the eyes.

"Lorenzo, please don't make this anymore difficult than it already is."

"Look at me! Look at me and tell me you want to throw twenty-four years away! Twenty-four years, Soleil!"

"Let go of me."

"No! Tell me! Twenty-four years, baby. I'm the man I am because of *you*. Can't you see that?"

Lorenzo searched Soleil's face for an answer. She finally found his eyes.

"If that's true, then, I've done an awfully poor job."

She pried his hands from her arms and began to walk out of the room. Lorenzo managed to grab hold of her right arm, swinging her back around. As swiftly as she swung back into her husband, Soleil jerked her hand from his grasp and slapped him viciously across the face with it. Lorenzo never saw the blow coming. And without missing a beat she said, "Expect your divorce papers in the mail." With those final words, she exited.

Fury consumed Lorenzo. He scoured the room to find something to throw or strike, but couldn't put his hands on anything. So he began to pace the floor until his eyes set on a wall nearby. And in the blink of an eye, Lorenzo leaped to the painted structure and punched it mercilessly until a massive hole evolved.

Karma listened to her parents' fight from her bedroom. She didn't know her mother had a speech impediment. *How could someone so beautiful be so broken?* She'd gone straight to her room, shut the door, and collapsed on her bed in heavy sobs. Her mother had, in few words, instructed her to stay collected in public, but she fell apart once they all got home. The way their voices carried throughout the house, rising and falling, upset her so. Karma had never heard her mother swear in English, not even when her grandfather was alive. Her uncle Victor would scold and belittle her sometimes in her presence, but Soleil had always remained calm. She'd seemed unfazed by his words. Karma guessed her mother acquired deaf ears over the years. She had no voice in her uncle Victor's life. He was the big brother and she was the little sister-the end.

So many years her mother had gone unheard. But this Easter, she found her voice and her father heard it loud and clear. The last thing Karma heard was the slamming of the front door. Her father was gone. There was an eternity of silence after that.

Karma laid on her stomach with her head buried in her tear stained pillow. Music from Queen Latifah's "Just Another Day" video played softly in the background. A gentle knock on the door sounded, disrupting her moment of grief.

"Go away."

"Karma, baby, it's Mommy. Let me in."

Karma lifted her head from the pillow and looked towards the door. She rose from the bed and unlocked it. Soleil entered as Karma walked back to her resting area, throwing herself down. Soleil closed the door behind her and sat down beside her daughter. She began to rub her back for comfort.

"I made dinner."

"I'm not hungry," Karma said with her face turned away from her mother.

Soleil's hand travelled from her daughter's back to her hair. She ran her fingers through her luxurious mane.

"You have to eat something, *mi amor*. You haven't eaten or been out of your room since this afternoon."

"I'm not hungry."

"Look at me, Karma." Soleil stopped fiddling with her daughter's hair.

Karma hesitantly lifted her head and turned to face her mother. Soleil's eyes were bloodshot and puffy. She knew her mother had been crying and she'd cried hard for the man she'd given her life to. There had only been one time before this occurrence that Karma had seen her mother's eyes so dimly lit.

She was eight-years-old and returned home from accompanying

Indigo to ballet class. When Karma ran inside the house, she found her mother standing at the kitchen sink holding on to it for dear life, her head bowed. Soleil had not heard the little girl calling for her when she entered the home. She had been startled, nonetheless, when Karma ran up to her and threw her arms around her waist. Instinctively, she began to wipe her wet eyes and face in an attempt to hide her evident pain, but Karma had already sensed a problem. When she asked her mother what was wrong, Soleil simply said, "Nothing, *mi amor*." Karma, not believing a word her mother uttered, asked her if she was sure. With a small, pitiful smile, Soleil swore that she was fine.

Later that night, Karma was awakened by the sound of her mother crying. She rose from her bed and followed the sound of the woman's broken heart. And when she found her, she was balled up in a fetal position in the middle of her bed. Karma, who had never seen her mother cry before, immediately became alarmed. She darted from the master bedroom door and called for her father while running through the house in search of him, but he was nowhere to be found. When she took a breath to call for him again, she heard her mother's voice flowing from her little mouth instead. It took a moment for Karma to realize that her mother was calling for her from the bedroom.

Again, she ran back, following the woman's cry.

When she returned to the room, Soleil was sitting on the edge of the bed; her feet nestled in the plush carpet, her legs slightly open. Her thick, black mane was beautifully wild with curls. And again, she was holding on to something-the mattress this time, beneath her, to keep her upright. It appeared as if she was trying to push against the weight of the cross she was bearing on her back. And she was visibly losing the battle.

"Come, *mi amor*," she said to her in a trembling whisper.

Karma obeyed. She trotted over to the woman who gave her life and settled between her legs.

"Mommy, what's wrong? Where's Daddy?" she asked on the verge of tears.

Soleil, noticing the panic in her child's tone, sniffled back a fresh set of tears that were brimming in her eyes before carefully answering her question.

"Daddy's gone to live somewhere else for a little while," she explained.

"Whyyy?" Karma asked in a small voice, her lips pouted.

"Because he and I aren't getting along right now," her mother replied regrettably.

"Why not, Mommy? Did Daddy do something wrong?" Karma asked with slightly furrowed eyebrows.

Soleil gazed into her baby girl's innocent blue, glossed eyes and sighed. She never thought she would ever have to share a moment like this with her child. Never did she think she would have to tell her little girl that her father hurt her mommy in such a way that it would most likely change her perception of men once she reached womanhood.

"Daddy hurt me," her mother managed to say before breaking down in heavy sobs.

Confused by not seeing any visible wounds, Karma went on and simply asked her, "Where?"

Soleil, in response, took her daughter's little hand into hers and placed it over her heart.

"Here," she murmured. "He hurt Mommy here."

Karma remembered watching her mother fall apart before her young eyes and not knowing what to do to stop her suffering. The first thing that came to mind was to outstretch her arms and wrap them around her mother's neck. So she did just that.

"Don't cry, Mommy," she begged with tears cascading down her flushed face. "Please don't cry. I'll be your band-aid," she offered. "God wants me to be."

From the mouths of babes. That night, Karma slept with her mother until her father returned home one year later. And for the next nineteen years of her life, she would continue to share her mother's bed as her father came and went. Serving his country would become his main priority, while her mother would become hers.

Now, here mother and daughter were again, broken without any hope of completely healing this time around.

"What happened today in church had nothing to do with you," she assured her.

"Did you know he had another daughter?"

Soleil nodded slowly. "Yes, I did. The...um...woman who you saw today phoned your father three weeks ago and told him."

"Did Aunt Maggie know?"

"Yes," she replied in a hushed tone.

Karma sucked her teeth in dismay. "How come nobody told me?"

Soleil sighed. "Because I didn't want anyone to tell you. *I* wanted to be the one...when the time was right."

"It's not fair."

"What's not fair, baby?"

"Everything! Doesn't Daddy love us? Did I do something wrong? Why does he need another daughter?" Karma began to cry again.

Soleil picked her child up in her arms and cradled her. She wiped her tear stained face with her hand.

"Listen to me. You didn't do anything wrong. You hear me? That child was not born to replace you. Your father went off and did something he had no business doing, and a child was conceived out of it. Now, we don't know if she's his yet, but once we find out the truth, your father and I will try to figure something out from there. He knows he made an unwise decision and he's paying the price for it."

"I hate 'im," Karma sniffled.

"Don't say that, baby. Don't hate your father. Don't hate him. This is why I was waiting for the right time to tell you about Mia, because I didn't want your father's doing to change the way you feel about him. I don't want your heart to grow cold like your uncles. They don't look at him the same anymore. They've lost all respect for him and there's nothing he or I can do about it. But you, my love, can continue to love him. Your father needs your love."

"Uncle Vic and Uncle Miguel are never gonna forgive Daddy." Karma was surprised her uncles hadn't killed her father after finding out what he'd done. She knew the only reason his life was spared was because of her. Her uncles adored her and did their very best to be positive male role models for her when Lorenzo was away on tour.

"One day they will…maybe. I don't know. I can only hope that they do."

"Mia…is that her name?" Karma wiped her tearing eye.

"Yes," Soleil softly replied as she rubbed Karma's head.

Karma clung on to her mother's hand and held it against her face.

"Mommy?"

Soleil looked down at Karma and frowned.

"Yes, baby?"

"Do you still love Daddy?"

Soleil stared into Karma's glossed eyes and breathed a sigh of despair.

"Yes…I do. I'll always love your father, which is why this hurts me so much. But I have to let him go. It's time."

Time. Soleil sat, legs crossed at the knees, in a small office looking at the time on her watch. She scoured the quaint room, admiring the many framed degrees, certificates, and brass awards placed around the office. A dish with peppermints sat on the physician's desk. Soleil leaned in, removed the top from the dish, and retrieved a piece of candy out of it. She placed the top back on the dish and proceeded to unwrap the peppermint. She placed it in her mouth savouring the cool taste as an older, frosted-haired African-American woman dressed in a white laboratory coat entered the room. Dr. Jenny Bridges, M.D. greeted Soleil with a smile and handshake. She walked around the desk and sat down, placing the folder with Soleil's records onto the desk. She leaned back in her chair crossing her hands over her stomach.

"Well, I'm so glad you could make the appointment this afternoon, Soleil."

"It wasn't a problem, Dr. Bridges. How are you?"

"I'm fine, just fine. I delivered a set of twins this morning."

"Really? That's something else."

"Yes, it was. First birth for both parents."

"Oh, well I'm sure it was an overwhelming experience for both of them."

"Indeed."

"She gave birth naturally or…"

"Oh, no. It was a caesarean birth. There was no way she was going to have those babies vaginally. They were big boys."

Dr. Bridges and Soleil shared a laugh.

"I'm sure."

"Enough about that. How have you been since I saw you last?"

"Well, considering the growths you found on my uterus two weeks ago, I've been doing pretty well."

Dr. Bridges raised her eyebrows and nodded. She sat up, pulled her chair closer to her desk, and locked eyes with Soleil.

"That's good…very good." She cleared her throat. "Well, now has come the time to talk about those growths I found on your uterus two weeks ago. I told you they could be anything from fibroids to benign tumors. And the abdominal swelling that you have been experiencing could be a possible result of the growths."

"That's correct."

"Well, the pelvic examination and CAT scan I gave you, both confirmed, that you indeed have tumors. The bloating you have is from metastasis, which is a build-up of fluid in the abdomen, which causes swelling. The type of tumors you have are epithelial tumors. Now these tumors have subtypes ranging from serous, mucinous, endometrioid, and cell tumors. You have the serous subtype. They account for forty percent of common epithelial tumors and are the most widespread form of ovarian cancer."

Dr. Bridges' words knocked the breath out of Soleil. She remained still. Her eyes and only her eyes reacted to the woman's heart-wrenching news.

"Ovarian Cancer. I h-h-have ovarian cancer?" The stuttering was back.

"Yes," Dr. Bridges said quietly.

Soleil looked away, then back at the concerned woman.

"Are they benign or…?"

"They're malignant."

Soleil cleared her throat and spoke, "H-h-how long have I h-h-had them? I mean, uh, the s-s-swelling hasn't occurred until r-r-recently."

"Well, you've had it long enough for my colleagues and I to see that you're in stage two of your cancer."

Soleil rubbed the space between her eyes.

"The second s-s-stage?"

"Yes."

Soleil breathed deep. This stuttering business was wearing on her. She wanted to concentrate on the situation at hand. She had to. She inhaled, then exhaled.

"Well, how many stages are there?"

"Three. Stage three is the most advanced phase of this cancer. The cancer has spread to more than one organ in this stage, but the tumors that you have only exist on your uterus."

"My mother died of ovarian cancer. Seventeen years ago."

Not only had Soleil inherited her mother's insecurity, but she'd inherited her cancer as well. She'd prayed for her mother's rotten soul when she passed, but she knew for sure, now, Ava was not resting in peace. She was very much so alive and kicking within the *cancer*. The monster was still with her.

"Well, I'm sorry for your loss. I, too, lost my mother to cancer. Look, I can't diagnose your life expectancy, Soleil. Not now. But I can treat you and hope that the treatment is successful."

"What has to be done?"

"The first form of treatment for epithelial cancer is surgery, including a total hysterectomy. Then after surgery, follow-up therapy will be necessary."

"Chemotherapy?"

"Chemotherapy, yes. By itself or chemotherapy with radiation treatment depending on your condition after surgery."

Soleil bit down into the dissolving peppermint.

"How soon will I have to have surgery?"

"I'd like to pencil you in for this Friday. We can't put this off any longer, Soleil. The sooner we treat this, the lesser the risk of the cancer spreading."

Soleil sat back and bit her bottom lip. She shook her head in disconcert. All she could think about was Karma. Her daughter was grown, yes, but she was still a child in her eyes. *Her* child. Every child needed its mother, especially little girls.

Leaving Karma here in this world alone wasn't an option.

"How am I going to tell my daughter?" she asked herself in a whisper.

"Speak to your husband first and then proceed from there. It may be best, for the both of you, to tell your daughter together. Relieve some of the anxiety."

"I suppose."

"It's never easy for physicians to tell their patients bad news. It makes our jobs far more difficult," Dr. Bridges admitted sorrowfully.

"I'm sure." Soleil allowed a warm smile to escape. Dr. Bridges returned the favor.

"I can't tell you not to be afraid, Soleil." She leaned forward and reached for Soleil's hand. Soleil placed her hand in the doctor's. "But I will tell you that you're not alone. We're going to get through this. We're going to fight it together."

Soleil walked into her dimly lit home through the kitchen. She placed her keys and pocketbook on the counter near the door. She could hear Lorenzo's muffled laughter resonating from his study in the distance. Even though she had asked him to leave days ago, he stayed anyway and slept in the guest room downstairs in the basement. Their paths never crossed.

Hearing his laughter, Soleil figured he was watching a *Sanford and Son* rerun.

A small stack of mail was sitting on the island top. She retrieved the mail and walked over to the den, which shared space with the kitchen and dining area. Soleil eased down on to the couch and leaned back. She struggled to keep her heavy eyes open as she sorted through the mail. Not seeing anything but bills, she flung the mail onto the coffee table before her. The weary queen decided to take her high heels off her worn feet, allowing the shoes to slide aimlessly along the floor. She sat motionless listening to her husband's joyous amusement. Knowing he was trying to enjoy himself, trying to find a little piece of happiness left over in his life brought a smile to Soleil's face. She wanted to hate Lorenzo, but she couldn't. She just hated the mistake he'd made. Her smile left as quickly as it had come. Lorenzo's life was about to take another turn for the worse and he had no idea. Soleil laid her head down to sleep. Before she knew it, the tears came and hushed her into a deep slumber.

Lorenzo walked into the den with caution. He spotted Soleil lying fast asleep on her side on the couch. He neared his stunning wife with quiet, steady footsteps. He gathered his thoughts as he sat down beside her on the edge of the sofa. He proceeded to rub her face with the back of his hand. Soleil slowly opened her eyes from the touch. Once she focused her eyes on the figure before her, she slapped his hand away.

"What are you doing?"

"I've been callin' you all day. You haven't returned any of my calls."

"So what?" she responded, wiping her eyes into focus.

"What do you mean, *so what*? We need to talk," Lorenzo stressed.

Soleil sat up slowly.

"We've done enough talking. I don't want to talk to you anymore. What part of that do you not understand?"

"I understand it perfectly," Lorenzo spat.

"Good. Then leave me alone," Soleil said with an upturned lip.

"You're avoidin' me," he acknowledged.

"Call it what you like."

Lorenzo looked at Soleil in amazement. He never saw this side of her before. She was distant. She was cold. She was her mother incarnate.

"You're unbelievable, you know that?"

"That's what they say." Soleil smiled smugly.

"Save the sarcasm, will you?"

"You came to me. If you don't like my attitude, you can leave. No one asked you to come in here, Lorenzo." Soleil ran her fingers through her loose mane.

"No, no. You're right. You are absolutely right. I'm sorry."

"I don't want or need anymore of your sorries," Soleil fired back.

Lorenzo balled his hands into fists. Soleil was testing his patience. This act she was putting on was too much for him to handle. He had no control over the situation.

"I want us to work through this. We've been through worse. Grant it, most of the stress brought upon this family has been from my doin'. I know that. I will take the blame for it, but I don't think a divorce is the solution to our problems, Soleil."

Soleil crossed her arms at her chest

"Really? I think it is. It's a solution to *my* problems. What you fail to realize, Lorenzo, is that *you* are my problem. *You* brought that woman into my life. My life was yours and vice versa."

"You won't have to worry about seein' her anymore. I've got that under control," he assured her.

"It doesn't matter whether I see her again or not, she still exists. That child still exists, Lorenzo. Look, I can't worry about you anymore. I've devoted my life to being a good wife to you and a committed mother to our child. But I just, I can't give you anymore than what I already have. If I continue to worry myself about us, a union that doesn't exist anymore, in *my* life, it's going to kill me. My main concerns are myself and our daughter."

"I'm not goin' to sign those papers," he stressed.

"I know you're not," she said wearily.

"And since we're talkin' about papers, paperwork, and all that, how was your doctor's appointment today?"

Soleil's eyes widened with confusion.

"How did you know I went to the doctor's?"

"Maggie called here about five minutes ago askin' me about your appointment, because she couldn't reach you on your cell."

"That damn Marguerite, I swear. The next time I see her, I'm going to stick a *platano* in her mouth."

Soleil nestled uneasily back into one of the couch's pillows. She felt Lorenzo's eyes on her. He wasn't smiling nor was he laughing at her joke. "She told me about the lumps they found in you, Soleil."

Soleil averted her eyes.

"She did?"

"Yeah, she did. How you've known about these damn things for two weeks now and haven't said a word about 'em. Why didn't you tell me?"

Soleil sighed.

"I didn't think there was any reason to. I didn't want you to get yourself all worked up over nothing."

"Well, I'll tell you. It's too damn late for that."

Lorenzo was serious and Soleil knew it. She could see the lines on his forehead beginning to appear. They always left him scarred from worry.

"I know. I'm sorry."

"What did the doctor say?"

Soleil sat up gingerly and took Lorenzo's hand into hers. She looked into his eyes and forced a smile. She began to pat it and cringe at the news she was about to deliver.

"Well...she told me...that the tumors I have on my uterus are malignant."

"Uteran Cancer?"

"Ovarian Cancer," she whispered.

Soleil squeezed Lorenzo's hand as he looked away and cleared his throat. He needed something to focus on in that room other than his wife. If he looked back at her, she was sure to see the fear in his eyes.

"She suggested that we tell Karma together," Soleil said as she looked into her husband's pain stricken face.

"What are they goin' to do for you? I mean, uh, what can be done?" he asked with averted eyes.

"I'm going to have a hysterectomy done this Friday and most likely, chemotherapy treatment afterwards."

Lorenzo's eyes snapped back towards Soleil. Chemotherapy caused chronic nausea. It brought about hair and weight loss. It was the reaper of death.

"If they remove your uterus with the tumors on it, what do you need the chemotherapy for?"

"She wants to make sure the cancer doesn't spread."

"Aw, naw. Naw, naw, naw."

Lorenzo completely lost his composure and broke down into an uncontrollable crying fit. He buried his head in his hands as Soleil turned away to find the strength within to carry this man. Never expecting her husband to react in such a way, she, herself, tried to refrain from crying, but failed from doing so. Lorenzo grabbed his wife around her waist. And like a frightened child, he helplessly buried his head in her lap. Soleil received him hesitantly before taking him into her arms and holding him close. She rocked her first love from side-to-side until their tears fell no more.

Chapter 6

F amily and friends gathered at the Alonso-Cruz family restaurant for Soleil's fifty-second birthday celebration. Guests danced, laughed, and talked over Elvis Crespo's *Suavamente* playing loudly over the wall speakers. A young handsome Latino disc jockey stood behind his laptop in the DJ booth mounted over the crowd below, while flirting with Karma as she sipped on an apple martini. The lower level of the restaurant was designed specifically for occasions like this one. The wooden dance floor was spacious and set before one huge television comprised of sixteen small television monitors. Wild colors and shapes danced on them, while the music blared throughout the crowded room. Marble pillars were placed meticulously around the room to support the upper level of the building and were often used as resting areas for many to catch their breath. Tonight, the hall was decorated with Soleil's favorite color pink, complimented by white and silver balloons, pink and white streamers, and pink and silver confetti.

A female and male bartender moved back and forth behind a large bar in the back of the room taking and placing orders. Soleil spun and twirled in the middle of the dance floor with Maggie, whose neatly dreaded hair sat high on her head and was wrapped with a colorful silk scarf. Soleil's sister-in-law was blacker than a thousand midnights and had teeth as white as an elephant's ivory tusk. Maggie was another beauty within her own right. She, too, had aged gracefully, glowing under the dancing lights. Soleil's older brothers, Victor and Miguel, who favored her so and whose figures towered over her and Maggie, cut in and took each woman by the waist. Miguel, the younger and heavier of the men, snatched Soleil from Maggie's grasp, allowing his brother to pull his lovely wife close. They all fell into step with each other and tore the dance floor up.

"Think you can keep up?!" Miguel asked his sister in a mocking tone.

"Try me, old man!" Soleil said, accepting the challenge.

As soon as Miguel prepared to bust a move, the salsa music made a transition into a mix of Soca and Calipso. Without missing a beat from the sudden music change, Miguel retrieved a handkerchief from his pants pocket and proceeded to wave it around in the air. Many of the other men and women followed suit and provocatively began to wind and grind their hips against one another.

Karma walked down the steel stairway leading down into the room in search of her mother. Embarrassed and feeling guilty for the way she acted earlier in the day, she scoured the room in desperate need to speak to her. As her eyes looked over the crowd, she spotted her mother fanning herself and walking off the dance floor towards the bar with Maggie in tow. Karma stepped into the sea of people and began to walk in the direction of her mother, but was grabbed at her wrists by her uncles. Karma did her best trying to explain to them that she didn't want to dance, but they both insisted she show the other young women in the room out. Karma knew her uncles were drunk and she kind of enjoyed their loud and unruly ways at the family functions. They were the life of the party. Karma knew her mother wasn't far from hindsight, so she didn't want to appear as if she was really having a good time if the birthday girl spotted her from the bar. But that was going to be hard, because her uncles were acting a damn fool.

Soleil and Maggie settled at the bar. Maggie took a handful of napkins out of a basket and wiped her face and chest off with them. She passed some over to Soleil, who wiped herself down as well. As Soleil lifted her hand to her face, Maggie noticed the sparkling diamond bracelet on her wrist.

"Soleil! Where in de hell did you get dat gorgeous bracelet from?!" she asked excitedly in her heavy St. Kittian accent.

Soleil smiled proudly and replied, "Karma got it for me! Isn't it beautiful?!"

Maggie took Soleil's wrist in her hand and studied the piece of jewelry in awe.

"It is absolutely gorgeous!" she screeched as she turned the bracelet with her index finger and thumb.

"And look!" Soleil screamed as she placed her hair behind ear. "She got me these too!"

Maggie's mouth fell open. She tried to catch herself, but it was too late. The jewels were absolutely breathtaking. Her niece definitely had exceptional taste. She placed her ageless hand on her chest.

"Oh me Gawd! You got a day at da spa, a diamond bracelet wit' earrings to match, a cruise, and a party?! You won dis round, gal! Hands down!"

Maggie and Soleil burst out into laughter.

"I told her it was too much!" Soleil expressed sincerely.

"Too much?! Sol, please. If dere's anyone who deserves all dat you got today, it's you. Shit, me can't wait to see what me goin' to get on me birfday next mont'."

Soleil shook her head and laughed again. Maggie was a piece of work.

"You're crazy."

Maggie sucked her teeth and replied, "Tell I someting me don't know."

Miguel and Victor's fancy drunken footwork amidst the heavy crowd on the floor captured Maggie's attention.

"Will you look at dose two fools out dere? Karma can't get away from dem."

Soleil followed her girlfriend's eyes. Although, she and Karma had that terrible fight earlier in the day, Soleil put it behind her. Everything Karma said was true. She had a right to be angry and she had a right to be hurt. Soleil was happy to see her baby out on the dance floor enjoying herself. Karma was getting down. Victor and Miguel could hardly keep up with her.

"Look at my poor baby. Now, that's a sad sight to see."

"You can say dat again. Dey need to get deir old asses off da floor. Look at dem tryin' to keep up wit' dose young people. And look at Karma. Look! Look!" Maggie yelped as she pointed at her sweat-drenched niece.

"Go Karma! Go!" she cheered her on. "Rude bois should be ashamed of demselves," she stated as she shook her head and giggled to herself.

"I don't know what happened. They could really get down back in the day." Soleil cringed at the sight before her.

"Dey got old is what happened. And look at Victor. Him look like him 'bout to have a damn heart attack. Papa just don't have it like him used to."

"Thanks to you," Soleil hinted.

"Excuse I?" Maggie asked with an attitude.

"You heard me. You know you've worn my poor brother out with your hot self. Look at 'im. Look at that limp he's got now. Only a fast piece of tail like you could give a fool a bend in his leg like that," Soleil teased.

"Post-menopause is a beautiful ting," Maggie bragged.

"That it is," Soleil beamed.

The girlfriends high-fived each other.

"Did Lorenzo call you today?"

"Yes, he did," Soleil blushed.

Maggie stepped back and folded her arms at her chest. She raised her eyebrows and prepared herself for the story of the evening.

"Ohhh, okay. And what did G.I. Negro Joe have to say?"

"He's officially retired," Soleil said calmly with a broad smile.

KARMA

Maggie's eyes widened. She knew Soleil was still in love with Lorenzo and vice versa, but the two had been talking about a possible reconciliation for years. It never came to pass...until tonight.

"Well, it's about damn time. Him been in de service since him was eighteen-years-old," she said disgustingly.

"I know," Soleil agreed in dismay.

"So, does dis mean you two are…?"

"Yes, it does," Soleil replied with a seductive smirk.

Maggie grunted in astonishment.

"Well, excuse I. Me sure hope him told his whore for de mont'."

Soleil chuckled at her friend's unadulterated humor.

"Now, you know he did, Mag."

"And what did miss-missy have to say?" Maggie pursed her lips in query.

"Well, he said she was a little upset about it, but got over it pretty quickly. She told him she knew this day was coming eventually. And that was it."

"Well, me sure hope Jimmy takes de news as well as ol' gal did," Maggie insinuated. She and Soleil knew he wasn't going to. He was going to be mad as hell and Maggie could only wonder how her sister-in-law was going to be able to handle his temper this time around.

Soleil waved her hand dismissively at her concerned friend.

"He knew what the deal was from the door," Soleil stated matter-of-factly. Jimmy knew Soleil was still married to Lorenzo when he met her. Soleil made that very clear when the two began dating. He also knew how much Lorenzo loved being a soldier in the Devil's army, so he wasn't worried about losing Soleil to him. She told him how there was no room in his life for her and Jimmy made sure Soleil would never feel the same way with him. He took pride in having her on his arm. And with Soleil in his life, his mindset changed. He'd forced himself to become "the man," the *only* man" in her life. Even though the two were still married, by law, he just knew it was going to end once he placed that ring on her finger that morning. Lorenzo was her beginning, and he was her end.

Maggie fixed her eyes on the crowd in search of Soleil's unforeseen boyfriend. "Where is de monkey anyway?"

Soleil sighed.

"Late as usual."

Maggie grunted again.

"You going to tell he tonight?"

"After the party."

Maggie nodded her head in agreement.

"Alright, now. You make sure you give de monkey one more good taste of de pum-pum before you turn he loose, gal."

Soleil bawled over with laughter. Maggie always found a way to drag her genitalia into their conversations.

All the while, Karma managed to break away from her uncles and traveled over to the bar. Soleil noticed the stress on her daughter's face, but tried her hardest not to show her concern. Maggie was unaware of the verbal disagreement she and Karma had that morning and Soleil didn't want to relive it by telling her what happened. Maggie would have berated Karma for disrespecting her mother the way she did in front of everyone and Soleil didn't want her party to be spoiled. She was going to handle Karma in her own way.

"Me know you're not tired, child!" Maggie exclaimed.

"Yes, I am, *Tia*. You can have Uncle Vic. I can't keep up wit' 'im," Karma responded exhaustingly.

"It's because you got dose damn heels on! Gal need to take dem off so you can mooove! Watch me now!" Maggie began to gyrate her wide hips explicitly to the music.

Karma smiled and laughed at the seriousness in her aunt's face. From the corner of her eye, she could see her uncle Victor watching his wife closely. There was lust in his eyes. Karma shook her head and continued to study her aunt's provocative moves.

"You got that, *Tia*."

Maggie winked at her niece before she caught the sight of her own daughter across the room. Indigo was dressed in her police uniform. She, with a wrapped gift in hand, stood beside a young, tall, dark-skinned man donning a police uniform as well. He ran his masculine hand over his closely cut Caesar as he scoured the room.

It didn't take long for his eyes to fall upon Karma. Indigo noticed her partner's entranced state and followed his gaze. She smiled at the sight he was mesmerized by. Her plan was in full effect. Unfortunately, the duo's focus was quickly broken by Maggie's abrupt approach. Indigo made a mental note to keep the conversation with her mother short, so she could execute the rest of her plan of introducing her partner to her beloved *single* cousin. Indigo introduced her ace to Maggie.

Officer Money Parks did his best to dip in and out of the ladies' conversation. He didn't want to appear rude or disinterested, but Karma's beauty had simply taken his breath away. He had to find out who she was. He was hoping she would look in his direction, so he could flash her with his thousand-watt smile, but Karma hadn't even noticed her cousin and her partner's arrival. She was too busy keeping her eyes cast towards the floor. Karma struggled to find the words to say to her mother and was succeeding at it. Soleil thought about how pitiful her one and only looked standing before her. It almost broke her heart to see Karma at loss for words. She knew her little girl was genuinely sorry and she didn't want her to put herself through anymore torture.

"Look at me, Karma," Soleil said sweetly.

Karma slowly lifted her head and met her mother's eyes. She rubbed her forehead nervously.

"I forgive you, baby," she continued with a sincere grin.

"Ma, I'm so sorry. I-"

Soleil held her index finger to Karma's lips.

"Mmm-Mmm. You don't have to say another word. I know you meant well. I'm not angry."

"You're not?" Karma asked in hesitation.

"No. I thought about what you said and you were right. You've been right for the past four years. All of you have. I was just trying to make Jimmy and I something that we weren't…better." She sighed heavily. "And I see, now, that's not going to happen any time soon." She shook her head. "It never will." She forced a smile and pinched Karma's cleft chin. "I love you, baby. You are my reason for living. My *only* reason for living. Don't you ever forget it."

KARMA

"I won't, Ma. I love you more," Karma professed through silent tears.

"Come here," Soleil instructed kindly.

Soleil pulled Karma into her close and hugged her with all of her might.

Karma returned the gesture with just as much need and power. She laid her head on her mother's shoulder the way she used to as a little girl. Then, she closed her eyes. Karma wanted to hold on to her mother forever. She could care less who saw her. Let them look. She truly believed deep down in her heart that it didn't matter how old she was, she was always going to need and want her mother. Every little girl needed their mother, whether at seven or twenty-seven.

"This is a straight up Kodak moment," Indigo teased, as she walked up on her aunt and cousin.

Soleil and Karma embraced in a kiss before parting, then turned their attention to Indigo. They both took turns in showering her with hugs and kisses. Indigo handed her gift over to Soleil as Karma and Money's eyes locked. All kind of thoughts began to run through Karma's mind. *When did Indigo get a new partner? And why didn't she tell her about him?* Before Karma could find any more reasons to get upset with her cousin, she gave Mister 5-0 a much-deserved once-over. Karma's eyes started at his huge feet, crept up his muscular legs, fell upon his flat stomach, outlined his broad chest, crawled up to his thick neck, and ended at his strong face.

Money's lips parted into a broad, blindingly white smile. Karma couldn't believe the specimen of a man that was standing only inches away from her. Needless to say, she was taken aback by his handsomeness. She never saw a man with such beautiful teeth. He had to have all thirty-two of them. His skin was as dark and smooth as milk chocolate. His lips were full and moist, waiting to be kissed. Karma had to catch herself from gawking at him any longer. She was sure her eyes were popping out of her head. She was certain she was salivating at the mouth and was convinced her panties were dripping wet. As hard as it was, Karma pulled her eyes away from Money and tried to refocus them on her mother. But Money wanted those beautiful turquoise-blue eyes back on him. He extended his hand out for her to shake.

"How you doin' this evening? I'm Money."

Karma stared back at Money in query while receiving his hand. *Had she heard him correctly?*

"Money? That's your real name?"

Money laughed lightly at her bluntness.

"Yeah. It's, uh, kind of a long story. My mother named me, but what about you? What's your name?"

Indigo jumped in before Karma could reply.

"Oh, Money, this is my cousin Karma."

Karma cut her eyes at Indigo. Indigo smiled mischievously in return.

"It's nice to meet you, Karma. That's a beautiful name for a beautiful woman."

Money smiled again showing off his pearly whites. Karma's face flushed with embarrassment. It wasn't the first time a man, or a fine man for that matter, called her beautiful. She'd heard it all of her life, but it was just something about Money that made her want to go crawl under a rock and hide. Maybe she was embarrassed because her mother was standing right there reading her like an open book. Yeah, that was it. It was only a matter of time before Soleil would bring Money's name up in future conversation. Karma twinged at the thought.

"Thank you. It's nice to meet you as well…Money," she sputtered still in disbelief at Indigo's behavior and Money's name.

"And this is my aunt Soleil. This is the one I was telling you about on the way over." Indigo introduced her aunt with an outstretched arm.

Money extended his hand again. Soleil received it without hesitation.

"It's nice to meet you as well, ma'am. And Happy Birthday. You don't look a day over thirty," he added before flashing his gorgeous smile.

Soleil turned red from blushing so hard.

"Well, thank you, honey. That's very sweet of you. I can't even remember the last time I received such a compliment."

"Well, if you don't mind me saying so, Mrs…" Money began.

"Walker. Mrs. Walker," Soleil insisted.

"Mrs. Walker. It won't be the last. Not as long as I'm around. And I will be around," he assured her confidently.

Karma rolled her eyes and sucked her teeth loud enough for them all to hear. She knew that last comment was indirectly made towards her. *Who said she wanted him around after tonight?* He didn't know her and she certainly didn't know him. Karma knew he was too good to be true. The nigga was conceited. She was turned off immediately. Indigo nudged Karma's arm as a warning to keep her from making any further offensive sounds. Karma crossed her arms at her chest and watched her mother melt in the palm of Money's hand.

"Well…I…" Soleil managed to say before seeing Jimmy emerge from the crowd, walking towards her. His steps were unsteady and he was sweating profusely.

"Hey, baby," he slurred as he kissed Soleil sloppily on the neck. He was drunk. She knew he was drunk. She could smell the whiskey on his breath and so could Karma. Party over.

"Hey…Jimmy," Soleil replied timidly.

Karma, Indigo, and Money sensed Soleil's discomfort, but said nothing. Indigo felt the heat rising in her cousin's body. Karma was fuming. It was only a matter of time before she went off on Jimmy for coming to her mother's birthday party pissy drunk. Indigo had to do something. She nudged Karma in the arm again.

"Don't say anything," she mouthed to her.

Karma looked over at her cousin from the corner of her eye and shook her head in disapproval. She then slowly turned her attention back to Jimmy and her mother.

"I'm sorry I'm late. Me and da boys got caught up in da game and shit. I lost track of da time," he admitted.

"It's alright. Listen, you want to go home? You look tired." Soleil was doing her best to handle this embarrassing situation with the little dignity she had left. The last thing she needed was for

Jimmy to do or say something disrespectful. All hell would definitely break loose.

"But I just got here, baby love. I wanna dance wit'chu. Don't you wanna dance wit'cha man?" Jimmy began to sway side-to-side.

"No, I've danced all night, hun. My feet are killing me," she lied while patting him on the stomach. "Let's just go home. I want to talk to you about some things. We need some alone time."

"Oh, hey, you don't have to say another word." Jimmy smiled and placed a wet kiss on Soleil's cheek. He then whispered something vulgar in her ear. Soleil closed her eyes in an attempt to keep her composure.

"Okay, go wait for me in the car, babe."

"You gonna drive?"

"Yes."

"Okay, 'cause I'm fucked up." Jimmy took the keys out of his pants pocket and gave them to Soleil. He excused himself from the group and proceeded out the restaurant.

Soleil turned her attention back to Karma.

"Baby, could you do me a favor and bring my gifts over to the house after the party's over? I'll leave the light on in the den so you can put them all in there, okay?"

"But, Ma…" Karma began.

Indigo signalled her cousin with the slight lift of her brow. Her eyes begged her not to say anything to her aunt that would upset her all over again. Karma informed her over the phone, while at the spa, about the argument she and her mother had that morning. It was Indigo who stressed to Karma that her mother was entitled to love whomever she wanted. She was a grown woman whose dues had been paid years ago and she deserved not only to be happy, if Jimmy was the one who made her happy, but to receive the utmost respect, love, and support from the most important person in her life-Karma. With that said, Karma submitted to her cousin's unspoken plea.

"Okay," she said quietly.

"Alright." Soleil patted Karma's face and smiled. "Indigo, my love, thank you for the gift." The two embraced in a warm hug.

"You're welcome, Auntie Sol."

"And Officer…" she paused as she extended her hand.

"You can call me Money, Mrs. Walker," he insisted.

"…Money, it was so nice meeting you. You take good care of my niece now."

"Yes, ma'am. I will," he nodded and shook her hand gently.

"Okay, baby," she turned to Karma.

"K, Ma. Call me when you get home so I know you got there safely."

"I will, *mi amor*."

Soleil and Karma embraced in another hug and kiss.

"I love you," Karma proclaimed coyly.

"I love you more." Soleil held Karma's face in her hands for a moment and stroked her cheeks with her thumbs. She gave her a reassuring look with her eyes before excusing herself and departing from the celebration.

Karma watched her mother kiss her uncles and aunt goodbye before ascending the stairs and disappearing behind the door.

"You gotta real beautiful relationship with your mother," Money chimed in disrupting Karma's distant thoughts.

She quickly snapped out of her trance and looked up at Money.

"Huh? Oh, um, thank you."

"You're welcome." Money looked around the room for an unseen destination. "If you don't mind me asking, is there a bathroom down here?"

"No, but there's one upstairs." Karma pointed in the direction of the stairway. "Once you go out that door, go straight down the corridor and make a left at the corner. The men's bathroom is right there."

"Alright. Thank you."

Karma nodded as Money walked away and up the stairwell. Indigo wrapped her thin arm around her cousin's tiny waist and bumped her playfully in the hip.

"I think someone likes you," she teased.

"Well, I don't like him. He's too cocky." Karma turned her lip up.

"No, he's not. Okay, maybe a little, but he's charming. He's really a good guy, cuz," she said truthfully.

Karma sucked her teeth and rolled her eyes.

"Whateva. I still don't like 'im."

"You shouldn't be so hard on him, K. Give the man a chance. It's been like, what, two years since you buried Joaquin? Which means it's been two years since you had any, right?"

"Indigo," Karma said sternly.

"Well, it's true." Indigo laughed to herself.

"You can't force me to move on. I'm not ready yet."

"I don't know, K. I don't think it's that you're not ready to move on. I think you just might not have found the right person to move on with," Indigo expressed sincerely.

"And I suppose that's with Money?"

Indigo shrugged her shoulders.

"Maybe. You never know."

"Yeah, right. What kind of fuckin' name is 'Money' anyway?" Karma twisted her lips and shook her head in disgust.

Indigo giggled at her cousin's sudden snobbish disposition.

"Damn, K, why are you so tight over the man's name? It's not like he can help it. He didn't name himself."

"I just can't believe his mother would name him somethin' like that. Even Stuff's name isn't Stuff," she protested.

"It might as well be. Negro's always asking for stuff."

"Nooo. He's always askin' for *your* stuff," Karma smiled slyly. The girls pushed each other playfully.

"I know! My baby's whipped isn't he?"

"Like Kraft's," Karma cracked.

The girls burst into hysterical laughter.

KARMA

Chapter 7

K arma quietly walked into her mother's softly lit home with Money in tow; his arms filled with an overflow of bagged birthday gifts. Karma closed the door behind Money once he settled into the foyer. She threw her keys into the dish set atop the endtable, then stepped to the side and removed her heels, placing them in the corner. As closely as he was watching her, Money caught on to what Karma was doing and followed suit. He placed his shoes neatly next to hers by the door.

"Where would you like me to put these?" he asked, balancing the mountain of gifts in his folded arms.

Karma pointed to the brightly lit open room to the left of them.

"You can put them in there."

Money nodded and moved to the spacious den while Karma remained in the foyer calling Indigo on her cell phone. Money placed the bags at the base of the fireplace and took in the room's dark red painted walls and white trimmings. The black leather couch, ottoman, and love seat filled the broad space. He admired the massive entertainment center that housed a wide screen television on its center spacing and photos of the family on the surrounding shelves. Money stood in the middle of the room impressed by the tasteful contemporary décor.

"Your mother's got real nice taste," he stated to Karma as she strolled into the room with the phone to her ear.

"I'll be sure to let her know," she answered gallingly. "Where the hell is she?" she said to herself, wondering where in the world Indigo was. She just up and disappeared after they closed the doors to the restaurant.

Focused on a photograph of a young Karma in the arms of her father in uniform, Money replied, "Oh, yeah. Indigo told me to tell you that she had to go make a quick run, but she won't be gone for too long."

"Did she now?" Karma huffed as she snapped the phone shut and flung it on the couch. She scratched her forehead in uncertainty of where to begin with sorting her mother's molehill of presents. She walked over to the mass and decided to begin in the middle.

"Mm-Hmm," Money responded keeping his eyes on the picture. "Who's this?" he asked as he picked the photo up for Karma to see.

Karma looked up and responded, "That's me and my dad."

Money looked at the picture again and shook his head up and down in admiration.

"Man, your pops is a soldier? That's alright. I bet he's fought a lot of wars, huh? A real black soldier. He *is* black, right?"

"Yes," Karma replied. She was going to kill Indigo when she got a hold of her. She wasn't in the mood to play hostess to this man. He was asking too many questions that had obvious answers. Money was getting under her skin and it really wasn't his fault. Jimmy's display of drunkenness left a sour taste in her mouth and she just wanted to sort the gifts, go check on her mother, and then take it down for the evening.

"And your mom's Cuban?" he continued.

"Yeah," she replied wearily.

"Indi said she was West Indian. How does that make you two cousins?" Money asked while placing the picture back on the mantle.

"Her mother is West Indian and she also happens to be married to my uncle, Victor, my mother's older brother. So that's how it goes. St. Kittian, Cuban, it's the same difference. Indigo just summed up her whole background into one thing."

"Alright, I got'chu. That's real." Money studied the rest of the photographs next to the one he just placed back on the mantle and picked up another one that caught his eye. It was a photo of Karma looking up into the eyes of a young brown-skinned man while clutched in his arms. The stranger's eyes returned her deep gaze.

"Who's this?"

Karma looked up at Money once again and her face changed from annoyed to pained. She rose slowly and gently took the picture out of Money's hand. She ran her fingers over her deceased love's face.

"This is…" she began before taking a big silent gulp. "…This is my ex-boyfriend…my fiancé."

Now he was getting somewhere. Money wasn't sure why Karma responded the way she did, but he wanted to know. He wanted to know everything there was to know about her. And Lord knows he was trying his hardest, but she wasn't giving him much to go on. He couldn't figure her out. His first thought was to ask Indigo about her, but he decided against it and took it upon himself to be the man he knew he was and squeeze into her life someway, somehow.

"What happened to him?" Money asked caringly.

Karma looked at Money and parted her lips to speak of what became of her love, but she closed them quickly. She placed the photo back on the mantle above the fireplace and rubbed her sweaty hand up and down her thick thighs in discomfort.

"Nothin'. Nothin' happened to 'im. I'm gonna go check on my mom."

"Alright," Money said as he watched her turn away and travel up the dark stairwell. She was built. *Karma is all woman in every sense of the word and then some*, he thought to himself. Money looked at the picture of the two former lovebirds before turning his attention to the other photos of Karma set on the mantle. As he reached for a sepia-colored photograph of Soleil holding an infant Karma, a blood curdling scream bellowed from the second floor of the house. Money turned towards the stairs and yelled, "Karma?!" He ran out of the den and scurried up the dark, narrow stairway. "Karma?!" he called out to her again.

With no answer from Karma, Money glanced into the master bedroom where there were no occupants or anything to cause her to scream the way she did. But he could hear her sobbing uncontrollably and screaming at her mother in the distance. He noticed an open door to a lit room down the hallway. Money sprinted towards the room flushed with terror once he reached the threshold. The horrific scene before him caused his heart to skip a beat. His eyes settled on Karma who was kneeling beside a brutally beaten Soleil. He watched her helplessly tug at her mother's limp arm and try to wrap it around her neck.

"Mommyyy! Mommyyy! Please, get up! Please! Mommy, get up!" Karma begged as she rocked back and forth. Her plea was unrelenting.

Her sonorous cries echoed in Money's head. He couldn't look away from the fallen woman who he'd met only hours ago. Soleil lay sprawled out on her back, eyes opened and glossed over. Her satin laced nightgown was torn straight down the middle from the struggle, exposing her bruised chest and ribcage. Her face was terribly battered and bloody, almost making her unrecognizable. Her skin was ashen from all the oxygen she'd lost over the time she'd been lying there dead. By the look of her daunting appearance, Money could tell she'd suffered greatly. He also knew whoever the culprit was behind her brutal murder wanted to make sure her face got the best of his rage.

Money couldn't move. His feet felt like they were being held down by blocks of cement. It wasn't until he saw Karma desperately trying to wipe away the blood from under her mother's broken nose and busted mouth that he snapped back into reality. He retrieved his walkie-talkie from his belt and called for back-up and an ambulance. Money placed the portable intercom back on his waist and walked over to Karma cautiously. He crouched down behind her and wrapped one arm around her waist. He leaned in close and whispered in her ear.

"Come on, Karma. She's gone. Let her go."

Karma tried to push Money away and pry his arm from her waist, but he kept a firm grip on her. "No, Money! No! Get off of me! Get off!"

Money couldn't help but feel for Karma. He'd only met her mother hours ago, but what he could gather from their meeting was that she was a genuinely kind and beautiful woman who welcomed him with open arms. She was a woman who had obvious pain in her life, but had been one of the very few to have been able to smile right through it all.

Money grabbed Karma's loose arms with his free hand and secured them tightly. As he predicted, Karma began to scuffle with him.

"Don't fight me. Don't fight," he stressed as he began to back away from Soleil's corpse with Karma in his grasp. She wrestled him until he lost his balance from her wild tussling, but found herself still in his arms as he scooted along the floor towards the doorway. As Money's back touched the door frame, he unwrapped the arm he had around Karma's waist and clasped it with the arm wrapped around her arms.

Sitting between his legs with no more fight left in her, Karma finally submitted to Money's will. Her strength was no match for his. She allowed her head to fall back and rest on his shoulder as her legs squirmed weakly beneath her. Money, in return, pressed his head against Karma's and whispered strained apologies in her ear for something he hadn't even done.

"My mommyyy! He killed my mommyyy! I can't...I can't...Mommyyy!" Karma cried aloud. She felt herself beginning to fade away. The air in her lungs had become too tight. The room was starting to close in on her. Karma's wild eyes looked for an escape, but couldn't stay set long enough to find one. She couldn't breathe suddenly and began to hyperventilate.

Money held on to her even tighter and urged her to take deep breaths.

"Breathe, Karma. Breathe."

Before he knew it, he was crying with her.

Sirens echoed in the distance. A daughter's pain and a lover's gain weighed heavily in the dark hours of that early autumn mourning.

Chapter 8

Popular Newark Restaurateur is Slain

By Christopher Allen
STAR-LEDGER STAFF

Newark Police are searching for a 56-year-old man who, when found, is expected to be charged with the first-degree murder of a 52-year-old woman, who, according to authorities, was beaten to death in her home yesterday.

Diane Wolfchild-Rutledge, a spokeswoman for the Essex County Prosecutor's Office in Newark, said James Hayes of Mount Prospect Avenue was linked to the 1:27 a.m. beating of Soleil Alonso-Walker, 52, of Highland Avenue.

"She was struck repeatedly in the face and upper-torso with, what could have been a blunt object or the suspect's hands," said police Capt. Anthony Pagano. "We won't know until the autopsy report is released."

Walker was found by her daughter, Karma Alonso-Walker, 27, and Newark police officer, Money Parks, both of Newark. At the request of the victim, who had been celebrating her fifty-second birthday last night, her daughter and Parks stopped by to check on her and drop off her birthday gifts. Walker was seen leaving the party early with a heavily intoxicated Hayes.

The relationship between Walker and Hayes was said to be a romantic one. The couple had been dating for the last four years.

After police and paramedics were summoned to the crime scene, officials immediately tried to resuscitate Walker.

"It was about 1:55 a.m. when we arrived at the victim's home," said DeAndre Pryor, one of the two EMT's who worked on Walker. "She was in full cardiac arrest."

Walker was pronounced dead at the scene at 2:15 a.m.

Walker, a Newark resident for over 29-years, was the co-owner of Afro-Cubana, one of the city's most highly-regarded restaurants and the proprietor of the Highland Estates chain in Orange, Montclair, and Newark.

"She was a businesswoman," said Chad David, a tenant of Walker's. "But she was a fair businesswoman. She wasn't like every other cold-hearted landlord. She had a heart of gold."

Walker was also well-known in her community for her human-itarian work. She opened her restaurant every Sunday, Thanksgiving, and Christmas to serve the homeless. And she also collected toys, clothing, and money for the women and children of Livingston's St. Barnabas Hospital Cancer Care Center.

"We're all heart-broken," said Jasmine Young, an R.N. in the hospital's Cancer Care Unit. "She didn't deserve to die. Not like that. Our hearts go out to her daughter Karma."

Walker's daughter, who, from 1994 to 1997, ranked #1 as New Jersey's fastest high school 100, 200, and 400-meter Track and Field sprinter and #3 in the nation, was once an Olympic hopeful. Once trained under UCLA Track and Field coach, Bob Kersee, who also trained Olympic gold medalists, Jackie Joyner-Kersee and the late Florence Griffith-Joyner, Walker was bound for great-ness. But early into her training, Walker quit to be at her mother's side, who at the time, was battling ovarian cancer. She would walk away from the sport altogether months later.

"Her mother was all she had," Young said. "And she was all her mother had."

Many predicted Walker, who was nicknamed "Wonder Woman" by the late Florence Griffith-Joyner, would have been the first high school sprinter in the Garden State's history to make the US Women's Track and Field team.

KARMA

The faint, barely legible ghost text visible at the top of the page reads approximately:

They're just not that into you. Maybe
you were too nice, which was her thing.
Maybe it was cold. You must've done it. If
not, it is your fault.

Still when she'd leave, I'd think of Vanessa
and how much I loved her. No, I love her still.
Hadn't even a day passed when I saw her sit there.
Until the next I'd feel

Chapter 9

I ndigo and Maggie gathered in Karma's sunlit kitchen. Rays from the sun peeked through the wooden blinds that donned the room's single window. The oven where Maggie stood preparing a Spanish omelette for her niece, rested against a wall next to the sink and the window that ascended over it. Indigo stood a couple of inches away from her mother with her back and foot pressed up against the counter. She nervously bit her nails while reading the article written about her aunt.

Soleil made the front page of the Essex County section of the *Star-Ledger* as well as the five and six o'clock morning news. The family had been bombarded by the local news stations upon arriving at her house last night. How the media learned of her death was anyone's guess. Indigo sighed heavily as images of her cousin walking and wailing beside the stretcher that her aunt's bagged body lay lifeless on played repeatedly in her head. Soleil was the victim of the second biggest murder in the city that year. And even though Newark was notorious for its high murder rates, its good people were always disheartened by the dire news.

Indigo sighed heavily again before closing the paper and turning her attention towards the meal her mother was preparing.

"She's not going to eat that, Mommy," Indigo spoke as she spat a cuticle out of her mouth.

"It's she favorite. Her has to eat it," Maggie replied without looking up. She had become so overwhelmed with shock and grief since Soleil's murder, the only way she knew how to deal with it was to keep herself busy. If she didn't, she was going to fall into a catatonic state just as Karma had.

"Well, she's not going to," Indigo continued. "You've been here. You see what kinda state she's in. She hasn't eaten in three days, Mommy. She hasn't changed her clothes. She hasn't spoken since…" Indigo's voice trailed off. "…since they questioned her down at the station that morning."

Maggie looked over at her daughter with a bewildered frown.

"Well, what do you expect, Indigo? Your cousin found she mother beat to deat' on she old bedroom floor. Would you have much to say had it been I?" she questioned her daughter with her eyes.

Indigo shook her head and responded, "No, I wouldn't. I just hate seeing her like this, Mom. I feel so helpless." Indigo sighed deeply. "We shoulda never let Auntie Sol leave early. Karma was about to say something to her about it, but I just…I just told her not to. It's all my fault." Indigo began to sob.

Maggie placed the spatula gently down on the side of the skillet and turned to face her guilt-stricken daughter. She lifted her head by her chin and wiped her tear-stained face with her long fingers.

"You are not to blame for your auntie's deat', you undastand I?" Maggie asked as she searched Indigo's glossed eyes. "And neiter is Karma. We all tried to help Soleil. God knows we did. But dat damn Jimmy…him had a hold on she. One tighter dan any jaw on a pit bull. Him found she weakness…she kindness and him worked on she. Him worked on she heart first," she stressed pointing to her own beating heart. "And when him broke dat, him moved on to she spirit. And when him broke dat…him took de only ting her had left in she. And dat was she soul." Maggie became choked up. She breathed deeply before continuing. "But dere is a God above. And we all have to answer to He someday." Maggie smiled through her evident pain and turned back to the food. She wiped a creeping tear away from her cheek before turning the stovetop off.

Indigo looked up at a clock hanging on the wall across the room. "What time is Uncle L's plane coming in?"

"Noon. Get I a clean glass out of de sink, please," Maggie asked politely.

Indigo walked over to the sink and retrieved a glass from the dish-rack as Maggie traveled over to the refrigerator and got a plastic container of cranberry juice out of it.

"Pour dat for I," she instructed Indigo as she placed the juice down on the counter.

Indigo did what she was told while Maggie placed the omelette on the plate in her hand. Indigo set the glass of juice down on the dressed tray her mother set upon the countertop. Maggie followed suit and placed the plate down beside the glass. She took the tray into her hands and moved towards the kitchen entryway.

"Indi, wash de rest of dose dishes in de sink for I, please," she asked as she walked out of the room.

"Okay," Indigo replied sadly as she turned to the sink to execute her task for the morning.

Maggie took a deep breath in, then released it before she knocked on Karma's bedroom door. No answer. She turned the doorknob slowly with her free hand and entered the dark room. She closed the door behind her after stepping inside. Maggie stood by the doorway trying to allow her eyes to adjust to the darkness. She patted the wall for the light switch, found it, and pressed the button. She watched the room take on a dramatic effect under the illumination. Maggie spotted Karma lying motionless in a fetal position under her sheets and comforter. She moved toward the bed at a measured pace and placed the tray of food down on the endtable beside it. The stuffiness of the room was overwhelming. Maggie stepped to the side of the nightstand and pulled the string connected to the window blinds. As the blinds rose and stopped in midair, she proceeded to unlock the window and open it to allow some much needed air to come in. She pulled the window's treatment string again and watched the shutters snap into place meeting the trim of the windowsill. Maggie stepped back around the endtable and sat beside her niece on the edge of the bed.

Karma stared blankly at the closed closet door across the room. She was aware of her aunt's presence, but showed no care or concern. Her mother was dead and no one could do a damn thing about it. She barely blinked or batted an eye as she reflected back to the day she visited her mother in the hospital after her hysterectomy. She remembered how scared she had been about losing her then to the ovarian cancer they both called the "monster." It was funny how the "monster" had taken another shape, another form, as a man, and eventually killed her mother anyway.

Soleil lay awake in her hospital bed draped with white sheets and blankets. An intravenous line inserted into her right arm bulged out as a pathway for the morphine drip she needed to ease her pain. Her breathing suffered from the heavy dosages of medication, labouring it. A clear strand of tape lied across the intravenous line. A wrist band with her name, age, and birth date clasped her left wrist. The surgery had taken a devastating effect on her. The large amount of blood lost during the procedure caused dark circles to form around her eyes and her complexion to lose the melanin it possessed.

Red roses along with crimson and cream "Get Well" balloons encompassed the room. Engrossed in conversation, Maggie sat at her sister-in-law's bedside rubbing her cold hand as Indigo stood at the head of the bed rubbing her aunt's head. A Motown classic played quietly on the radio set on the windowsill. Unable to speak with conviction or volume, Soleil signalled to Indigo with her hand to retrieve a cup of water for her. Indigo moved to another side of the room and found the pitcher of water and cup on a tray. She poured the liquid into the cup and crossed back to her aunt, giving her the drink. Soleil sipped the water, then passed it back to Indigo for her to hold until she was ready to take another swig.

Maggie began to rock side-to-side in her chair and hum a gospel song. She then paused and said, "Me would have tought Karma would have been here by now. Me sure hope nutting happened to me gal."

"I don't think anything happened to her, Mommy. She's probably bracing herself before she comes to see Auntie Sol. You know she hates hospitals," Indigo confirmed.

"Well, me can't blame she. Me hate hospitals meself," Maggie admitted as she checked her watch. "Her driving in today?" she asked her only child.

"Mm-Hmm, she's supposed to be driving in from the airport."

"Lord have mercy. Gal should have been here by now. Oh, Lord. Did me say dat already?" she asked with her hand placed over her heart.

Soleil shook her head up and down.

"Uh-huh," Indigo said with a smile.

"Lord, me mind is going," she exclaimed distressfully.

"Why don't you…go take a walk, Mag. Clear your mind…a little," Soleil urged, struggling to breath and speak.

"Me making you nervous dere, gal?" she asked worriedly.

"Yes," Soleil spoke softly.

"Me sorry, honey." Maggie was doing her best to stay strong for her best friend, but it wasn't working. She was a nervous wreck. Karma was coming in from Los Angeles, California this morning and she was already running an hour late. She'd wanted her niece to be present prior to her mother's surgery and afterwards, but God only knew where Karma was.

"That's …alright. I know you mean well…but…I don't have the strength to get myself…worked up. Just calm yourself down. She'll get here…when she gets here," Soleil said soothingly.

Maggie closed her eyes and shook her head. She was overwhelmed with emotion and decided to send a special prayer up to the Almighty for her niece. But her moment of prayer was cut short as a result of the door opening. Karma entered the room with a handful of balloons and a teddy bear. She smiled as her eyes met with her cousin's, aunt's, and mother's. She kicked the door closed with the heel of her foot. Indigo ran over to her cousin and greeted her with a hug and kiss on the cheek. Maggie rose thereafter and embraced her goddaughter with a firm hug and long kiss on her forehead.

"We were just talking about you. Worrying ourselves sick," Maggie uttered.

"As you always do," Karma replied with a sly smile.

"Yup," Indigo cosigned without hesitation.

Karma placed the teddy bear on the nightstand next to her mother's bed and allowed the assortment of balloons to float up to the ceiling. She bent over the railing of the bed thereafter and embraced her mother with a kiss on the lips. Soleil gradually brought her hands to her daughter's face and held it for a moment. She studied her round, blue eyes and smiled. She hadn't seen her only-born in three days.

Karma left for UCLA to train under Bob Kersee the very same night she'd broken the news to her. Her little girl cried and begged to stay, but Soleil insisted she go and run for glory. She didn't want Karma to be a waste of talent. She'd already packed her bags a week ahead of time to make the inevitable separation easier on them both. Soleil prepared herself for the long haul, but it didn't ease the longing she had for her only child. She remembered watching Lorenzo drag Karma out the front door kicking and screaming for her. Soleil was only trying to do what she thought was best for her daughter. She never wanted to be the cause of her child's anguish. Yet, here they were in a hospital 'recovery' room awaiting her fate.

Mother and daughter shared another warm peck on the lips.

"Hey, Ma. How ya feelin'?" Karma asked in concern. She looked her mother over and studied the subtle change in her appearance. She'd expected her to look like someone she wouldn't recognize, but that wasn't the case at all. Soleil was still incredibly beautiful to her-dark circles and all.

"I'm better now that you're here," Soleil cooed.

Maggie and Indigo noticed the difference in Soleil's speech pattern the moment she spoke to Karma. Before she arrived, it had been chopped and strained. But as soon as Karma respired, her mother took in her air and exhaled. It was as if mother and daughter were sharing the same breath.

"Indi, come. We got to let your auntie and cousin talk for a little bit," Maggie instructed as she reached into her purse and retrieved a pack of cigarettes. "Me need to have a smoke."

"What I tell you about that smokin', *Tia*?" Karma asked in jest.

"What me tell you 'bout dat tongue?" she jested back.

Maggie tried not to smile at her niece's quick wit, but failed.

"Auntie, you want us to get you anything while we're out?" Indigo asked sweetly.

"A fresh pitcher of water, please."

"One pitcher of fresh water coming up," Indigo replied playfully.

She walked back over to her aunt and kissed her on the cheek before exiting the room with Maggie. Karma seated herself in her aunt's chair and shifted it to a more comfortable angle to view her mother.

"How was your flight?" Soleil asked.

"Bumpy. Very, very bumpy. I thought we were never gonna land. I see Aunt Maggie's nerves are still shot."

"Indeed, they are."

An urge to laugh came over Soleil, but it was cut short by an overwhelming amount of pain. She winced. Noticing her mother's suffering, Karma jumped out of her seat and searched the bed for the button to release a dosage of morphine. She found it and pressed it to release Soleil from her torture.

"How's that, Ma? Better?" she asked as she held her mother's hand.

"Mm-Hmm. Thank you," she whispered with her eyes closed.

Karma kissed her mother's pallid hand. She held on to it as she grabbed one of the legs of her chair with her foot and pulled it closer to the bed. She sat down and kissed her mother's hand again.

"I'm sorry, baby." Soleil opened her eyes and looked over at her daughter's strained face.

"Sorry for what, Ma?" Karma asked confusingly.

"I'm sorry for getting sick...and making you...come all the way back here."

"Why would you even say somethin' like that? It's not your fault. It's not," Karma said just above a whisper as she rubbed her mother's head.

"Because...I know...they need you," Soleil responded in a shortened breath.

Hearing her mother's broken speech tore Karma up inside. Seeing her in so much pain was almost unbearable, but she was determined to stay strong. Her mother wouldn't have wanted her to be any other way.

"Ma, no one needs me more than you right now and you didn't *make me* do anything. I'm supposed to be here. Indigo won't be able to take care of you, because she doesn't know how to. And Aunt Maggie has enough on her plate with Uncle Vic and the restaurant. You come first. Runnin' is not my life. It's my job, but it's not my life," Karma stated sternly.

"How long...are you on leave for?" Soleil looked up into Karma's eyes and watched her search for an answer to her question.

"Coach told me to stay as long as I need to," she began. "But the next time I speak to 'im, I'm gonna tell 'im to find a replacement for me. I'm hangin' up my cleats. I don't wanna run anymore."

Soleil's eyes widened. She searched for the untruth in Karma's face, but it didn't exist.

"What do you mean you *don't want to run anymore?* That's what you've always done, Karma. I want you...to run," Soleil nearly begged.

"I can't, Ma. I don't enjoy it like I used to. All I've ever done was run and I'm tired of it. How many of Indigo's birthday parties have I missed? How many tears have I not wiped from your eyes when I should have, but couldn't because I was in Virginia, Pennsylvania, or South Jersey? How many fights could I have broken up between you and Daddy? Jesus Christ, Ma, I couldn't even be here with you when they admitted you this mornin'." Karma shook her head and looked away in disgust. She was all her mother had since her father's affair and she had been in California for only a couple of days now training for the next Summer Olympics. She wasn't happy with herself and she wasn't comfortable being so far away when her mother needed her the most-even though it was Soleil's idea to send her to the other side of the country to train.

Soleil sighed deeply. Karma had thrown a curve ball. She hadn't expected her daughter to say what she'd just said. Karma never expressed any displeasure with running or anything else in her life up until that point in time. Soleil felt guilty. Her child was putting her life on hold for her. Even if the end of her life was nearing, she didn't want Karma's life to end with it. It wasn't worth it.

"Karma, I told you the day you decided you wanted to run professionally that it would be your life. Did I not?" Soleil queried.

Karma sucked her teeth in response.

"I asked you if you were absolutely sure about the decision you were making. And what did you say to me?" she asked knowingly.

"Yes, Mommy, I'm sure," Karma sighed.

"That's right," Soleil nodded. "And then what did you say to me?"

Karma pursed her lips and looked away.

"I know that I'm gonna have to make a lot of sacrifices, but I don't care-"

"-because I'm willing and ready to do whatever it takes to be the best," Soleil said, completing Karma's confession. "I know you're not a hurdler, but you're going to have to look at my illness like it is a hurdle and jump over it. You're an athlete, *mi amor*...whether you like it or not. Accept it. You are a gifted runner and you are my daughter. I love you very much, but I didn't raise you to be a quitter."

"I'm not quittin', Ma," Karma huffed.

"Okay. Well, then, what do you call it?" Soleil asked, folding her hands over her stomach.

"I call it 'closin' one chapter in my life and startin' a new one'," Karma replied proudly.

"Alright, so you don't want to run anymore. What do you plan to do then, with the rest of your life?"

"Well, I decided to talk to Uncle Vic about takin' on a managerial position at the restaurant since I plan on gettin' a degree in Business Management and one in Business Law anyway when I get to college. Workin' at the restaurant would give me great exposure and hands-on experience before I get to school. He thought it was a great idea and he also thought it would be in your best interest that I stand in for you as the landlord of your buildings until you get better," Karma hinted with a grin.

"Did he now?" Soleil asked suspiciously.

"Uh-huh. I mean, I already know everything there is to know about real estate and entrepreneurship because you taught me. Now, of course, I'll get the necessary licenses that I'll need after I graduate from college so when I stand in for you, it'll be legal. And, you know, I also took Indi's feelings into consideration about her wantin' me to come back home and stay, so I figured, why not? Uncle Vic offered me the job after his "interview"…" Karma laughed to herself. "…and I took it. That's what was takin' me so long to get here. I was meetin' wit' him. I'll move back home with you and I promise I'll try not to get on your nerves. I'll be there when you need me and still make time to do what I want on the side. So you see, Ma, everyone's happy."

Soleil closed her eyes and shook her head in disapproval.

"Everyone is not happy. *I'm* not happy. I want you to run, Karma. You're still young. You have so much more to offer before you decide to retire...now."

"My mind's already made up, Ma." Karma crossed her arms at her chest.

Soleil sighed wearily.

"I don't want you to have any regrets, *mi amor*. I don't want you to have any like I do. Please? I don't know what the outcome of this whole thing is going to be, but if I should succumb to it-"

"Nope," Karma interrupted while shifting uncomfortably in her chair.

"Karma," Soleil countered softly.

"No, Ma. I'm serious. I'm not gonna sit here and listen to you talk about that," Karma stressed with tears in her eyes. "Nope. We are not havin' that conversation today," she said, shaking her head. Her mother dying was *not* an option. And Karma surely didn't want to hear her putting the possibility of her doing so out into the universe.

"Well, I'm sorry, baby girl, but we are having that conversation today," Soleil replied earnestly. "I want to be able to rest in peace knowing you, at least, took what I said into consideration, Karma," Soleil said carefully.

"Okay, first of all, you're not gonna die, so you can stop alluding to that now. And second of all, you're not listenin' to what I'm tryin' to tell you. I'm not gonna have any regrets. I *don't* have any regrets just like I don't have a reason to run anymore. I don't love it anymore. I mean...what have I got to run for if the love is already gone? And if the love is already gone, there's nothing left, right?" Karma said, pleading her case. "Runners have souls, Ma. And I hate to say it, but I lost mine a long time ago. So what reason do I possibly have to keep runnin'?"

"Me."

Soleil and Karma's eyes locked. The door opened and Indigo entered the room with a pitcher of fresh water in hand. Maggie was close behind. As she settled beside Karma, Indigo noticed the heavy silence in the room between mother and daughter. She placed the pitcher on the windowsill as Maggie retrieved her coat from the back of the chair Karma was sitting in.

"Well, me tink me better go now and catch up on some work," Maggie exclaimed.

Soleil slowly turned away from the unspoken battle between her and Karma and drew her attention to Maggie. The two best friends shared a warm smile.

"Alright, sweetheart. Thank you for staying with me."

"Anytime, me love. Anytime." Maggie bent over the railing and embraced Soleil with a careful hug and kiss on the cheek.

"Okay, Mommy, I'll stop by to see you and *Papi* later," Indigo said as she walked over to her mother and hugged her.

"Don't forget, Indi," she warned with wary eyes.

"I won't," Indigo responded, waving her hand dismissively at her mother.

Maggie sucked her teeth in disbelief. She then turned and waved at her niece who returned the favor.

"Bye, *Tia*."

Maggie exited the room, closing the door quietly behind her. Indigo crossed back to Soleil's bed and admired the teddy bear Karma bought for her.

"Auntie, can I lay with you?"

"Sure, baby."

Indigo found the button that released and lowered the bed railing. She carefully scooted onto the bed beside Soleil and laid her head on her chest. Soleil rubbed her niece's face with her hand as Karma looked on. She remembered the days when climbing into bed with her mother were a necessity. But those days were long gone. Reaching for her wasn't an option now. She couldn't bring herself to be vulnerable. The chair she was confined to was her place of consolation and she was determined to stay there. She allowed herself to live vicariously through her cousin for the moment.

"Have you eaten anything yet, Ma?" Karma asked.

"Just a couple of saltine crackers. They won't give me anything else until the doctor says it's alright."

"Oh."

Indigo studied her cousin's uneasiness.

What's wrong? What happened?" she queried, looking back and forth between her aunt and cousin.

"Nothing," the two women responded in unison.

"Oh, yeah? Then, how come you two were so quiet when me and Mommy came in?" she asked as she raised her perfectly arched eyebrow.

"Well, *nosey*, she and I can't agree on what the new color scheme of the coffee house should be," Karma answered convincingly.

"I think it should be left alone," Indigo replied as she laid her head back down on Soleil's chest.

"Why?" Karma asked with furrowed eyebrows.

"Because there's nothing wrong with it. If it isn't broken, then don't fix it. I love that mural. If you two try to get somebody to paint over it, I'll never forgive either one of you," Indigo proclaimed dramatically.

Karma couldn't help but chuckle at her cousin's overreaction to the lie. Indigo was so serious it was sad.

"Fine, you big baby," Karma teased with raised eyebrows and a smirk.

Indigo and Karma shared a laugh that came to a swift halt when a knock on the door sounded.

"Come in!" Indigo yelled.

The door opened. Lorenzo peeked his head in before entering the room with a bouquet of pink roses. He closed the door behind him and remained there, unsure of what to say or think. Karma rolled her eyes and turned her attention back to her freshly manicured nails. Soleil's eyes shot back and forth from her daughter to her husband. She'd told Lorenzo not to come today, yet here he was. He was hard-headed, a trait she disliked most about him. World War III was about to begin in her recovery room and everyone there knew it.

"Hey, Uncle L," Indigo said hesitantly.

"Hey, Indi. How's my favorite niece?"

Karma grunted aloud, forcing all eyes to fall upon her. Unaware of the glares, she kept her focus on her nails.

"You brought Auntie Sol some flowers?" Indigo questioned the obvious. She was trying her best to break the tension in the room.

"Uh, yeah, yeah. Pink roses. Her favorite."

Karma watched her father closely as he walked over to the bed and gave Indigo a kiss on her forehead, then handing the bouquet of flowers over to Soleil. He kissed her softly on the lips. Soleil, in return, forced a smile and raised the flowers to her nose to smell them. The aroma was divine.

"Thank you," she said sweetly.

"You're welcome," he responded suavely.

Lorenzo cleared his throat as he walked over to the windowsill and sat down. The tension in the room was stifling. Lorenzo caught Karma's cold glare from across the room and held onto it.

"You invite him here, Indigo?" Karma asked without taking her eyes off her father.

"No, he-"

"If you have somethin' to say to me, Karma, then say it. But don't talk about me like I'm not here," Lorenzo stated tersely, cutting Indigo off.

"I don't have anything to say to you. And if I did, I still wouldn't waste my breath on the likes of you," Karma shot back.

Indigo slowly rose from her lying position into a perch.

"No matter how you feel about me, I'm still your father and you're *goin' to respect me*." Lorenzo's eyes widened with his last five words. He was serious. This was not the time, nor was it the place to fight with Karma.

"Respect you? Respect you? You gotta be kiddin' me. How can I respect you when you don't even respect yourself or the rest of the people in this family? If you've taught me anything, it's how to *disrespect* myself and the ones I love."

"That's enough, goddamnit!" Lorenzo screamed as he jumped off of the windowsill.

"Lorenzo, please," Soleil begged weakly.

"Naw, fuck that, Soleil! She's way outta line! I didn't come here to be disrespected by my own goddamn daughter!"

"Fuck you!" Karma shouted back. She jumped up out of her chair so fast, the piece of furniture collapsed onto the floor behind her.

"Fuck me?! Fuck me?!" Lorenzo rushed over to slap Karma, but Indigo jumped down from the bed in time to run swiftly between her uncle and cousin. She decided to make an attempt to restrain Karma, but it was useless. Karma pushed her out of the way and began to invade her father's space.

"You wanna hit me, nigga?! Hit me, den!" she taunted.

"You better back the fuck up, Karma! I'm serious!" he warned.

"Or what?! You gonna hit me?!" she taunted again.

"I said BACK THE FUCK UP!" Lorenzo's voice shook the

room.

"Uncle L! Karma! Please?! Stop!" Indigo begged as she jumped in between them again. She managed to push Lorenzo away from Karma. And without a struggle, he started to back away.

"You're a fuckin' disgrace to this family!" he cried, pointing his finger at his unmoved daughter.

"You would know, wouldn't you?! I am my father's daughter!" Karma sneered.

Unable to raise her voice, Soleil squirmed in her bed as she looked around for something to bang up against the railing. She managed to get her hands on the remote control for the television overhead. She gathered every bit of strength within her and banged it against the railing.

"You're no fuckin' daughter of mine! I'm finished wit'chu!" Lorenzo hollered from across the room.

"Good! Good! I can't stand your bald-headed black ass anyway!" Karma hollered back. They were two of a kind; Karma and her father.

"You're dead to me! You hear me, Karma?! You're cut the fuck off!"

"I don't give a fuck! You just did me a favor!" Karma grabbed her belongings and stormed out the room, slamming the door behind her.

Indigo covered her hands over her tear-stained face and collapsed in the chair next to the one her cousin left unleveled. Lorenzo began to pace the floor. With his hands clenched in tight fists, he tried to calm down. Soleil allowed the remote control to fall aimlessly out of her hand. She ran her hands over her closed eyes and sighed. Lorenzo's pacing ceased as his niece's sobs broke him out of his maddened trance. He walked over to Indigo, bent down in front of her, and attempted to console her.

"I'm sorry, angel. I didn't mean it. I didn't mean what I said."

Indigo looked up at her pitiful uncle and rubbed the running snot from her nose with the back of her hand. She rose from her chair unexpectedly and exited the room, slamming the door behind her. Lorenzo stood up from his crouched position and fell into the empty chair. Soleil watched from her bed as he rested his head in his hands.

"I didn't mean what I said. I love Karma. You know I do. My temper..."

He looked over at Soleil. Her face was etched with abhorrence.

"The pain I've been left with from this surgery is nothing compared to the pain I'm feeling right now after seeing what I just saw. You shouldn't have come, Lorenzo. I asked you not to come."

"I know you did, baby. But I needed to see you. I needed to make sure you were bein' well taken care of," he insisted.

A wave of pain washed over Soleil once again. She retrieved the clicker for the morphine drip underneath her arm and pressed the button. As the medication began to take its effect on her, she took a deep breath in, and then released it.

"This family...cannot...go on like this. There's so much hatred...within our child. And we...are the only ones to blame for it. As for Indigo...she should not...have to feel as if she's caught...between you...and Karma. I will not stand for it...any longer. I won't, Lorenzo. The fighting has got to stop," she asserted as she closed her eyes.

"I wasn't goin' to stand up here and let that girl speak to me any kind of way, Soleil. She was way out of line. I don't care how she feels about me; she was wrong for talkin' to me like that."

"And your choice of words was...better? Laying your hands on her was going... to resolve the problem?" she asked grimly.

"She would have known her place," he replied adamantly.

"And she would have ended up...in the hospital...like she did the last time...as a result of your temper. None of this would have happened...if you hadn't come, Lorenzo." A tear fell from Soleil's eye. "If I ask you not to be somewhere, please respect my wishes and stay away."

"Why are you pushin' me away, baby? Why?" Lorenzo strained to get a decent answer.

"Because it hurts...too much...for you...to have to see me this way," Soleil whispered. She turned her head and peered out the window. It was raining outside. She always hated the rain. It rained the day she came into this world and her mother never let her forget it. She'd told her God pitied her little soul and He cried for her. He cried for all of His unwanted children. God felt sorry for Soleil. He'd felt sorry for her then and He was feeling sorry for her now. Her mother, after all these years, made her believe it. Rain was God's tears and Soleil didn't have a tissue big enough to dry them.

The tapping of the raindrops against her windowpane brought Karma back to the present. She remembered that day in the hospital like it was yesterday. It wasn't the first time she would see her mother laid up in a hospital bed fighting for her life. Nor was it the last. Newark's University Trauma Center had become their second home since Jimmy came into their life. She wondered where he was and how he could do such a thing to her mother. A woman whose only crime was loving him.

Maggie rubbed her niece's back.

"Karma..." she began slowly and carefully. "...Me know, right now, it seems like your whole world has come crashing down on you, but you can't stop living. Me know Mommy doesn't have dat choice anymore, but you do. And you know it would break she heart if her saw you like dis."

Tears began to fall from Karma's eyes. Maggie moved her hand from Karma's back to her matted hair and went on to rub it as well. Karma closed her eyes and sniffled at the touch of her aunt's gentle fingertips running along her scalp. She opened her eyes again and reset them on the closet.

"Me don't expect you to speak to anyone anytime soon, because me know you will in your own time. But dere is business dat you have to take care of now concerning Mommy," Maggie confessed. She moved her hand from Karma's scalp to her swollen eyes. She brushed over them gently and placed her backhand on her wet cheek. "De medical examiner released she body dis morning to Woody's," she continued sullenly. "Your uncle Vic and me have an appointment to meet wit' de funeral director at noon. Now, your daddy's coming in at de same time and me know him really wants to see you. Uncle Vic and me would love for you to come wit' us and help make arrangements. But me know you haven't seen your daddy since Christmas. Whatever you want to do, we'll support you."

Karma thought about her aunt's proposition for a moment and slowly wiped her puffy, bloodshot eyes before placing her hand back underneath her cheek.

"I wanna go to the funeral home," she answered quietly.

"Okay, angel heart." Maggie smiled kindly.

"But I don't want you or Uncle Vic there," Karma continued in the same small voice.

Maggie looked down at her in confusion.

"Me don't undastand, baby. Why not?"

Karma looked up at her aunt with intense eyes. Maggie suddenly became unsettled by the glare. It caused her to shift her weight.

"Because my mother is my responsibility. I tried to protect her and keep her whole while she was here, but I failed. It's only right I give her the homegoing she deserves. It's the least I can do for her…now," Karma admitted as she rested her head back on her clutched hands.

"Karma, me undastand what you're saying, but, dear heart, you know nutting about funeral preparation. It's more dan just picking out a pretty casket and a dress for someone," Maggie emphasized.

"I know that, *Tia*," Karma sighed.

"Well, den, let I and your uncle, at least, go wit' you and sit in. We want to make sure de business is handled correctly."

"I know how to handle business," Karma said curtly, looking up at Maggie. "Or have you forgotten?"

"Karma-" Maggie began.

Karma shrugged her aunt's hand off her arm and gradually rose from her fetal position. She sat up and threw her legs over the side of the bed. Maggie noticed Karma was still wearing the blood-stained clothes she'd worn on the night of her mother's slaying, but said nothing. She just followed the young woman with her deep brown eyes as she made her way over to the dresser in search of something fresh and clean to wear for the day.

"*I* run the restaurant, remember?" Karma said, interrupting her aunt's thought. "And now I own my mother's half of it. *I* oversaw this building when my mother wasn't able to," she said, pointing to herself. "When that muthafucka beat her up so bad to the point where she couldn't even stand up straight, *I* was the one who held this building down, right along with the others. Whenever a tenant made a complaint, *I* took care of the problem. *Me*. And now…I own this bitch too. And let's not forget about my mother's house. I own that as well," Karma stated smugly.

Maggie threw her hands up in surrender. "Me not trying to insult your intelligence, baby. Me just saying dat dey may try to take advantage of you because you're young and you're vulnerable right now. We just want what's best for Mommy."

Karma ran her fingers through her uncombed hair. "No disrespect, *Tia*, but I don't remember you or Uncle Vic ever comin' to my mother's rescue when Jimmy was beatin' her ass. Yeah, you let her cry on your shoulder from time to time and all dat, but you weren't really *there* for her, you know what I'm sayin'?" Karma asked with wild eyes. "I don't remember either one of you ever takin' any of his punches for her. I know I did. Uncle Miguel did." Karma abruptly began to laugh as she took her aunt back to one of the many "special" times in the family's life. "Remember last year when he pressed those charges against me? Aggravated assault in the second-degree. I *still* can't believe dat shit. I hit 'im in the head with a bottle so he would get off of her. What else was I supposed to do?" Karma's asked her eyes glazing over.

"I heard her screamin' from downstairs. I never heard my mother scream like that before, so I knew somethin' was wrong. I ran up those stairs so fast I don't even remember climbin' 'em. Her bedroom door was closed, but I could still hear her screamin'. She was beggin' him to stop, but he wouldn't. When I opened the door and saw what he was doin' to her, *Tia*…" Karma paused and shook her head. "…I swore to God I was gonna kill 'im right then and there. She was lyin' across the bed on her stomach and he was on top of her. She was tryin' to get away from 'im, but he was too strong. I could see the blood runnin' down her legs. I could *smell* it. He had his left arm wrapped around her throat and her hands were pinned down above her head. He was like an animal. He was lickin' her face and smilin'. He wouldn't stop. It was like, the more she screamed and cried, the more aroused he got. He was callin' her all kinda bitches and tellin' her how every bitch needed to be broken in sooner or later. He kept sayin' how tight she was and how he should have fucked her up the ass a long time ago, it felt so good. I found the closest thing to me and bashed 'im in the head with it. He got off of her, then turned on me. But I didn't care, 'cause I finally got 'im to stop." Karma sniffled back tears. "And when the police came…he forced her, my own mother, to tell them I attacked him for no good reason at all. And they sent me to Clinton for a whole weekend on a bum-ass charge. All I was tryin' to do was pro-tect my mother…and they arrested *me*…not him," she said snif-fling. "I came out of there Monday mornin' with you and Indi tellin' me he put her in the hospital again."

Maggie watched her niece reflect back on that day. It broke her heart to see Karma relive that moment. The rest of the family could only fathom how Karma felt that night seeing her mother being raped and sodomized by her own boyfriend. None of them knew what he'd done to her after she hit him. Karma never said. And none of them knew if anything happened to her during her stay at the woman's correctional facility either. But it was obvious that Karma was a different person than she was when she went in the day she walked out. She'd grown cold and distant over the course of hcr stint there and hearing about her mother's hospitalization added more fuel to her fire. Maggie remembered the severe dam-age Jimmy left on Soleil's rectum. Her tissue was torn and terribly inflamed. She had to have emergency surgery that very weekend to repair her broken skin. It was a crying shame. Soleil was left mak-ing bowel movements through a colostomy bag for three months after that incident.

Maggie knew Karma was right. She and Victor did very little to help Soleil when she needed them the most. Victor gave up on try-ing to help her after the first time Jimmy laid his hands on her. He was very vocal about his disapproval of the relationship from the very beginning and he would do nothing for his sister until she let Jimmy go. Because she hadn't, his only concern was Karma. Unfortunately, Maggie found herself torn between her sister-in-law and her husband, and eventually sided with her husband. Not because she wanted to, but because of principal. He reminded her of their vows, especially the "honor and obey" part.

"Your uncle did he best to get you out of dere as quickly as possible, angel. Him did all him could do for you. You have no record because of he. Him did you a favor," she stated firmly.

"And I'm grateful *to* him *for* that, even though I wasn't in the wrong, *Tia*. But that doesn't excuse him for not being there for my mother," Karma replied defensively.

"Dere wasn't much him could do for she then, Karma," Maggie responded in a defeated tone.

"And what about now, *Tia*? Huh?! He was a fuckin' police captain. You tellin' me he has no pull, none whatsoever, with the people he worked with for over thirty-somethin' years? As crooked as these muthafuckin' cops are out here, he can't find somebody to ice that bitch ass nigga? He can't do that, but he wants to take part in layin' my mother to rest?" Karma smiled disgustingly. "No. I can't let 'im do that."

Maggie sat on the edge of the bed, wiping her wet face. The guilt set in. She had not expected to be read like an open book this morning, but it happened. Karma saw right through her. Karma noticed her aunt crying in her mirror's reflection. She shut the opened dresser drawers and carried a black top and pair of dark denim blue jeans over to the bed. She gently threw them down and kneeled at her aunt's feet.

"*Tia*, don't get me wrong, okay? I don't have anything against you. I love you. I do. You were my mother's best friend and the sister she never had, but I ain't no fool. You and Uncle Vic can't make up for what you didn't do for her when she was here now that's she's gone. If you two want forgiveness, you're gonna have to ask for it. Not from me, but from her and God. Okay?" Karma asked with heavy eyes. She took her aunt's hands into her own and held them tightly.

"Okay," Maggie nodded.

Karma rose from her squatting position and retrieved her clothes from the bed.

She turned to walk towards the door, but stopped in mid-step. She turned back around and faced her distraught aunt. Maggie looked up and met her faintly blue eyes.

"Thank you for the breakfast. You remembered," she said, giving her a half-smile.

"Why wouldn't I? It's your favorite," Maggie countered genuinely.

Karma nodded, opened the door, and walked out of the room. Maggie remained both shaken and awestruck by her niece's steadfast strength.

Chapter 10

A handful of patrons sat sporadically around the Alonso-Cruz family's coffee house sector of their restaurant. The coffee house was built as the forefront of the family's business and the only quarter open this afternoon. The restaurant, which could be found by walking down a lengthy hallway to the back of the building, was shut down for the week. It was being used to house the outpour of cards and floral arrangements the family were receiving during their difficult time.

The coffee house was a quaint space. The walls were painted a chocolate brown with white trimming. The flooring was a tanned brown granite. The counter tops shared the same color granite with walnut and maple wood facing. An Afro-Cuban mural stretched around a great portion of the room. A huge menu with traditional hot and cold Cuban drinks, savory foods, and sweets hung behind the cashier counter. The Cuban art deco furniture and track lighting created a relaxed atmosphere. To complete the Caribbean-like experience, music from the islands played softly overhead.

Maggie moved diligently from behind the cashier's counter to serving customers on the floor while Miguel restocked and took inventory in the back. The chime of the bells attached to the front door captured Maggie's attention. Victor entered the building with a handsome, brown-skinned man walking behind him. Master Sergeant Lorenzo Walker was a force to be reckoned with. He stood at six-foot-four with mahogany colored skin, a bald head, a meticulously trimmed goatee and wide muscular arms and legs. Lorenzo was a black man who had aged well, an image of timeless masculinity. His full figure was accentuated by a heavy black velour jogging suit. He wore a pair of black aviator sunglasses over his eyes to hide the indescribable pain he was feeling from the loss of his beloved wife. Lorenzo rubbed his masculine hand over his scalp as he scoured the room.

As Maggie finished serving a content customer, she wiped her hands on the apron she was wearing over her clothes and walked over to Victor just as he was showing Lorenzo the coffee house's renovations. She greeted them with a warm smile and they received her with the same.

"It's about time you two got here," she said as she kissed Victor softly on the lips.

"I know, baby. I know. But it couldn't be helped. The traffic was bumper to bumper on 280. It was ridiculous," Victor stated disgustingly.

"Me not surprised," Maggie replied as she licked her lips in hope of savoring the remnants of her lipstick. She looked over at Lorenzo and mustered up another smile. It was nice to see him again standing before her. Regardless of his past transgressions, he was still a good man. It pained her to see him so broken.

"Hello dere, Lorenzo," Maggie said sweetly as she embraced him with a hug.

"Hey, Mag. How are you, love?" Lorenzo asked in his deep baritone voice.

"Me alright. Today's a good day. How about yourself? How are you holding up?" Maggie's voice was dripping with pity. She was trying her hardest not to come off feeling sorry for the man, but she was failing successfully.

Lorenzo rubbed his nose and cleared his throat before he spoke. "Ahh, I'm holdin'. I'm just tryin' to wrap my mind around it all, you know?"

Lorenzo spent the entire plane ride from North Carolina to New Jersey crying silently to himself. Every time he thought about Soleil and how much she'd suffered before she died was tearing him apart inside. And the thought of Karma finding her put him over the top.

Maggie nodded, "Me sure do."

Victor decided that was the perfect time to move on from everyone's uncomfortable greetings and focus on something else.

"We're going to go take the booth in the corner and talk, baby," Victor expressed to his wife.

Maggie knew what her husband meant by "talking in the corner." It was the spot where Victor always went to speak to someone when he didn't want her to hear what he was talking about. Maggie, knowing her place, nodded and smiled.

"Okay. Well, do either of you want anyting? A Café con Leche maybe?"

Both men replied, "No, thank you."

"Alright, den," Maggie said as she and the boys departed in two different directions.

Lorenzo and Victor took their seats at the chocolate leather booth in one of the corners of the house. Victor rested his elbow on the table with his chin resting in his cupped hand while Lorenzo sat back and wiped his lined forehead.

"Run everything by me again, man. Because I still haven't comprehended what you were tryin' to tell me in the car."

Lorenzo was still in a state of shock from everything Victor told him about Soleil's case on the ride over. Nothing made sense and he was sure it still wasn't going to make sense to him once Victor reiterated what he'd already said in the car.

Victor sighed heavily.

"They found his car in his company parking lot, but there were no signs of him. They took the car in and traced it for blood and hair samples. His blood, as well as Soleil's, was found in the upholstery, but there were no footprints, tire prints, or anything to lead the boys in a direction. They questioned his employees, but none of them have seen him since the morning of Soleil's birthday."

Lorenzo ran his massive hand over his mouth and rested his index finger and thumb on his chin.

"Well, he can't hide for too long. He's gotta business to run. Man's gonna have to call in eventually to supervise his men and those trucks," he said, trying to convince himself that Jimmy would eventually come out of hiding.

"The company isn't under his name, L," Victor replied hesitantly. "It's under his general manager's name. The permits, the insurance, everything. *Maricon's* had his shop set up from the very beginning." Victor looked away, then looked back at Lorenzo. Lorenzo's eyebrows furrowed.

"The man is no fool," he admitted.

"Nope," Victor agreed. "Slick muthafucka," he mumbled under his breath.

"So what about his record? What do they have on him?" Lorenzo continued.

Victor sat back gradually and began to rub his aching knuckles.

"He's got no prior assault or battery charges on his record, because Soleil never filed any complaints. *Chupaverga's* only got drug possession, distribution, and a sex trafficking charge on there."

"He didn't serve any time for any of that?" Lorenzo asked in puzzlement.

"Yeah, a ten year bid for the sex trafficking. And the only reason he got locked up for that was because he was tied to that *cutre* drug lord, Owl. Remember him?" Victor hissed.

Lorenzo's mouth twisted with disgust.

"Yeah, I remember him alright. A nigga who was never seen, but was always heard. Sent his messengers out to speak on his behalf and shit. Yeah, I remember that muthafucka," he sneered.

"Well, I hate to tell you this *hermano*, but no one still knows where the fuck he is or what the fuck he looks like," Victor replied with an inappropriate chuckle.

"Well, what the hell are they doin' over there at the precinct?

What happened to the undercover squad in the operations bureau? They stopped sendin' men out into the field to scope him out? They got nothin' on him…nothin' on his employees? Everybody's just given up? Is that what you're tellin' me, Vic?" Lorenzo asked furiously.

"A lot's changed since you've been gone, L," Victor confirmed.

Lorenzo shook his head in disbelief. His wife was murdered three days ago and the man who killed her completely vanished without a trace. This was ridiculous. Lorenzo felt himself getting hotter by the second. Victor wasn't giving him any leads, any accounts, or any hope that Soleil would be given the justice she so well deserved.

"Vic, you gotta be kiddin' me, man. Please tell me you're jokin'," he begged with a smirk.

"I wish I was, Lorenzo. But the fact of the matter is…Owl still reigns as king up here. He's got all of Essex County on lockdown and he's making big moves to take over Philly, too."

"He's still the top boss after three decades?" Lorenzo asked.

"Yeah, and he'll probably have that spot for three more," Victor guessed.

Lorenzo removed his sunglasses and placed them on the table. Dark circles surrounded his wide doe eyes, almost giving him a racoon effect. He hadn't slept since hearing the news and the lack of rest was wearing on him. Lorenzo closed his eyes, placing his index finger and thumb in the corners of them.

"You think he had anything to do with Soleil's death?" he asked wearily.

"No. But I do think Jimmy ran back to him, told him what he did, and he shipped his punk ass off somewhere. Probably to South America or the West Indies. There's no telling where he could be right now," Victor responded honestly.

"I can't believe this," Lorenzo spoke as he rubbed the corners of his eyes.

"Nobody can," Victor stated miserably.

"They're goin' to close the case, aren't they?" Lorenzo asked already knowing the answer.

"Eventually," Victor said as he crossed his arms at his strong chest. "It doesn't matter that I used to be one of them. I'm retired now. And I was a spic first, a man second, and a cop last. My sister, your wife, is going to be put down in the books as just another statistic and we can't do a damn thing about it."

Lorenzo opened his eyes and stared at his brother-in-law from across the table. It was a shame how a man could give his life to serving his community or country, in Lorenzo's case and receive nothing in return. He wanted to find some untruth in his comrade's statement, but he couldn't. Soleil was going to die in vain just like the many other victims of domestic violence.

Lorenzo shook his head in despair.

"She never told me. In the four years she was with him, she never said a word to me about him puttin' his hands on her. She and I would talk on the phone, I'd ask her if she was alright, and she'd tell me yes. Karma never said a word either."

"That's because she was handling it," Victor replied seriously.

Lorenzo looked over at Victor and held his gaze.

"I want you to tell me that this is all a bad dream, man. That my wife isn't really gone and that my daughter still has her mother. Tell me, Vic. Tell me," he demanded with water-filled eyes.

"I can't," Victor responded, his voice cracking. "I can't," he repeated in a whisper.

Lorenzo sniffled to fight off his urge to break down and cry.

"My daughter's without her mother, man. My little girl's gotta look at the world through her own eyes now." He cleared his throat. "How much longer do you think she and Indigo will be at the funeral home?"

"Indigo told me she'd call me as soon as all the arrangements were made," Victor said kindly.

"Okay," Lorenzo nodded.

"And trust me when I tell you Karma's much better today. She had us all a little worried there for a minute. I'm not going to lie to you. We had her on suicide watch, but she came out of her room this morning ready to take charge." He smiled.

"She's got her game face on, huh?" Lorenzo beamed proudly.

"Oh, yeah…without a doubt. She's all you." Victor nodded.

The men shared a much needed laugh, but Lorenzo cut it short. He suddenly thought about Karma, the only person he had left in this world. He was wondering how she was making out at the funeral parlor. *How much had she changed since he saw her last? How were they going to get through this?* Lorenzo regained his composure and became serious once again.

"I gotta get Karma out of here. If not permanently, then, at least, for a little while."

"You can try, man, but I don't see that happening. Maggie told me she's very adamant about sustaining Soleil's position behind the condos and the restaurant. She's even going to move back into the house. Despite everything that's happened, she's going back home," Victor said, nodding.

"I figured that much, but she still needs a break. She's gonna run herself into the ground if she doesn't slow down," Lorenzo professed worriedly.

"Well, talk to her after the funeral. Maybe you two can work something out," Victor suggested.

"I will. I will definitely do that," Lorenzo replied as he put his sunglasses back on.

Karma and Indigo stood outside a project complex. The ten-storied red and brown sun-dried bricked building was a typical architectural design for the housing of those on a fixed income. Along with its shameless concrete sidewalks and dilapidated streets, Newark was built on a man's vision of the solidity of bricks.

Clay is the foundation for making bricks. Once the clay has been dug out, it is grounded and mixed with enough water to allow it to be shaped to form bricks. They are then dried slowly and fired in a kiln at high temperatures. The clay becomes metamorphosed, the water that once settled within it is driven off, and new minerals are formed. A dehydration reaction evolves and the bricks fire once again. The brick then becomes interlocked, causing the iron that exists inside of it to form the red-brown iron oxide haematite. Like the minerals living within the clay, the people of Newark morph into beings who more so compliment their city than censure it. Its people exemplify hardship with their faces set in stoned grimaces and their hearts formed into cold blocks of ice. They, like iron, bleed red giving the city, its streets, its sidewalks, and its buildings their red-brown coloring. Welcome to "The Bricks."

Karma leaned up against Indigo's silver 2007 Honda Civic with her arms folded across her chest, while Indigo stood a few feet away from the car looking at herself in a compact mirror. Karma watched her apply another coating of lip gloss to her small lips.

"You need to chirp Stuff's ass again and tell 'im to come the hell on instead of puttin' more of dat shit on your face. We been standin' out here for ten whole minutes," Karma sucked her teeth with a scowl.

Indigo closed her compact and placed it back in her pocketbook.

"Damn, Karma. Don't get your panties in a bunch. He'll be down in a minute, alright? My baby's probably just checking himself over in the mirror or something. You know he's gotta make sure he looks good for me."

Karma knew if there was any other person in the world more vain than Indigo, it was her boyfriend Stuff. She couldn't imagine what it was like to see them getting ready in the morning. She often wondered who stayed in the mirror the longest.

Karma looked down at her watch and sighed.

"Did you tell 'im we had other business to tend to?" she asked in an annoyed tone.

"Yes, Karma. I did," Indigo replied exhaustedly as she walked over to the car to stand beside her cousin. "He'll be down in a minute. I promise. This is just his routine," Indigo reassured her.

Karma cut her eyes at her cousin and began to laugh to herself. It was the dead of autumn and they were standing outside of one of the city's worst housing projects waiting for her cousin's drug dealing boyfriend.

"You know what? You two were made for each other. But what I don't understand, is how you gonna be a cop with a drug dealer for a boyfriend?"

Indigo grinned guiltily, "Stuff's profession has got nothing to do with me."

"Oh, no?" Karma asked in astonishment.

"No," Indigo replied nonchalantly. "I've been a cop for nine years now and he's been in the game for how long?"

Karma chuckled, "You gotta point."

"Thank you. But, uh, enough about me and my boo." Indigo paused and grinned devilishly. "A certain officer has been asking about you." She waited for Karma's reaction. Indigo was aware that her cousin hadn't seen or spoken to Money since the night they found her aunt. She knew Karma found it difficult to reach out to him after that night. The man had seen her at her worse, but she was too afraid to face him after everything that happened.

Karma looked over at her cousin in uneasiness.

"Oh, yeah?" she asked as she averted her eyes to the ground.

Indigo smiled at her cousin's sudden childlike demeanor.

"Yup! He's been wanting to know how you're doing."

"That's…that's sweet of him. Tell 'im I'm doin' alright the next time you see 'im," Karma was able to muster.

"Nooo, you can tell him that yourself when he calls you," Indigo teased with her gap-toothed smile.

Karma's head snapped in the direction of her gloating cousin.

"You gave 'im my number?!" Karma screamed in disbelief.

"Unh-unh, who do you think you're getting loud on?!" Indigo asked with the roll of her neck.

"You!" Karma exclaimed.

Indigo fell into a fit of laughter.

"No, you're not! I did you a favor!" she replied matter-of-factly.

Karma scratched her brow and shook her head.

"I can't believe you did that, Indigo."

"What?" Indigo asked with shrugged shoulders. "He asked me for your number, so I gave it to him. He just wants to talk to you, Karma. Damn. There's no harm in talking to the man, is there? It's not like you have feelings for him or anything, right?"

Karma remained quiet and avoided eye contact with her cousin. Money, like her mother, was an uncomfortable topic for her to speak about. She, indeed, had feelings for him, but felt this was an inappropriate time to express them to Indigo, Money, or anyone else. Karma believed she was supposed to be mourning her mother's death. There was no room to feel anything else. Joy was not an option. Yet here she was being put on the spot for liking a man she barely knew. This was wrong.

Indigo studied her cousin's silence and averted eyes. Karma's discomfort finally sent her a signal.

"Oh, nooo! You do have feelings for him!" she yelled as she jumped up and down clapping her hands.

"Shut up, Indigo," Karma warned through clenched teeth.

"Awww, yay! That's so sweet!" Indigo continued.

"Shut up, Indigo," Karma warned her again through clenched teeth and bulging eyes.

"Why? I think you guys would make a beautiful couple. Money's sexy, *mamita*. I know he's my partner and everything and I got a man, but the truth is the truth," Indigo smirked.

Karma closed her eyes and sighed.

"And Money's a good catch if I've ever seen one," Indigo continued. "He's good at what he does, he's got his own place, his own car, he's got a great relationship with his mom, and most importantly…" Indigo paused with a wicked grin. "…he's got his eyes set on you."

Karma sucked her teeth, "Indigo, please. I'm sure Money's got women throwin' themselves at him everyday."

Indigo nodded in agreement, "You're right. He does. But, trust me when I tell you, he doesn't pay them any mind. His mind is occupied on you and *only* you." Indigo nudged her cousin in the arm.

Karma waved Indigo off with her hand as a tall, medium muscular man with butterscotch colored skin descended the stairway of the building. His head was covered with a white du-rag while the rest of his body was enveloped in a dark denim blue jacket and pant-set overlapping the crisp, white, oversized T-shirt he wore underneath. A fresh pair of white Airforce Ones completed his outfit. Shawn "Stuff" Davis approached his girlfriend and comrade with open arms.

"Ayyy!" Stuff exclaimed with his slight overbite smile. He scooped Indigo up with one swift move and hugged her tightly. He placed her gently back on the ground and proceeded to kiss her passionately on the lips. Karma looked on in disbelief. The gentle giant standing before her eyes got his moniker as a little boy from always asking other people if they ever had any stuff for him i.e. candy, toys, money. She and Indigo had known Stuff since they were little girls. They all went through elementary, junior, and high school together. Stuff had been raised by his father. His mother passed after giving birth to him. And even though he never knew her, he missed her just the same. Stuff's father was a good man who worked honestly as a garbage man for the city of Orange, another city in the county of Essex. Mr. Davis never remarried, solely believing Stuff's mother was his one and only true love.

Unfortunately, Mr. Davis died of a heart attack four months after Stuff graduated from high school. Stuff strongly believed that his father died from working too hard for too little and he didn't want that type of life for himself. Left alone to fend for himself in the world, Stuff pushed his dreams of becoming an Electrical Engineer to the side and became a pusha man.

For as long as Stuff had been in their lives, Karma knew he'd always been in love with Indigo. And even though it took her cousin, what seemed like forever, to finally come around and love him back, she did and they've been together for almost ten years. Karma was happy for the two lovebirds. They deserved each other and by the looks of things, they had no intentions of separating. Why they weren't married by now was anyone's guess. But what Karma did know was that their explicit public display of affection could put any porn star couple to shame. It was disgusting.

Karma cleared her throat to snap the couple out of their world and back into reality. The two slowly pulled away from each other smiling.

"Love you, girl," Stuff said softly.

"Love you too, baby," Indigo responded in a whisper.

Stuff gently pulled out of Indigo's embrace and turned his attention towards Karma. He wrapped his long arms around her and hugged her tightly. Stuff felt for his best female friend. He had not known his mother, but like Karma, he'd lost her just the same. And he could tell, just by the way Karma tensed up in his embrace, that she felt responsible for her mother's demise, like he did for his own. Stuff kissed Karma sweetly on the forehead, then pinched her cleft chin.

"What up, Karma Sutra?" he asked jokingly to alleviate her anxiety.

Karma slapped Stuff's hand, "Don't even go there, nigga."

Stuff stepped back laughing.

"Nah, nah. I'm just playin', sis. But for real dough, on a serious tip. I wanted to tell you how sorry I am to hear about ya moms. She was a real beautiful lady, nah mean? Lovely. Me and da fellas are real fucked up ova it. We gonna miss her."

Karma blinked back tears and smiled, "Thanks, Stuff."

Stuff gently brushed his thumb across Karma's cheek.

"No doubt, fam. If there's anything you need, just let ya brotha know."

That's all Karma needed to hear. She knew who Stuff worked for and the pull he had. He was high in rank and that made a world of difference. If the police weren't going to find Jimmy, Stuff's boss would.

"Actually, there is. I need you to do me a favor," Karma admitted.

"Aiight," Stuff replied as he threw his arm around Indigo's neck.

"I need to have a meetin' wit' ya boss," Karma expressed sternly.

Indigo gave her cousin a quizzical stare.

"For what?" she blurted out.

Before Karma could answer her, Stuff replied, "I don't see dat happenin', K."

"Why not?" Karma asked in annoyance.

"'Cause Owl don't conduct business wit' nobody outside da fam." Stuff shook his head.

"Well, who does?" Karma asked in confusion.

"Hawk."

"Well, then, set up a meetin' for me and Hawk," she suggested. Stuff rubbed his nose nervously.

"What you need to talk to him about?"

"Jimmy," she answered coldly.

Stuff nodded slowly.

"You want dat nigga dealt wit'?"

"Mmm. But, see, Owl and Jimmy used to run together back in the day," she informed him.

"Oh, word?" Stuff asked in astonishment. "Den, I don't know what to tell you now, K. Cuz Owl ain't gonna lay his own mans out. It's dat O.G. loyalty thing, ya feel me? It goes against da code of da streets and shit, nah mean?"

Karma waved her hand dismissively, "I know all dat, Stuff. Okay? Now, see, that's where you come in. When you go and talk to Hawk, you're just gonna tell 'im one of your peoples needs a favor. Someone very close to them was killed and they need help findin' the muthafucka who did it. You don't need to use my real name, nor do you need to tell 'im my mother's real name. If Jimmy and Owl still talk, tellin' Hawk our names is gonna fuck up my whole operation."

Stuff ran his hand back and forth over his du-rag, "Yo, Karma-"

Karma cut Stuff off before he could finish his thought.

"This city takes bodies everyday, Stuff. *Everyday*," she emphasized with her hands. "Hawk and Owl shouldn't suspect anything if you just stick wit' what I'm tellin' you to say."

Stuff looked away in uncertainty, and then looked back down at Karma.

"You puttin' me in a fucked up spot, K. Dis is my job, nah mean? Dis is my ass on da line."

"You said *anything*, Stuff," Karma responded with pouted lips.

Stuff dropped his head and smiled. Karma got him every time with that pout.

"I did. I did. I know I did."

"Please, Stuffy?" she asked in a childlike voice.

Stuff raised his head and looked into Karma's pleading eyes. They were so pretty. But when did they turn gray? He always thought they were blue. He had to stop smoking soon because he was sure his mind was playing tricks on him. Whatever the case, he gave in.

"Aww, man. Well, if Hawk does decide to meet wit'chu, sis, he's gonna wanna know ya name."

"Tell 'im it's 'Doll'," Karma replied without hesitation.

"I can't believe this," Indigo mumbled under her breath. She'd been standing there the whole time and Karma hadn't looked her way not once. She didn't know what her cousin was up to, but whatever it was, she wasn't going to the right people for help. Indigo knew the men Stuff worked for were dangerous, especially Owl. No one knew what he looked like, not even his workers. However, when he needed to make an example out of someone, his point came across loud and clear to the people of Essex County.

"You serious?" Stuff asked Karma.

"As a bitch in heat," she smirked.

"Dem niggas is gonna want somethin' in return for their services, K," he warned.

"That I already know. And we'll cross that bridge when we come to it, now won't we?" she replied with a half smile.

"Aiight, sis. I'll talk to him," Stuff confirmed.

Indigo looked back and forth between her beau and her blood in disbelief. She was an officer of the law, and here these two were discussing a potential meeting with a well-known drug lord in her presence.

Karma stroked Stuff's muscular arm and smiled.

"Thank you, Stuffy."

"Yeah, yeah, yeah," he teased as Karma laughed to herself.

Indigo pressed the unlock button on her remote control to give Karma entry to the passenger side of the car. Karma opened the door and sat down. Stuff closed the door for her thereafter. He then walked Indigo around to her side of the car and locked his eyes with hers. Her face was strained with concern.

"You're really going to go talk to him about this?" Indigo asked.

"Yeah, baby," Stuff shrugged. "I mean, I ain't really gotta choice, ya dig? I'm a man of my word. You know dat."

"And you think Hawk is going to meet with her?"

"No, I don't think. I *know* he will," he chuckled. "Nigga's weak when it comes to you females. He gets off on dat damsel in distress shit. Nigga thinks he's fuckin' Captain Save-a-Hoe or some shit. No disrespect to you or Karma of course."

Indigo sighed heavily. She wasn't comfortable with what she was about to say, but Karma's mind was made up. Indigo was about to go against her better judgement.

"I swear to God, Stuff…you better not let anything happen to my cousin."

Stuff cupped his love's face in his massive hands.

"Neva dat, mami. You know I ain't gonna let nuttin' happen to her. Dat's my word." Stuff reassured Indigo with a stern nod. She gently grabbed his face and pulled him down to her level for another sweet kiss on the lips. After the two parted, Stuff opened the door for his better half, allowing her to retrieve a box of White Castle burgers from her seat. She handed them over to him and grinned as he accepted them graciously. Stuff kissed Indigo again before she settled down behind the wheel. He closed the door for her and backed away from the car as she revved it up and took off down the street.

Karma walked into her brightly lit condo rubbing her heavy eyes. It was after ten o'clock and she was dead tired from all the running around done today. After spending three hours at the funeral home putting everything in order for her mother's homegoing, Karma could care less how the family was going to lay her to rest once she passed on. They could wrap her up in a white sheet and bury her under an unmarked tree somewhere for all she cared. She had no idea it took so much time and money to prepare a wake, funeral, and a repast for someone. A person had to pay to live and pay even more to die. It was depressing.

Karma walked into the living room and placed her pocketbook and leather coat down on her cushioned chaise. She noticed the couch was pulled out into its convertible bed with a fitted sheet, blanket, and two pillows upon it. The coffee table that usually sat before the couch was pushed to the side. A large box of pizza, a small box of hot wings, and a two-liter soda sat atop it. The television was on its highest decibel. Karma grabbed the remote control from the pull-out and turned the volume down on the flat screen.

"Daddy!" she yelled as she rubbed her eyes again.

The door to the bathroom opened. Lorenzo stepped out into the room with a pair of flannel pants on and a gray T-shirt with "ARMY" scrolled across his chest in big black letters. A broad white smile grew along Lorenzo's face. He hadn't seen his little girl in nine whole months. She was just as beautiful as she was the last time he saw her, but she appeared to be much older now. The glint in her eyes was gone. She'd seen too much, too soon. She'd seen the two most important men in her life walk out on her and fight for the respect of a country that didn't respect them back. She'd seen her mother lose herself behind a man who showed his love through his fists and eventually loved her to death. She'd seen her eyes change color overnight and hated the way they looked like the rain that always made her mother cry.

"Hey, baby doll," Lorenzo said sweetly as he embraced his only daughter in a long hug. He pulled away slowly when he noticed she hadn't hugged him back.

Lorenzo held Karma's small face in his massive hands and kissed her on her nose. He rubbed the dark circles that surrounded her eyes with his thumbs and kissed her again on each lid. Karma looked up at her father and smiled tiredly.

"Sorry I'm late. I didn't know I was gonna be gone all day."

"It's alright," he reassured her.

The two made their way over to the pull-out. Lorenzo sat down on the edge of it and patted the space beside him for Karma to occupy. She did willingly and took another look around at all the junk food her father bought for the evening.

"Daddy, what are you doin' wit' all of this junk food? You know you have high blood pressure."

"A man can't watch the game without his necessities, baby doll," Lorenzo replied with a broad smile.

"He can't watch the game from the grave either," Karma spat.

Lorenzo grabbed his chest in jest.

"Ooo, that was a low blow. My feelings are hurt."

Karma shrugged and shook her head.

"I'm sorry, but you know you're supposed to be watchin' what you eat. Eatin' junk like this was the reason you had that heart attack two years ago."

"I know, I know," Lorenzo responded in defeat. "I'm done for the night, alright? I'm full anyway."

Karma smirked. Her father's three weaknesses were her, her mother, and junk food. The inside joke was, they were all liable to kill him. Karma had to laugh to herself at the thought of it. She'd tried to laugh a lot in the past couple of hours to keep from crying. So far, so good.

Lorenzo cleared his throat, disrupting the uncomfortable pause in the conversation.

"So, um, how'd everything go at the funeral home?"

It was only a matter of time before her father would ask about her day at the funeral parlor. It was bad enough she had to sit through something like that on behalf of her mother, of all people. But talking about it was much worse. Speaking about the experience would force her to face the reality that her mother was truly gone. She would have to accept it and she didn't want to. Karma wasn't ready to.

"It went smoothly," she said with a sigh. "I picked out a...a nice lilac and gold casket for her. The bedding is a pale pink, so it should go nicely with her pastel pink pant-suit."

"Her favorite one," Lorenzo whispered.

"Yeah." Karma ran her fingers through her spiked hair. "Indigo helped me pick out the program and prayer cards. We got the laminated bundle. You know how they have the prayer on the front and a picture of the loved one on the back?"

"I do," Lorenzo nodded.

"Well, we got those."

Another loud silence fell, suffocating their conversation. Lorenzo cleared his throat again while he rung out his large hands.

"Are we goin' to be able to have a viewin'?" he asked as he slowly looked over at his expressionless daughter.

Karma breathed deep. She wanted to be careful with her words. Her father was liable to break down and cry at any moment. She could tell by the way he cleared his throat before he spoke. He was literally choking back his tears. Karma wouldn't look at him. She couldn't look at him.

"The funeral director said…um…he said they'll do the best they can with her, because…Jimmy broke most of the bones in her face and it swelled up pretty badly."

Karma paused. "He said her jaw can be reset…so can her cheek bones. But her nose and mouth might be a problem."

Lorenzo wiped his face over with his hand.

"Because they're made of cartilage and palates. Shit."

"After we discussed that, he gave me copies of all of the paper-work…includin' her autopsy report. He wasn't supposed to, but he did," Karma admitted regretfully.

Lorenzo looked over at his daughter in shock.

"Baby Doll, you don't need to have somethin' like that in your possession," he insisted.

"But I needed to know what killed her, Daddy," Karma replied in a desperate tone. She looked over at her father and turned her eyes away again. "There were fingerprints on her chest. And I needed to know if they had anything to do with her death. And I was right. The funeral director told me...that nigga…punched my mother in her chest. And because the blow was so hard…her heart went into shock, then, sudden cardiac arrest." Karma looked over at her father grimly.

Lorenzo looked towards the ceiling and exhaled deeply. His wife's death was just as much his fault as anyone else's in the family; everyone except for Karma. The guilt was killing him. Tears brimmed in his eyes. He sniffled them back.

"Your mother's heart was what I loved most about her. It was made of gold. And it carried a heavy weight of patience. Your mother and I, even though we were separated for the past seven years, never stopped lovin' each other. And I know that's why we never divorced. Debbie and Jimmy just kind of happened. They were relationships of convenience. But, she and I always knew, once I put my sword and shield down, it was goin' to be me and her against the world again. And I did it, baby doll. I finally retired from the Army."

Karma looked over at her father in wonderment. She never thought he'd ever resign from his job. Her father was a soldier to the core. If there was anything he took seriously, it was his place in the Army.

"You did, Daddy?"

"I sure did. It was a long time comin'…way over due. But I did it. My last day was on your mother's birthday. And I told her that day. We were goin' to tell you the good news next week, but…I was gonna fly up and surprise you. We had it all planned out," Lorenzo admitted sadly.

"That would have been a nice surprise," Karma said softly. It saddened her to know her mother wouldn't be able to experience having her one and only true love back in her life. It wasn't fair. As happy as Karma was to hear of her father's retirement, she wished he'd done it a little sooner, like nineteen years ago when he slipped and had that affair with the nurse in his unit. She wished he'd hung up his fatigues after her mother was stricken with cancer, but he hadn't. When the two most important women in his life needed him the most, Lorenzo had only given them half of himself…half of his time, half of his attention. Karma would forever be scarred from it.

Lorenzo began to get choked up. He'd been doing so well up until that point. Soleil sounded so happy to hear the good news and was more than willing and ready to welcome him back into her life. He had been looking forward to seeing her beautiful face again, holding it and kissing it. He never wanted to forget his wife's face. He had even been nervous about making love to her again after all of these years. Soleil had that effect on him. She made him feel like the shy little boy he'd once been so many years ago. Soleil was intimidating, but she was all his. It was a shame Lorenzo would have to meet her in his dreams now.

Karma placed her hand on her father's back and began to rub it softly. She was much better at comforting than being comforted. Her mother's touch was the only one that calmed her spirit. Karma hoped she'd passed it on to her.

"I've hated myself for a long time," Lorenzo continued. "Mostly because I put the Army before my family...the mistake I made with Brenda. I didn't blame your mother for wantin' to separate. A woman can only take but so much. I was very selfish." He sniffled. "I loved your mother. I want you to know that, baby doll. I loved her more than life itself."

"I know you did, Daddy. She loved you, too. And she missed you," Karma said coyly.

Lorenzo stared into his daughter's charcoal gray eyes.

"I want you to come back to North Carolina with me after the funeral."

Karma removed her hand from her father's back and rested it back in her lap.

"Daddy, I would if I could, but I have too much business to take care of up here. There's a lot of things that need to be sorted out before I decide on takin' any trips."

"I undastand," he nodded. "But just think about it. Okay? For me?" he asked with pleading water-filled eyes.

"Okay. I will." Karma smiled weakly.

"Thank you," he muttered.

"You're welcome," she replied in a yawn. Karma leaned over and kissed her father on the cheek. "I'm goin' to bed." Karma rose from the bed and retrieved the boxes of junk food. She placed them in one hand and the soda in the other.

"Get some sleep."

"Alright," Lorenzo said as he watched his daughter walk out of the room and into her bedroom with his treats. Lorenzo made himself comfortable underneath the sheets and comforter on the pullout. He discovered a manila folder lying at the foot of the bed. He leaned forward and reached for the folder. Once he opened it, he found a black and white portrait of Soleil holding Karma as a baby. His eyes connected with theirs. He remembered the day his wife and daughter took that photograph. Lorenzo insisted that their beauty be captured on film. He was convinced that his "two favorite girls" deserved to be seen in all their natural nude glory…from the waist up of course. All in all, the picture was tasteful. Soleil's milk-filled breasts were hidden behind her arm and Karma's chubby body. Lorenzo smiled at the memory. But it soon faded as he brushed his thumb over Soleil's face again. It was the face he fell in love with over thirty years ago on the campus of Hampton University.

Lorenzo was in the ROTC program while Soleil was enrolled as a business management major. He was walking along the waterfront with his roommate when he noticed her sitting alone on a bench by the water's edge. Soleil was reading a book about the Argentine guerrilla Che' Guevara. Lorenzo wasn't sure if it was her hair, her complexion, or her interest in history that transfixed him, but he wanted to know who she was. So he told his roommate to go wherever it was they were on their way to and Lorenzo walked up to the unknown beauty. When Soleil looked up at Lorenzo with her eyes, those gems that reflected the sunrises and sunsets of his beloved Orange, New Jersey, he blushed. He outstretched his hand and introduced himself as the man she was going to wed. Soleil kindly dismissed his superciliousness with a smile and received his hand. When she spoke, her strong southern Cuban accent hit Lorenzo like the beat of the Samba. Lorenzo had fallen in love with Soleil right there on the spot. He sat down beside her and the rest, as they say, was history. From that warm spring day by the waterfront, a thirty-something year long love affair sprouted.

Lorenzo looked back at the face in his hand. It was the face he held at night when his body was united with hers. It was the face he lied to when he slipped and got caught up in another woman's rapture.

Lorenzo placed the photograph back in the folder atop the newspaper clipping regarding Soleil's slaying, her death notice, the signed contracts from the funeral home and the autopsy report before closing it. He intertwined his fingers and held them under his chin. Losing his wife had only come across his mind that one time when she was diagnosed with cancer. But Soleil had beaten it. She was the better half of him and now she was gone forever. Lorenzo's jaw locked as he placed the folder down onto the coffee table. As he settled himself down for a much needed night's rest, he said his prayers and wiped a creeping tear away from his eye.

Chapter 11

1997. The evening of Soleil's hysterectomy recovery. Indigo awakened from a restless slumber. The thought of her aunt succumbing to the chemotherapy treatment she was going to start receiving for her cancer disturbed the slightest subconscious feeling or mental notion. The Walker home was dark and Soleil's absence weighed heavily on its foundation. Lorenzo decided to stay at his wife's bedside for the evening, leaving the girls alone. Indigo wiped her eyes as she threw her legs over the side of her uncle and aunt's bed. She walked out of their bedroom and travelled down the hallway to the kitchen. She noticed a single light on in the room, but could not make out where it was coming from. As she entered the darkened kitchen, Indigo looked over to see Karma sitting up against the door to the freezer. The door to the refrigerator was wide open. With her head hung, knees bent, and legs gaped open, she placed the green bottle of Heineken to her lips.

"Karma?"

Karma slowly looked up and over at her cousin through her long, heavy eyelashes. She allowed her head to fall back against the freezer while a smile grew along her sweat glazed face.

"Hey, Indi. What you doin' up?"

Indigo walked over to Karma and crouched down beside her.

"I couldn't sleep."

"Me either." Karma took another swig of her beer.

"When did you start drinking beer? You're not twenty-one yet, Karma. And how many have you had?" Indigo asked in concern. She was not used to seeing her cousin in such a state. She was unaware Karma drank at all since she was an athlete. She understood her cousin's discipline and her strength. But in this dark hour, Karma possessed neither one.

"I don't know. Three...four...the whole pack." Karma laughed at her self-pity. "I don't usually drink like this. Just tonight. I needed somethin' to help me forget what happened today."

Indigo sat down beside her cousin.

"Why did you attack Uncle L like that?"

"I don't know. I saw him and I just went off. See, when your heart is consumed with so much hate, it's hard to control it. It takes over. It takes over your soul. It takes over your life."

"I don't know how to hate Uncle L. I don't want to hate him. I love him."

"That's good and you don't need to hate him. Daddy...my daddy disowned me today. Didn't like what he saw, so he closed his eyes and shut me out."

She took another sip of her beer.

"He didn't mean what he said. He told me so."

Karma shook her head in disbelief.

"Well, I meant what I said. Every word. And I'm not sorry for it."

"I think you hurt his feelings," Indigo admitted.

"You think so?" Karma asked with raised eyebrows.

"Yeah, I do," Indigo nodded.

Karma laughed to herself.

"Good."

"You're just like him, you know," Indigo said softly.

Karma cut her eyes at her cousin and tightened her lips.

"Your words aren't enough to fight with. You gotta fight with your hands too. You and Uncle L are two of a kind," Indigo continued.

"You know what? You are absolutely right. I got the worst of my father and our grandmother. And you, you got the best of her. I'm sorry you're not my mother's child. Shit, I ain't even my mother's child. She didn't give birth to this monster. Nope...Grandma Ava created this."

"I don't understand what you're talking about, K."

"It's nothin'," she said quietly before placing the empty bottle of liquor down between her legs. "I look at you, Indi, and even though you're my cousin, you got my mother written all over you. And you don't even know it."

"That's not true." Indigo shook her head.

"Mm-Hmm. Yes, it is," Karma nodded. "You got her beauty, her brains, and her talent. And most importantly...her heart. You got it all."

"I can't believe you just said that. You possess the same qualities I do, and then some."

Karma looked up to the ceiling and shook her head.

"But you can dance, Indigo."

"So what? Everyone can dance."

A loud silence befell. Karma turned her head and locked eyes with Indigo. She raised her hand and placed it on the top of Indigo's head and left it there.

"I don't want you to be just like me. I want you to be better than me. Don't ever feel as if you have to compete with me, Indigo. Or that you aren't enough. You are enough. And believe it or not, you're gonna go far in this life. Farther than me or anyone else in this family."

"No, I won't," Indigo said as she averted her eyes downward.

"Yes, you will. My mother knows it. I know it. Your parents know it. Humph. I can't run forever. If my old injury comes back...that's it." Karma paused with a sigh as she thought back to the day her right Achilles tendon tore during a weight training session.

KARMA

A female member of her high school track team "accidentally" dropped a ten pound free weight on the back of her right foot, snapping her Achilles tendon in two. The extensive trauma caused to her muscle hindered Karma from running the rest of the season. She, the only freshman on varsity, had been chosen to be the anchor for the girls 4 x 4. It was unfortunate Karma missed her first Penn Relay as a result of the senior's jealousy.

She snapped out of her trance and focused back on the matter at hand.

"You know, I was so afraid to come to the hospital today. I don't know what I was expectin' my mother to look like. Death, I guess…or Grandma Ava. But she didn't. She still looked beautiful."

"Auntie Sol's the most beautiful woman in the world," Indigo said with a smile.

"Yup," Karma smiled back. "Hey, when's the last time you listened to her heart beat?"

"The night before she went into the hospital."

"That's good. You know, I used to listen to it too when I was a little girl. It's the most beautiful sound I've ever heard," Karma spoke proudly.

"Yeah. It is beautiful," Indigo replied.

"Don't ever forget that sound for as long as you live. Promise me," Karma responded with sharp eyes.

"I promise. Karma?" Indigo asked.

"Yeah?" Karma replied as she played with the empty bottle in her hand.

"Do you think she's gonna die?" Indigo asked hesitantly.

Karma sighed and closed her eyes.

"No…not from this. She's still got some work here to do."

"Like what?"

"Well, she has to see us graduate from college. She's waitin' to see the day I get married, but that's not gonna happen. Not if Joaquin gets himself killed over there in Afghanistan." Karma sucked her teeth in disgust.

"Don't say that. He's going to come back for you. He just has to get all that *"I'm a Soldier"* mess out of his system."

Karma smiled at her cousin's kind gesture.

"And when he does come back, you two are going to start knocking the boots again, and then the babies will come. And they are going to be sexy!"

"Shut up, Indigo!" Karma cried through hysterical laughter.

"They are!" Indigo said with her wide smile.

"I guess you're right," Karma submitted. "My mom's *got* to stay around for that. She has to see her grandchildren and great-grandchildren born. I mean, someone has to teach me how to be a good mother, right? She's already taught me how to be a good wife. So I guess those are more than enough reasons to show that she's not gonna die. We need her here. I need her…here. And I think God knows that. And so does she," Karma convinced herself by shaking her head up and down.

"Karma?" Indigo asked sweetly.

"Yeah?" Karma replied with a belch.

"Can I sleep with you tonight?" Indigo asked hesitantly.

"If you want to. But my heart doesn't play the same melody as my mother's," Karma admitted.

"That's okay. Mine doesn't either," Indigo agreed.

KARMA

Chapter 12

T he wooden cathedral doors of St. Rocco's Roman Catholic Church were opened by two husky male ushers. They stood outside the sanctified building holding the doors with their weight. The sun shone by itself earlier that morning just like the weather man on the news said it would. But it was a little after one o'clock and the sun was now accompanied by light sprinkles of rain. The sun shower was uncommon for the fall in New Jersey, but it was a beautiful sight to behold. If anyone looked a little deeper into the rare spectacle, they would have probably thought God was having mixed feelings about calling Soleil home so soon. Only He knew.

A faint rainbow appeared and spread across the sky just as the Alonso-Cruz family filed out of the church behind Soleil's casket. Four pallbearers, along with Victor and Miguel on each side of the casket, walked unhurriedly down the concrete steps. The family were all dressed sharply in simple black pant-suits with the exception of Lorenzo who wore his suited army uniform complete with his stars, stripes, strings, and other awards he'd earned over the course of his time in the service. He and Karma, with the other remaining members of the family standing behind them, stood beside Father Pacella at the top of the church's steps and watched the pallbearers place Soleil's casket into the hearse. Lorenzo was visibly shaken. His body shook lightly as he cried silently to himself. Karma, whose arm was interlocked with her father's, tightened her grip and kept her head cast toward the ground. She didn't know when she would look up and face the world again.

At Karma's request, her mother's wake and funeral were both held at the church that day. She thought it necessary to arrange the homegoing as such to make it easier on herself and the family. The only thing that didn't sit very well with Karma was having to see her mother for the first and last time that day. She couldn't bring herself to view her mother prior to the services, so Indigo decided to go to the funeral home the previous day to make sure her aunt was impeccably done and acceptable for viewing. When Indigo arrived at Karma's home later that evening, she reassured her cousin, through tear-filled eyes, that she would be pleased with her appearance.

The family met at Karma's condominium around ten o'clock, said a prayer with the funeral directors once they arrived, and then filed out of the building into the black stretch limo that was waiting for them outside. To the family's surprise, many of the tenants were standing outside in the crescent-shaped driveway waiting to give them their final condolences. Little conversation took place inside the limo. Guilt spoke for everyone. The family mostly looked out of their windows, watching the other cars speed past them on Route 280. When they finally arrived at the church, the first thing that greeted them was the glorious sounds of the church's band playing the instrumental to Richard Smallwood's *Total Praise*. The choir had not yet been cued by the director to lift their voices. That was his plan. It was all about the timing. The choir was to sing the moment the family reached the doors. And so it was granted. The choir sang their praises to the Lord the exact moment the Alonso-Cruz family arrived.

Karma could feel her heart beating faster and faster the longer they stood outside the church's humungous doors. She hadn't stepped foot into that basilica since her father's one night stand disrupted Easter service ten years ago. Unlike Indigo, who continued to attend the church every once in awhile, Karma became a parishioner of the streets. God was no longer her salvation. It was in *His* house where He let a whore disgrace *her* mother's name before *His* people. And it was the same house she was standing right outside of. Her mother's soul was being offered up to the man who had promised He would always be there when they'd call. *But where had He been when Jimmy took her mother's life? Why hadn't He picked up the phone?*

"Total Praise" was playing loudly behind the gateway to her mother. Karma was sure the song was going to set her off. It was her mother's favorite song and she remembered how it always made Solcil cry. Indigo, Maggie, and Miguel were already crying behind her. She could hear her uncle consoling her aunt and Stuff consoling her cousin and other uncle. If she turned around to look at them, she was sure to break down as well. The black Jackie Onassis sunglasses she was wearing were doing their job of hiding her red, swollen eyes. Karma hadn't slept at all the night before. She was too afraid to close her eyes. Dreaming had become a distant memory. And why should she ever dream again when she was living a nightmare? She remained still and forward with her arm clutched with her father's.

Then it happened. The doors swung open and a house full of grief-stricken faces came into view. All eyes were on them…standing and waiting for the family to walk down the red carpeted aisle. Karma couldn't believe how packed the church was. She knew her mother touched a lot of lives, but never actually saw her work in the flesh. There were so many faces. There were faces of people she didn't even know, but she knew they were present out of respect.

Father Pacella made a sign of the cross in the air and preceded the family down the aisle. Everything seemed to move in slow motion. The walk felt more like a death march to Karma than a celebratory step to honoring her mother's life. There were so many floral arrangements surrounding her mother at the pulpit, it looked like she was sleeping in a garden. It was all so surreal.

Karma couldn't believe her eyes once she and her father reached her beloved mother. Soleil was an image of perfection. There were no signs or scars of the battle she'd lost so many days ago. Her face was meticulously painted with warm browns and a touch of pink on her high cheek bones and lips. Soleil's mouth and nose, the two features on her face the funeral director was uncertain of mending, were set flawlessly. Her hair was pulled back into a low bun. A pink rose was set underneath her hands that were laid one on top of the other upon her stomach.

Karma's chest became tight. Her heart was pumping ten times harder than normal, fighting the pain and loss that was invading its space trying to suffocate it. As much as she wanted and tried to make herself believe that her mother was in a much better place, freed from years of pain, Karma couldn't. Her eternally still, beautifully broken mother had been taken away from her too soon...too violently. She'd been given wings of faith to fly away to be at rest. But she'd left her little girl behind. And now, here Karma was standing before her with a set of her own broken and tattered wings, wondering when they'd be replaced so she could fly away too. Fly to be with her mother again.

Father Pacella stepped out of Karma's way, settled on the other side of her and wrapped his arm around her tiny waist.

Lorenzo, who'd been holding up fairly well until that moment, slowly removed his hat from his head, bent down, and placed a long kiss goodbye on his wife's lips. He whispered something in her ear that only he, God, and Soleil could hear, then broke down unexpectedly. His resonant cries could be heard and felt throughout the entire church. Karma, standing on the little strength she had left, looked away as Father Pacella comforted her with words of encouragement. Two female ushers, dressed in white, escorted Lorenzo to the family's appointed pew.

Father Pacella talked Karma through the moment. And she, in return, nodded in response to everything he said. As his words came to an end, she finally looked back down at her mother. She wanted to go with her so badly, but she knew she had to stay and take care of her father. Karma slowly removed her sunglasses, folded them, and held them in the clutch of her hand. She gradually bent down thereafter and laid her head upon her mother's chest like she'd done so many times as a little girl. She listened and waited for her heartbeat, but it never sounded. She lifted her head afterwards and studied her mother's peaceful face for the final time. She gently placed her hands on each cheek, leaned in, and kissed her softly on the lips. Karma closed her eyes as she turned her face to press her cheek lightly against her mother's lips so she could kiss her back. But when Soleil didn't, Karma began to choke back a fresh set of tears that were brimming in her eyes. She slowly pulled away from the woman who gave her life and walked over to the family's assigned pew. She sat down next to her father and let his head fall onto her shoulder. She leaned her head against his and stroked his face as they watched the rest of the family say their final goodbyes.

The family made their way down the church steps once Soleil's casket was locked and closed in the hearse. As they stepped off the final step and onto the sidewalk, something propelled Karma to look up. When she did, she saw a figure standing across the street looking directly at her. Money, dressed in his suited police uniform, stood in an about-face position. He closed his white gloved hand into a fist, raised it slowly, and placed it firmly over his heart. Karma released a visible heavy breath in response to her secret love's silent declaration. She bit down on her quivering bottom lip and stepped into the tinted window limousine. Her mother hadn't left her to walk alone after all.

Three months passed and the family was getting back to living life with as much normalcy as possible. They managed to survive their first Thanksgiving without Soleil and before they knew it, December rolled in with its frigid air and strong winds. The streets were sheeted with white snow. Newark, New Jersey was a winter wonderland. The city's crime was at its all-time low and the citizens were enjoying the peace and quiet that came with it.

Several patrons sat in the Alonso-Cruz family's spacious lunching room engulfed in conversation. Light Caribbean jazz music played softly over the mini speakers hung in each corner of the space. Busy waiters and waitresses shifted between taking orders and serving customers their meals. Karma, among the many present, made her rounds seeing that every customer was enjoying their stay. To her satisfaction, many were pleased with the service and the cuisine. She often received well wishes and condolences for her loss. Karma, in return, thanked everyone humbly.

Miguel walked into the room in search of his niece. He noticed her engaged in an entertaining conversation with two elderly Cuban men. His face automatically changed to a grim expression once he realized he would have to approach the group. Miguel crossed to the other side of the room and placed his strong, plump hand on Karma's shoulder. She turned her head to see who the hand belonged to and smiled knowing that it was her uncle's. Karma knew her uncle didn't like the two old timers because they would occasionally get fresh with her. But Antonio and Manuel would get fresh with all of the women working at the restaurant. A female waitress would eventually tell Miguel. He'd come out of the kitchen, reprimand the men and remove them from the establishment. But they always returned, behave for a little while, and then start trouble all over again. Miguel forced a smile as he looked the senior citizens over.

"*Como somos nosotros hoy? Hemos otorgado nosotros su cada deseo?*" he asked in a professional tone.

"*Si, si. Usted ha otorgado la mina,*" Antonio replied happily.

Miguel smiled in satisfaction.

"*Acabamos del Karma de decir que el alimento es delicioso, pero probaria major si ella lo servia,*" Manuel jested.

The two men burst into hysterical laughter. Miguel could feel his blood boiling. Manuel's slick reply was exactly what the waitresses complained about. Miguel's face flushed to a deep crimson. He looked over at a grinning Karma and shifted his weight.

"*Ah, si. Si,*" he nodded. "*Eso es chistoso. Muy chistoso. Pero yo me pregunto como Lupe y Vera se sentirian acerca de que desea ungranted suyo. No seria una vista bonita si dijimos, ahora lo hace?*" he asked with a sly grin.

The smiles on Antonio and Manuel's faces faded quickly.

"*Ahora si usted dos caballeros nos dispensarian,*" Miguel said politely.

He gently placed his arm around Karma's waist and pulled her away. The two settled at the entrance of the dining hall.

"Take no prisoners, *Tio*," Karma spoke through a hardy chuckle. She loved her uncle Miguel so very much. He was the quieter of her two uncles and the sweetest. She could tell he took after her grandfather more so than her grandmother because of his laid-back demeanor. Nothing bothered him...nothing except his sister's murder. Miguel was handling her death well. He had his moments where he'd break down and cry at any given time or place, but all in all, he was a trooper. When Karma looked at her precious uncle, she saw the Pillsbury Doughboy. Miguel was shaped just like him. From the spherical shaped eyes right down to his small feet, her uncle was the little doughboy incarnate. She always wondered why he never married. He was such a great catch. Karma figured he probably didn't want to get caught up in any female drama. Who could blame him?

"It's not funny, Karma. It's hard enough to keep my eyes on Maggie and Indigo when she's here. I don't have time to look after you, too. I've asked you time and time again not to let those two back in here," he uttered in frustration.

Karma ran her fingers through her uncle's curly mane.

"I know you have, *Tio*. But Antonio and Manny have been eatin' here since the very first day we opened. They're loyal and so are their families. You and I, both, know they've been very good to us over the years. We can't just turn them away now," Karma stated matter-of-factly.

Miguel sighed heavily in response to her declaration.

"I know you don't like 'em, *Tio*, but this is business. We have to be professional at all times. To allow the disdain you have for certain patrons to show on your face and in your actions is unprofessional and unacceptable."

Miguel placed his hands on his hips and shook his head.

"I don't care. I don't like the way they joke with you. I don't like it."

Karma waved her hand dismissively and said, "Oh, they're harmless, *Tio*. If I took every inappropriate thing a male customer has said to me personally, you and I would *both* be locked up right now."

A smile crept along Miguel's pale face. He began to laugh at the stated fact.

"Aww, see," Karma said as she poked her uncle in his potbelly. "There you go. There's the laugh I love to hear," she cooed.

"I don't know what I'm going to do with you, *mija*," Miguel admitted.

"Unfortunately, *Tio*, you're not the only one," Karma confessed.

Miguel pinched her cleft chin. It was nice to see his niece smile again.

"*Ah mi Dios*, if my sister could see you now. She'd be so proud."

Miguel never saw anything like it before. Karma was doing better than anyone could have ever expected. Considering all the stress that was accompanying her mother's left over bills and other legal documents, Karma was handling all that came her way with resolve and grace. There was little time to feel sorry for herself. She wasn't the only one in the world who'd lost her mother. The circumstances were unfortunate, but she had to move forward and take care of business. Justice would be served for Soleil eventually.

A loud silence fell between uncle and niece.

"Did you open the letter yet?" he asked hesitantly.

Miguel had given Karma an envelope containing a letter her mother had written to her last year while recovering from Jimmy's sodomy. She'd instructed her favorite baby-faced brother to give it to Karma if, and ONLY if, she'd succumbed to Jimmy's abuse. Miguel had placed the sealed envelope in Karma's hands at the repast they'd held at the restaurant after Soleil's funeral.

"No," she admitted solemnly. "Not yet. I don't know if I'm

ever goin' to."

"Okay. Well...," Miguel began. "...there's an Officer Parks waiting for you out front."

Karma batted her gray eyes in surprise.

"Really?"

"Yes. He says he's a friend of yours?" Miguel asked in confusion.

"He is," Karma confirmed.

"Okay. Well, go. Don't keep him waiting," he insisted.

"Okay." Karma smiled at her uncle before exiting the room.

Karma walked into the front of the building and watched Money observe the world outside of one of the huge picture windows. Money had become a permanent fixture in Karma's life. He had called to check on her the night of her mother's funeral and a respected friendship had evolved. They talked on the phone for hours every night and had gone on a couple of dates here and there, but nothing serious. Seeing Money standing at the window in his police uniform caused a chill to run down Karma's spine. She studied his masculine legs through his uniform pants and wondered how many squats he did a day to get those legs. He was a beautiful man, simply beautiful. Money, with his hands in his black bomber jacket pockets, shifted his weight back and forth from one foot to the other. Karma cleared her throat to capture his attention. Money turned around and smiled at the sight of his love interest.

"Hi," Karma said softly.

Money walked over to her and the two embraced in a friendly hug.

"Hi," Money responded.

"Sorry I didn't call you back last night. I fell asleep," Karma said regretfully.

"That's alright." Money shrugged. "I figured you did after spending all day moving your stuff into your mom's house, getting a new carpet for your old room and all of that. Did they get a chance to put it down for you?"

"Yeah, they did. It looks nice in there. Maybe one of these days you can drop by and take a look at it," Karma teased with a seductive grin.

Money blushed.

"For real?" he asked coolly.

"For real," she smirked.

Money scratched his chin and smiled at Karma's flirtatious ways. He never saw this side of her, but he was surely enjoying it. Her flirting, to him, meant that he was one step away from capturing her heart. Karma was reeling him in and Money was going to make sure he took *all* the bait.

"I can do that," he nodded. "I can definitely do that. I might even go out and get you a little house warming gift. You like surprises?" he asked with his deep brown eyes locked on her. Money loved looking at Karma. He couldn't help himself. He felt it was a sin for any man to not look her way. Her golden hair always smelled sweet, her lips were full and even more inviting when she wore lip gloss. She fit perfectly in his arms when he held her close, and her eyes, her eyes reminded him of two mood rings. They were clearly blue when he met her, then they'd suddenly shifted to a dark gray the night her mother was killed, and now they were a lighter gray with a green tint. Money thought all of the colors suited her well.

"Only good ones," Karma admitted.

"I hear that," Money replied. "So, I mean, are you busy right now? I'm on my lunch break and I wanted to talk to you for a little bit."

"No, I'm not too busy that I can't step away for a little while. Just let me go get my things and tell my uncle I'm leavin'," Karma expressed dutifully.

"Okay. I'll wait here, then."

Karma turned and walked away with Money watching her closely.

Money and Karma strolled down one of the many paths in Newark's notoriously dangerous and beautiful Branch Brook Park. Few people were in the park, but enough passed the couple by.

Karma outlined the bare limbs on the tall trees that hovered above. She tried not to notice Money staring at her, but couldn't help but look over at him from time to time herself. Gradually, Money's stride began to shorten and he finally came to a complete halt. Karma followed suit with furrowed eyebrows.

"Is there somethin' wrong?" she asked in concern.

Money looked down into Karma's eyes with apprehension. Karma watched the man before her struggle with his words. His mouth was moving, yet there was nothing coming out of it. Karma couldn't imagine what was possibly keeping Money from expressing himself. He was always so sure of himself. And here he was standing before her nervous as a little school boy. She didn't know whether to laugh or cry. Money let out a sigh of uncertainty before speaking.

"I'm really digging you, Karma. I'm talking about on a level I never even knew existed. I've been digging you since..." Money paused. He wasn't sure if he could continue knowing Karma stole his heart the very moment he laid eyes on her. Under the known circumstances, he was uncertain if saying how he truly felt was appropriate.

Karma nodded and waited for Money's unspoken proclamation.

"Go on. You can say it," she insisted. "I'm not gonna break down and cry or anything," Karma reassured him with her dimpled grin.

"Okay. Well, I've been digging you since the moment I saw you at your mother's birthday party. It was one thing to see you from across the room, but to have gotten a chance to see you up close and personal was a whole 'nother story." Money hesitated and watched Karma nod for him to continue. He had her undivided attention. Money smiled at the thought and continued. "I know you didn't like me at first because I came off cocky, but it's a part of me. It's not all of me, but it is a part of me. And by no means am I vain, but I do take pride in taking care of myself, may it be by the way I dress, speak, or conduct myself. All I know is I *am* that nigga. We've been talking now for three months, we've gone on a couple of dates, and I've really enjoyed the time we've spent together. So, I guess what

I'm trying to say is…I'd like for us to be more than just friends."

Karma's eyebrows raised in surprise. She hadn't expected Money to pour his heart out to her like this. The attraction between the two of them was obvious, but Karma wasn't ready to pursue a relationship with him or so she made herself believe. Money was a police officer. He was her only cousin's partner. And to make matters worse, Karma's nerves were already shot from worrying about Indigo's safety night after night. She'd lost, both, her fiancé and her father to the war on the streets of foreign lands. She wasn't sure if she could handle another man in her life throwing his safety out the window for the sake of others on their own territory. And then there was her mother. Karma still had unfinished business to take care of regarding Soleil. A man, especially the one standing in her presence, would get in her way of executing her plans.

Karma bit down on her bottom lip and grinned sadly.

"Money, don't take what I'm about to say to you out of context, okay?"

Money placed his hands behind his back and nodded.

"I know we've been talkin' for three months now, but it's still too soon for me to even think about gettin' into a relationship with you or anyone else for that matter. I'm in no position to be your woman. The emotional and mental state I'm in right now would keep me from givin' you what you need. And that's just not fair to you. I've gotta lotta things that I'm tryin' to take care of right now and I don't want you to get caught up in it. You *are* that nigga. Any woman can see that. But I am *not* that bitch."

Money's lips turned into a frown. He couldn't believe Karma had convinced herself into believing that she didn't want to be with him as much as he wanted to be with her. He understood the daily struggle she had with her emotions and thoughts regarding her mother, but Money also knew Karma was stronger than she may have believed. Any woman who could still laugh and smile only a few months after burying her mother was one strong individual. Money thought back to the weeks that just passed and how gruelling and stressful the job had unexpectedly become. He'd call Karma and tell her about his day, she'd listen quietly and patiently, then calm him down with words of wisdom or a kind email to get him through the rest of his weary days. Money had a feeling Karma was afraid. She was afraid to love and lose again. She was holding herself back. She was her own worst enemy and Money decided he'd put an end to it that moment.

"Well, I know you're not that bitch, because you're not a bitch at all. You're a queen. And you know, just as well as I do, that you are *that* woman. So you can feed yourself those lies if you want to, but they don't move me. I want you, Karma. And I'll take you if I have to," Money confirmed with the tilt of his head.

Karma's mouth dropped open. She couldn't believe Money just read her through and through. He'd pinpointed her fear and dismissed it completely all in the same breath. Karma was aware she no longer had the upper hand in the situation, but she wasn't going to lose without a good fight. Money didn't want to give up easily, that was fine with her. She would make him work even harder to earn her love and affection.

Karma stepped back and crossed her arms at her chest.

"Is that right?" she asked with a smirk.

Money stepped into Karma's space, tilted his head, and looked deeply into her eyes.

"Right it is," he spoke smoothly. "Look, I only know half of what you've been through. But I'm here to learn the rest. And, in time, you'll learn just as much about me as my woman," Money said matter-of-factly as he licked his full lips.

Karma looked up at Money and shook her head in disbelief. She was definitely losing this battle. He'd topped his confession off with licking his lips. How could she say no to those lips and that tongue of his?

"Money-", Karma began.

Money gently grabbed Karma's cleft chin and held it with his thumb and index finger.

"Indigo told me what happened to Joaquin."

Karma looked away, but Money turned her face back to him.

"He got caught up in the hype of this war," he continued. "He's no different from the next soldier. He signed his life away and it was taken from him. Make peace with it, Karma. Because what I've heard from you, by the way you've been talking, you got your own war to fight. I don't know what it is, but make sure it exists and it's worth fighting."

Karma's cell phone rang breaking her focus away from Money. She retrieved it out of her pocketbook, flipped it open, and placed it to her ear.

"Hello? Oh, hey, Stuffy."

Money looked on in confusion. He'd never heard Karma talk in such a high voice. He questioned her with his eyes. She, in return, put her index finger up as a signal to him that she wouldn't be on the phone much longer.

"No, I'm just takin' a walk in Branch Brook. Yes, I have someone with me," she said with a smile. "What's up? You did? Tomorrow night? Yeah, I can do that. Good lookin' out. Alright, ma dude. Bye." Karma closed her phone and placed it back into her pocketbook. She stepped back over to Money grinning widely.

Money smiled back and asked, "Stuffy, huh?"

"You teasin' me?" Karma asked in jest.

"No," Money lied.

"Yes, you are," Karma insisted.

"No, I'm not. It's cute though. I didn't know you gave out pet names," he insinuated.

"I don't *give* out anything. I take," Karma stated with the raise of her eyebrow.

"Oh, yeah?" Money asked in a low, seductive voice.

"Yeah," Karma confirmed sweetly.

"Then, show me what you take," Money demanded sensually as he leaned down and prepared his lips for a long awaited kiss. Karma moved in close enough to touch Money where he wanted to feel her ever so badly, but quickly turned her face and etched her mouth to his ear.

"I take niggas' hearts and run wit' 'em," she said in a whisper. "Catch me if you can." Karma broke out into a hysterical laugh and sprinted down the pathway. Money stood in shock for a moment before he realized he'd just been played for a fool. Once his senses returned, he ran after Karma for his much desired kiss of confirmation. Unfortunately, he never got it. The large hot tea and box of Dunkin Donuts he'd scarfed down earlier in the day kept him from achieving his goal. Money accepted his defeat like a man, but vowed he'd get Karma in his arms sooner or later.

KARMA

Chapter 13

K arma sat on the edge of her mother's former bed with the cordless phone resting between the crook of her neck and her shoulder. She listened to Indigo rant and rave about the meeting she was going to have with Hawk in a couple of hours. Karma rolled her eyes as she slipped her feet into her suede knee-high boots. She made sure the sharp heels were in tact before rising from the bed and heading over to check herself over in the mirror. The rye-colored cable knit dress Karma wore accentuated every curve in her sculpted body. Karma retrieved a large brown leather belt off the dresser and wrapped it around her petite waist. She buckled and centered it thereafter.

"You are so lucky I'm on duty tonight, because if I wasn't, I swear to God, you and I would be rolling on the floor right now," Indigo spat on the other end of the phone.

"You are such a drama queen, Indigo. I swear," Karma laughed. "I really think you chose the wrong profession," she said as she analyzed her hair in the mirror. She fixed a stray piece and set it back into place.

"And I think you're making a bad decision by going to meet with that old fart, Hawk, tonight," Indigo retaliated.

Karma cringed at the sound of her cousin's domineering tone. Indigo was way out of line. In life, a girl had to do what she had to do and Karma was a firm believer in that.

"Well, what would you rather me do then, Indigo?" Karma asked furiously as she spun around and sat against the dresser. "Sit around and wait for you and your buddies in black to do somethin', because you're not. My mother's been in the ground for three months now and ya'll still haven't found Jimmy's ass. And you wanna know why? Because ya'll ain't lookin' for 'im." Karma felt her blood boiling. She knew her cousin meant well and was only concerned for her safety, but Indigo's approach was far too aggressive for her liking.

"This is some bullshit. I don't have time for this," Indigo huffed.

"Oh, no, you have the time. You have plenty of time," Karma spoke into the phone with widened eyes. "You had enough time to call me up to try to talk me out of my meetin' with Hawk. So you have enough time to deal with what we're talkin' about right now."

Indigo sighed into the phone. The last thing she wanted to do was upset her cousin and she'd done exactly that. The conversation wasn't going the way she'd planned it and there was no way of fixing what was already broken. The two were way too deep into their disagreement. Indigo was well-aware of how dangerous the men Stuff worked for were. She couldn't imagine Karma getting caught up in some mess she wouldn't be able get out of. Although, she knew her cousin could hold her own, the drug game was a whole different story. It was a world within itself and it was no place for a woman. God only knew what Hawk would make Karma do for or to him in an advance to finding Jimmy's whereabouts. Her cousin was beautiful and she had great sex appeal, no matter how much she tried to downplay it. The thought of the plans Hawk could possibly have for Karma sent chills through Indigo's body. She sighed again in dismay.

Karma looked up to the ceiling and rubbed her forehead.

"Just separate yourself from bein' a cop for one minute, Indi. Okay?" she begged. "You're in police mode right now. I need you to be Indigo, my cousin, whose aunt was murdered by her boyfriend three months ago. I need you to be my cousin, a citizen of Newark, New Jersey and the girlfriend of a drug dealer who knows the game like the back of her hand because of him," Karma said in a disgusted tone as she looked towards the carpeted floor. "I want you to tell me, with all of your heart and soul, that I can and I *should* put my trust in the 5th precinct," she continued in a softer tone. "You tell me that and I swear on my mother, I will hand it over to them. If you know they've made her one of their top priorities, I will cancel my meetin' with Hawk, direct my attention elsewhere, and keep it movin'. I'll leave it alone."

A sniffle sounded from the other end of the receiver. Karma closed her eyes and shook her head in shame. Indigo was crying and it was all her fault. She never meant to make her feel guilty for caring about her well-being, but her mind was already made up. She was going to meet with Hawk whether Indigo liked it or not. Her mother was *not* going to die in vain. And Karma would not rest until Jimmy was found and punished for what he did.

"Indigo?" Karma asked timidly.

"I can't tell you any of that," Indigo managed to mutter between sniffles. "I wish I could."

"I know you do," Karma responded regretfully. "Look, I know you're worried about me, okay? If I didn't know what I was gettin' myself into, I wouldn't have gone to the extremes of settin' up this meetin'. You have to trust me on this, Indi. I need your support."

The doorbell rang interrupting the girls' conversation.

"Listen, your boo's at the door," Karma continued as she travelled over to her closet and retrieved a sable fur jacket. "We should be home no later than three-thirty," she went on to say as she put the jacket on crossing back over to the mirror to give herself one last glance over. "I'mma leave the spare key under the doormat for you. Come by if you feel you need to check on me, okay?"

"Okay," Indigo responded meekly.

"Alright. I love you," Karma replied sweetly.

"Love you, too," Indigo said in return.

Stuff and Karma entered the crowded reggae club in deep conversation. Stuff was making sure Karma had her story straight and that every aspect of her tale of lies could be justified by anything Hawk may ask her in the meeting. Stuff knew his boss well enough to know he liked to know the ins and outs of his clientele. Hawk asked the questions and the client was expected to answer them. Karma was growing tired and frustrated from the constant questioning. Stuff had been testing her from the time they left her house to the time they pulled up to the club. Stuff explained that their safety depended on there being no holes in her story. Karma eventually surrendered and changed her bothered disposition to a more pleasant one.

The massive crowd was shown under dimly lit red and pink lights from above. Stuff assisted Karma in removing her fur jacket and held it over the crook of his left arm. As the two moved through the crowd, men and women alike, turned to watch the known drug dealer and the mystery woman make their way to the back. Stuff dapped hands and smiled at some while giving threatening glares to others. Karma, unmoved by the catcalls from the sea of men around her, continued to move forward with unbroken concentration. She and Stuff walked to the back of the room where they stopped to speak to a bouncer who was blocking a black door. The bouncer and Stuff embraced in a half-hug before the large man took Karma's hand into his and kissed it. The gentle giant opened the door allowing the two to trail up the flight of steps. Once Stuff and Karma reached the top of the stairway, they immediately stepped into a black carpeted hallway. The brick layered walls created an uncomfortable frigidness in the foyer. Muffled laughter sounded from behind a door the two were walking towards. Stuff, knowing the familiar laugh, knocked on the door and waited for a response. A voice from beyond the wall beckoned the young man to enter.

"Wait here for a minute," Stuff instructed Karma.

"Okay," Karma replied with a nod.

Stuff entered a brightly lit brick-layered room. He closed the door behind him as he locked eyes with a silver-haired man who was reclining in his leather swivel chair behind a large wooden desk. The man's pointed eyebrows accentuated his old eyes. The large gap between his two top front teeth was hard to ignore as he smiled. Hawk handed over a white envelope to another older gentleman who was sitting across from him in one of the guest chairs. The man, who went by the name "Slick," ran his hand over his freshly permed hair and pulled at the low ponytail that hung at the nape of his neck. He retrieved the envelope graciously and placed it inside his suit jacket. He and Hawk, who were both expensively dressed in navy blue suits, turned their attention to Stuff who had not moved from the doorway.

"Stuff-Like-That! My main man. Step in a little closer," Hawk insisted with his gap-toothed grin.

Stuff walked a few feet away from the door and nodded at both men.

"Hawk. Slick."

"Stuff, what's happenin'?! How's it hangin', soldier?" Slick asked in jest.

"All da way to da floor," Stuff replied with a straight face.

Hawk and Slick fell out into hysterical laughter.

"Now, that's what I like to hear! We trained this muthafucka good, didn't we?!" Slick asked Hawk proudly.

"Sure 'nough," Hawk said with a nod and grin.

"I can't believe this nigga is up in rank. Nigga been wit' us for what?" Slick looked from Hawk to Stuff for an answer.

"Twelve years," Stuff replied.

"Twelve muthafuckin' years! Goddamn, I'm old as hell!" Slick exclaimed.

The three men shared a hardy laugh.

"Sure 'nough," Hawk said again.

"Aww, nigga, I know you ain't sqauwkin'," Slick spat, offended by his friend's last comment.

Hawk raised in hands in surrender.

"Time is a bitch," Slick continued as he shook his head in disbelief. "For real. Goddamn, it seems like only yesterday when we recruited your ass. And now you're a muthafuckin' lieutenant colonel. How you likin' your status, young blood?"

"I'm lovin' it, nah mean," Stuff replied with a humble smile. "All day, everyday."

"That's good. Keep doin' what you doin' and you'll be a sergeant sooner than you think," Slick confirmed.

"Aiight," Stuff nodded.

Hawk leaned forward on his desk and began to drum his fingers along the massive structure.

"What can I do for you, Stuff?"

"I got my peoples here wit' me. You and her got dat meetin' tonight," Stuff reminded his boss.

Hawk's eyebrows furrowed in confusion, and then reset themselves once he remembered what matter Stuff was speaking about.

"Oh, yes. Yes. I almost forgot. Is she outside?"

"Yeah," Stuff replied.

"Well, alright. Bring her in," Hawk instructed.

Stuff turned away and walked out of the room. Hawk and Slick picked up from where they left off in the conversation they were having before Stuff arrived. As the door to the office reopened, Stuff stepped back into the room and positioned himself on the side of the door. The conversation between the two kingpins ceased as soon as they set their eyes on Karma. Karma entered the room with her jacket hung over the crook of her left arm and her head held high. Her mother's pride rested on her shoulders and with that she immediately locked eyes with Hawk.

"Goddamn!" Slick blurted out before he could catch himself. He shook his head in utter disbelief as Hawk swivelled from side-to-side in his chair. Their eyes outlined every inch of Karma's statuesque body.

"Gentlemen," Hawk spoke sternly to Stuff and Slick with the raise of his eyebrows.

Slick rose from his chair without argument and strolled past Karma taking in every inch of her before exiting the room with Stuff. Karma remained where she stood and kept her eyes on

Hawk. He was the man she was there to see and he was the man she was studying.

"May I?" Karma asked as she gestured toward the guest chairs.

"You may," Hawk nodded.

Karma walked slowly over to the chair opposite of the one Slick had occupied, placed her jacket on the arm of it, then sat down. She turned her attention back to Hawk. By the lustful way he was looking at her, Karma knew she had him right where she wanted him. Acknowledging the fact he hadn't taken his eyes off her since she stepped into the room, Karma took advantage of the moment and decided to cross her legs in a slow, sensual manner. She showed off her warm dimpled grin thereafter.

Hawk cleared his throat in discomfort. He'd been in the business for over thirty years and many women had come to him seeking justice for slain loved ones. But never before had any of those women, young or old, been as beautiful as Karma. Although, Hawk did know of one woman, a friend of his brother-in-law's, that he'd met on a couple of occasions who was as stunning as the young lady sitting before him. She was, too, uncomfortably gorgeous and shared the same fire in her eyes.

"How may I help you, Miss…?" Hawk began.

"Cruz. It's Cruz, but you can call me Doll," Karma insisted.

"That name suits you well," Hawk complimented.

"Thank you. I'm sorry I can't say the same," Karma replied apologetically.

Hawk smiled widely. Karma's ladylike demure was incredibly attractive for someone so young.

"Well, Miss Doll, if you must know, I was named for my keen sense of sight. My vision is the strongest of my five senses."

"I can tell," Karma admitted.

"You can? How so?" Hawk asked as he tilted his head back.

"By the way you're trying to look through me," Karma replied with a smirk.

Hawk laughed in amazement.

"You're very observant, Miss Doll. You don't miss a thing. That's good. That's very good." Hawk folded his fingers under his chin. "Stuff spoke very highly of you. He said you've known each other since you were kids."

"Yes, we have. Since elementary school. He's like a brother to me," Karma confessed humbly.

"I'm glad you said that, Miss Doll, because I am a firm believer in family. Stuff is like a son to me. He's been a part of this family for twelve years now and never once has he ever come to me or Owl for anything…until now." Hawk unfolded his fingers and leaned back in his chair. He placed his index finger at his temple and allowed his chin to rest on his thumb. "I know he must have great love for you to put his pride aside to come and ask me for this meeting. I think you will agree, Miss Doll, that it takes a humble man to ask for help."

"Yes, it does," Karma responded with a straight face.

"If you don't mind me asking, what do you do for a living? I only ask because I like to know a little something about the people I'm dealing with," Hawk confirmed.

"No, no, I understand," she replied shaking her head. "I'm into real estate. I invest in commercially and privately owned businesses, particularly restaurants, bakeries, and coffee houses. Most of my clients are located in the Iron Bound section of Newark. I'm currently in negotiations with a new proprietor who is interested in opening a coffee house in the Downtown section of the city, right on Broad and Market Street," she said proudly.

"A coffee house?" Hawk asked perplexed.

"Yes, sir. A coffee house," Karma repeated.

Hawk began to bounce back and forth in his chair. He was still bewildered in understanding the significance of a coffee house in the city.

"Tell me more about these coffee houses, because, by no means am I a stupid man, but I am quite ignorant of these little houses of coffee you're speaking of."

Karma laughed to herself.

"The coffee house is a prominent productive sector in the Hispanic community, especially in the Cuban community. Most of the islands in the West Indies thrive on major goods like: fruit, sugar cane, and coffee beans."

"I see. Well, you definitely know your history. Tell me, have you ever thought about expanding your horizons and venturing into the nightclub scene?" Hawk asked sincerely.

Karma folded her hands in her lap.

"No, I can't say that I have, sir. The business never really appealed to me, nor has anyone ever approached me with a proposition that interested me."

Hawk's pointed eyebrows rose highly.

"Well, I can change that for you. You obviously know what you're talking about and dipping into the business wouldn't hurt your pockets. It would only help them."

"I'm flattered, but again, the club scene never appealed to me and it still doesn't. I will keep an open mind though," Karma replied with her broad white smile.

Hawk leaned forward into the desk. He placed his hands back onto the desktop and folded them.

"Good, I'm glad to hear that. And I'm glad to see a woman who knows what she wants," he said with a warm smile. "Now, with that said, Miss Doll, how can I be of service to you this evening?"

"I need assistance in finding my mother's killer," Karma stated without blinking.

"I see. Well, there's a few questions I need to ask you before we continue," he uttered.

"That's fine," Karma said with the shrug of her shoulders.

Hawk opened one of the desk drawers and retrieved a notepad and pen. He shut the drawer thereafter and placed the items on the desktop.

"What is your mother's name?"

"Marisol," she replied without hesitation.

"Alright," Hawk continued. "And how long ago did the murder occur?"

"This past July," Karma lied.

"Cause of death?"

"She was stabbed to death," she confirmed with an expressionless face.

"Okay. Do you have any idea who may have wanted to kill her? Did she have a boyfriend or…?" Hawk questioned her with his sharp eyes.

"No, she was happily married to my father," Karma said sadly. She could feel her face starting to flush. She was sitting before a man who seemed very sincere about wanting to help her find her mother's killer and she was lying to him with a straight face. She and Stuff hadn't discussed the consequences they'd have to deal with if Hawk found out they were being untruthful. The two hadn't even discussed how Karma would continue or what she would do after her end of her bargain was met. That bridge the friends had not yet come to was surely approaching and quick.

Hawk proceeded to write the last bit of information down on the pad. He completed his last note and pushed the pen and paper to the side.

"Well, first, I want to extend my condolences to you and your family."

"Thank you," Karma replied with a nod.

"You're very welcome. It truly is a shame. Now, do you mind if we proceed with business?" Hawk asked.

"No." Karma shook her head.

"Alright, well, look, Miss Doll. I'm not going to beat around the bush with you. I like you and you seem like a woman who can hold her own. We don't do for you until you do for us. That is our one and only rule," Hawk stated sternly.

"I see. Well, now that we have established your rule, it's time to establish mine," Karma answered authoritatively. "I pay my dues as I go…with the exception of fucking, sucking, or licking anyone. And I expect nothing less than the credit I deserve for my services. In this case, my mother's killer," she said with the raise of her perfectly arched eyebrow.

Hawk sat back in his chair astounded by Karma's commanding and astute response. She was very serious about her position in his arrangement, but had enough sense and respect for herself to refuse degrading her body in return for his request. Karma was definitely one in a million. The many women before her never told Hawk what they would or would not do. Why, he did not know. He guessed they were way too desperate to dispute his rule. Nonetheless, he accepted them for who they were. Karma, on the other hand, put her desperation to the side and was handling business with no care or concern of losing anything but her self-respect.

Hawk nodded and smiled at Karma with great adulation.

"You're something else, Miss Doll. I haven't come in contact with a woman like you since my wife," he said as he chuckled to himself.

"Is that a good thing or a bad thing?" Karma asked in puzzlement.

"It's a good thing…a very good thing. I'm very impressed to say the least. And you'll be pleased to know that we can and we will accommodate you. You have a sharp mind and a quick tongue. I like that. I like that very much." Hawk smiled.

"Thank you." Karma smiled back.

"Tell me, Miss Doll. Do you drink? And if so, can you hold your liquor?" Hawk asked with a sly grin.

Karma entered her bedroom with her boots in hand and Stuff trailing behind her with a bowl of ice cream in his clutches. The room was lit by the picture on the big, flat screen television. The volume on the tube was turned down to its lowest decibel. Karma caught sight of Indigo sleeping heavily on her stomach beneath the mounds of covers on her bed. Her snores were baby-like and Karma hoped they would stay that way as she rubbed her heavy eyes and walked over to the bed to sit down. She retrieved the box for the boots from beneath the bed and placed them neatly back inside of it. As she pushed the box back underneath the bed with the heel of her foot, Indigo let out a loud, abrupt snort. It caused Karma and Stuff to snap their heads in her direction and stare at her in disbelief.

"Unh-unh, Stuff. Get ya girl," Karma demanded as she shook her head in disgust.

Stuff laughed at Karma's outburst and traveled over to the side of the bed where Indigo was sleeping. He set his bowl of ice cream down on the floor, carefully bent down, and kissed his love sweetly on the cheek.

"Baby?" he whispered.

Indigo squirmed a little in response to Stuff's call.

"Baby, come on," he continued. "Wake ya sexy ass up."

Indigo's eyes slowly opened. Once her other half came into full focus, she acknowledged him with a smile.

"Hey, boo. What time is it?" she asked sleepily.

"It's a little afta three," he established.

"Oh," Indigo replied blinking her eyes slowly. "Where's Karma?"

"She's sittin' ova dere on da otha side of da bed," Stuff pointed.

"K," Indigo whispered before sleep overtook her once again. Her snoring started up again and Stuff looked up at Karma with pitiful eyes. Karma, unaffected by Stuff's pathetic, vulnerable state, pointed to the door with her thumb.

"Ya'll can sleep in one of the guest rooms."

"Aiight," Stuff replied gratefully as he pulled the covers off Indigo.

Karma made her way to a chair set in the corner where her flannel pajamas were waiting for her. Stuff bent down and picked Indigo's petite body into his lean arms. She, unconsciously, wrapped her arms around his neck and buried her head into his chest. Stuff crossed around the bed and made his way towards the door.

"Can we stay in da blue room? I love dat room, yo," he admitted to Karma with pleading eyes.

"Yes, you can stay in the blue room, Stuffy," Karma said with a smile.

"Dat's what I'm talkin' 'bout. Thanks, Karm," he replied walking out the door.

"Anytime," Karma said with the wave of her hand. "And, Stuff?"

Stuff spun around carefully.

"What's up?"

KARMA

"I know how you two get down in the mornin'. Take the sheets, towels, and anything else you plan on doin' da booty on and please throw them in the washin' machine after you are through," Karma instructed with a smirk.

"Damn, Karm. Why you tryna play us? You sayin' we're messy or somethin'?" Stuff asked sincerely.

"That's *exactly* what I'm sayin'. And I'm also sayin' you two are nasty as hell. My cousin's got but so many holes for you to fill, okay? You follow?" Karma asked playfully.

Stuff laughed to himself.

"Ya mind is worse den a dude's, Karm. On da real. But, you right. I got'chu."

"Okay. Goodnight."

"Goodnight." Stuff turned and walked out of the room leaving Karma to giggle at the vulgar thought and reflect on the days when Stuff and Indigo were far more careful about the disposal of their bodily fluids.

KARMA

Chapter 14

Indigo sat in one of the cushioned bar stools at the island in her cousin's kitchen eating a hot bowl of Cream of Wheat. She watched Stuff cut a banana into pieces over a huge bowl of Frosted Flakes. Stuff could feel Indigo's eyes on his back from across the room. He turned around and smiled at her with the bowl of cereal in hand. Stuff placed the knife into the dishpan in the sink before walking over to the bar stool beside Indigo and sitting.

"You're an old man, you know that?" Indigo teased with creased eyebrows.

"What'chu talkin' 'bout, girl?!" Stuff asked in surprise. "My great-grandmotha used to put bananas in her cereal all da time. How you think she lived to be ninety-seven? You betta start doin' dis shit too so you can be around for dat long," he exclaimed while placing a spoonful of cereal into his mouth.

"Who said I wanted to be around for dat long?" Indigo asked with an attitude.

Stuff gave his girlfriend a look of disbelief. He wasn't sure if she was playing or not. Whatever the case, he took another bite out of his breakfast before speaking again.

"Let me find out you not tryna be around for our great-grand-children."

Indigo couldn't help but smile at the serious undertone in Stuff's joke. Of course she wanted to live to see their great-grand-children, but Stuff hadn't even asked her to marry him yet. Even though the two lovebirds had known each other all of their lives, it wasn't until Indigo turned eighteen that they became a couple. Stuff was three years older than Indigo and the only thing she ever asked of him was to respect her wishes of not pursuing a relation-ship until she was of legal age. Stuff, in return, did what he was asked and waited.

Only her cousin could have predicted she and Stuff would still be together nine years later. The thought of it was somewhat surre-al. Indigo giggled at the thought of her love's plans for them, their future children, grandchildren, and great-grands. It was nice to know she would still have a place in his life fifty years down the line.

"Whatever, crazy," she teased.

"Yeah, I'm crazy alright. Crazy about'chu, girl. Lean ova here and give ya man a kiss wit' ya sexy self," Stuff demanded with puckered lips. Indigo met her boyfriend half-way and placed a deep kiss on his thick pink lips. The two found themselves lost in anoth-er passionate embrace, completely oblivious to Karma's entrance.

Karma walked into the room in a terry-cloth robe. Her hair and body were still wet from the shower she'd stepped out of only a few moments ago. As she looked on at another one of her cousin and best friend's infamous x-rated kisses, she sighed and cringed in despair. Karma couldn't understand how two people, who woke up engaging in sex, were about to start something she assumed they finished upstairs a half an hour ago. She came to the conclusion her cousin and best male friend were definitely nymphomaniacs.

Karma cleared her throat loudly as she proceeded to make her morning chai latte. Stuff and Indigo smiled at each other as they parted lips and turned their attention to Karma.

"Hater," Indigo spat with a sneer.

"Eat me," Karma sucked her teeth and rolled her eyes.

"No, thank you. That's Money's job," Indigo responded sharply.

Karma smirked and stuck her middle finger up at her cousin who returned the gesture.

"Goddamn, you two go at it everyday. Do I need to go get my belt?" Stuff asked, looking back and forth from Indigo to Karma.

"Shut up, Stuff!" the girls yelled in unison.

The doorbell rang breaking the trio's discomforted morning gathering.

"I'll get it." Indigo hopped off the stool and made her way to the front door. She opened it and was greeted by a young Asian delivery boy holding a wrapped basket of Hershey chocolate bars and kisses. The delivery boy looked down at his electronic pad and read the name on it.

"This is for a: Ms. Karma Walker."

A huge smile grew along Indigo's face.

"Alrighty."

The delivery boy handed Indigo the pad to sign. After she completed her signature, she handed the pad back to the boy who gave her the basket of goodies in return.

"Thank you," she said looking over the massive basket of treats.

"You're welcome. Have a nice day, ma'am," the delivery boy uttered as he turned and walked away.

Indigo closed the front door and locked it. She strolled back into the kitchen with a mischievous smile on her face. She and Karma's eyes met as she placed the basket on the island.

"You have a special delivery, *Ms. Walker*," Indigo mocked.

Karma put her hot cup of tea down on the counter and looked to her cousin for an explanation.

"Dat sure is a lot of chocolate," Stuff said with a mouth full of cereal.

Karma made her way around the island and probed the basket with her hands and eyes.

"Did the delivery man say who it was from?" she asked her beaming cousin.

"Nope." Indigo noticed a card stapled to the back of the basket as Karma continued to turn it. "Wait a minute," Indigo interjected. "The card's right here." Indigo removed the small red envelope from the basket and gave it to her cousin. Karma took the envelope, opened it, and pulled out a simply designed card. She opened it and allowed her eyes to run over the words written upon it. A grin appeared on her face soon after.

"Well, what does it say?" Indigo asked excitedly.

"Yeah, inquirin' minds would like to know and shit," Stuff added.

Karma laughed to herself. Indigo and Stuff were a trip.

"It says, 'YOU CAN RUN, BUT YOU CAN'T HIDE FROM MY KISSES LOVE, MON$Y.'

Indigo's mouth fell open. She was so happy her cousin was on her way to being loved and loving another man again. Karma deserved Money and he deserved her just as well. It warmed Indigo's heart to see her cousin's face light up after reading that card. Money's face lit up the same exact way whenever she spoke of his soon-to-be love. Indigo laughed to herself as she watched Karma read the card over and over again.

"I like dat. Nigga sent a whole basket of Hershey kisses ova here and topped it off wit' a metaphorical note and shit. Dat's peace, yo," Stuff said as he drunk the rest of the contents out of his bowl.

Indigo and Karma burst out into hysterical laughter.

"You definitely have to give him some now, K," Indigo validated.

Karma frowned and playfully threw the card at her cousin. Money. He'd gone beyond the call of duty and surprised her with her all time favorite pastime-chocolate. Karma knew Money was thoughtful, but who would have thought he was just as creative underneath that badge of honor?

Christmas was right around the corner. Karma immediately began to think of different things she could get Money for his favorite day of the year. But no sooner than the wave of gift ideas came, they left. Karma had more important things to do...like figure out the best way to thank Money for his generosity. Then it hit her. She was going to pay him a surprise visit.

Karma pulled up in front of the two-story home next to Money's humble abode. She squinted her gray eyes to get a clearer view of the spectacle that was taking place outside of her car. Money was screaming in the face of a young, dark-skinned woman who was dressed in filthy, tattered clothing. Karma couldn't make out the woman's face from where she was sitting, but she noticed how small the denim jacket the woman was wearing over her holed, mismatching outfit every time her arms flailed in the air. It was frigid outside. Karma knew only a crackhead would be dressed the way that woman was in such weather. She didn't know who the woman was, but was going to make sure to ask Money what her relationship was to him when the woman left.

Karma watched the woman hold her own as she yelled back into Money's twisted face. Uncertain if she should get out of the car or not, Karma decided to do so anyway. She shut the door behind her, walked around to the front of it, and leaned up against the hood zipping up her red parka as the dispute between Money and the drug addict continued.

"What the fuck did I tell you, huh?! What the fuck did I tell you?! I told you to keep ya skank ass away from my goddamn house!" Money screamed through flaring nostrils.

"I wanna see my daughter!" the drug induced woman screeched back.

Karma couldn't believe her ears. Money had a child. For the three months they'd been speaking, the man never said one word about having a child, let alone the mother being a crackhead. Karma didn't know whether to stay or leave after hearing that. Money's level of rage was the second thing that took her by surprise. She never saw him so angry and she never heard him swear. The temper, he also never spoke of, was in full effect. How could Money tell her everything else about his life, but leave something as important as having a child out? She wouldn't have treated him any differently. Karma actually enjoyed the company of children. They were so innocent and it was their purity that made her love them so. Betrayed...that was an understatement.

"You ain't gonna see shit! You ain't got no muthafuckin' daughter!" Money spat viciously.

"You can't keep me from seein' my child! That's my fuckin' daughter in there, Money! She's mine, too!" the woman exclaimed through fallen tears. She suddenly made an attempt towards the steps. She tried to bum-rush Money, but failed. He grabbed her arm spinning her around to face him and proceeded to shake her violently.

"Where the fuck you goin', huh?! What the fuck you think you doin'?!"

The young woman managed to break free from Money's deadly grip and began to throw wild slaps and punches at him.

"Fuck you, Money! Fuck you! I'm her mother! I'm her mother!" she repeated with a heavy tongue.

Money tried his best to get a hold of his ex's wildly swinging arms, but could not. He, unexpectedly, lost all control and brutally pushed her to the ground. His daughter's mother hit the cold concrete with a loud thud.

"Get the fuck up!" Money screamed, standing over her.

Karma remained by her car watching in total shock. She couldn't move and to hell with jumping in the middle of their quarrel. She'd stay put and wait until the fight was over.

"I'm her mother!" the woman cried, scrambling to her feet.

"Get the fuck out of here!" Money spat, shoving his ex away from his property.

The woman accepted her loss for the day and scurried away from Money. But as she walked past the neighboring house, she spotted Karma leaning up against her car. She walked up to her rubbing her running nose.

"Excuse me, ma'am, do you have any spare change?"

Karma couldn't speak. The young woman looked so awful. Her skin was blotched and covered with pock marks. Her lips were in terrible need of moisturizing. Her eyes were sunken in and full of sadness...desperation. Karma knew that look all too well. The woman was a victim of loss and she'd eventually given up on living. Karma felt sorry for her. They had to be around the same age. It was just a shame the woman was too far gone to get her soul back.

"Please, ma'am?" the young woman begged with a frail hand extended and bouncing on the tips of her toes.

Karma opened her mouth to speak again, hoping something would come out, but noticed Money charging in their direction. The woman followed Karma's eyes.

"A, yo! Get the fuck away from her!" Money screamed angrily.

Before he could reach the two women, the drug addict made a quick dash down the street. Karma watched the woman disappear around a corner. She, then, slowly turned her attention back to Money who was pacing back and forth on the sidewalk.

Money sat on the bottom step of his stoop with his hands interlocked on the back of his hung head. Karma stood with her arms folded at her chest and her left leg resting on the second to last step of Money's stoop. Her face was tight with rage.

"How old is she?" she asked, looking out towards the street.

"Three," Money mumbled.

"Three, huh?" Karma shook her head. "And her name is Mimi."

"Yeah," Money replied without looking up. He never felt so horrible in all his life. He wanted to tell Karma about his little girl the moment they officially started seeing each other, but he'd been too afraid of her reaction. Money's "baby mama drama" was the epitome of them all. If he wasn't sorry for not telling Karma about Mimi in the beginning, he was surely sorry now.

"That's a pretty name," Karma admitted genuinely.

"Thank you," Money replied softly.

Karma repositioned the fleeced hat on her head.

"Can I ask you a question?"

"Yeah," Money muttered hesitantly.

"Why didn't you tell me about your little girl and her mother when we started talkin' back in September?"

Money slowly looked up at Karma with remorseful eyes. She'd

asked a valid question. It was a question that deserved a just answer. Rejection was Money's worst fear in life. It was the greatest fear for many men. Money breathed deep and released his breath. Could he be man enough to admit he was afraid she'd leave him if he told her?

"'Cause I didn't know how to," was all Money could muster.

"You didn't know how to?" Karma asked in a calm annoyance.

"No. I mean, what was I supposed to say, Karma?" Money asked desperately.

"I don't know." Karma shrugged her shoulders and looked deep into Money's eyes for an answer. "Maybe somethin' like, 'I have a daughter. Her mother and I aren't together and haven't *been* together in however many years mostly because of her addiction to drugs'."

"And you would have accepted that?" Money asked with a look of distrust.

"Yes, I would have. It would have been an honest answer," Karma replied sternly.

Money ran his hand over his goatee and shook his head.

"It's not that easy, Karma. I'm not proud that my daughter's mother is a crackhoe and got eight other kids by seven other dudes. I'm not proud of that shit."

"You shouldn't be," Karma confessed. "It sounds like to me, you didn't know what type of chick she was when you started fuckin' wit' her."

"I didn't." Money held his forehead in his hand. A severe migraine was forming. He could feel it. "I knew she smoked weed and she liked to drink and club occasionally, but I didn't know she was an undercover fiend. She didn't look like that when I met her. And she didn't mention anything about having kids."

"And I understand that. But I'm not gonna stand here and take pity on you, Money. Look at me," Karma stressed. Money lowered his hand and gave Karma his undivided attention. "You're a grown ass man and you had the choice to strap your shit up when you ran up in that girl. But you didn't." Karma looked away briefly shaking her head. "I do admire you, though," she continued as she looked back at Money. "Just for the simple fact that you've been raisin' your little girl all by yourself. That's somethin' else. I commend you for that."

"Thank you," Money replied humbly.

"No problem." Karma became tickled with laughter.

Money looked up at her in confusion. Nothing was funny to him. Having Mimi and a crackhead for an ex was either going to make or break their relationship.

"What's so funny?"

"This is just unbelievable. Your baby mama drama is on a whole 'nother level. I don't even know how I should feel about all of this," Karma admitted through an inappropriate giggle.

"I know. I apologize," Money said pitifully. "I understand if, uh, if you want to recline or whatever."

The grin from Karma's face disappeared. Didn't she tell him she wasn't taking pity on him? And was he not sitting at her feet swimming in it? Karma's face grew tight again.

"Please, don't do that. I hate when people do that. Don't force unsought thoughts and feelings on me, okay?"

"No, I'm just saying-" Money began.

"No, I know what you're sayin', Money. So please stop while you're ahead. You're startin' to piss me off," Karma warned.

Money waved his hand dismissively.

"Fine. Whateva."

"Don't 'whateva' me either. Alright? Don't disrespect me like that," Karma advised him with widened eyes.

"What you mean *'don't disrespect you like that'?*" Money asked mockingly. "Did you hear me come out my face and call you out your name or some shit?"

"No, I didn't," Karma admitted.

"Alright, then," Money countered.

"But you didn't have to," Karma argued. "The way you said 'whateva' was enough. I know what the hell 'whateva' means and so do you."

"Oh, yeah? What the fuck does it mean then?" Money looked up at Karma with his head tilted and his lips tight.

"It means 'fuck you'. That's what it means," Karma replied with furrowed eyebrows.

"You're right," Money countered with an insincere smile. "You are absolutely right, Karma."

"Don't patronize me, Money." Karma saw her relationship with Money dwindling right before her very eyes. He was wrong and she was right. They both knew it and he was sitting there trying to make her feel guilty about 'potentially breaking up' with him because he had a daughter. The thought of her ending their relationship never even crossed Karma's mind. Money was playing mind games and Karma was not trying to entertain him by any means.

"I should have just came right out and said that shit then, right?" Money went on to say smugly.

"Yeah, yeah, you should have," Karma snapped.

A loud silence fell between the couple. Karma looked down at Money, then his house, and then the street. Her heart was taking on the life of the tree lined block; cold and empty. She laughed disgustedly at the thought in her mind.

"You know what? It doesn't even matter, 'cause none of this shit got anything to do wit' me anyway."

"Oh, no?" Money asked in amazement.

"Nope," Karma muttered with the roll of her neck.

Money nodded his head and rose slowly from the stoop.

"So you're not a part of me now? Is that what you're sayin'?"

"What you gettin' up for?" Karma asked indignantly. Karma hoped this man didn't think she was afraid of him, because she wasn't. She'd seen and been through too much to be afraid of him or anyone else for that matter. She saw how Money threw his daughter's mother to the ground, but Karma would be damned if he was going to try to pull the same stunt with her. She hoped Money was prepared for her to fight back, because that's what she planned on doing. Let him put one finger on her and see if she didn't call her uncles and Stuff for backup. Karma was fearless. Her mother's death made her that way. She stared death, that son-of-a-bitch, right in its face and fought its partner, mourning, every day of her life. Money could try her if he wanted to, but he'd better think before he made a move he'd later regret.

"Answer the fuckin' question, Karma! This shit here ain't got nothin' to do wit'chu?!" Money roared with bulging eyes.

"Hell, no, muthafucka!" Karma bellowed back. "We've been talkin' all this time and I'm just now findin' out you have a daughter?! That should have been one of the first things you told me from the jump! This shit is none of my business, 'cause you didn't make it my fuckin' business!"

"I don't fuckin' need this shit!" Money turned his back and began to walk up the stairs.

"Yeah, walk away like a little ass boy!" Karma taunted.

Money spun around and pointed his finger down at Karma.

"I ain't no little boy! I'm a man!" he blared hitting his chest for emphasis.

"Nigga, you ain't shit!" Karma waved her hand dismissively. "You were the one who ran up in that bitch raw, not me! Don't take that shit out on me 'cause you can't deal!"

"Ay, yo, do yourself a favor and step the fuck off my stoop! Fuckin' bitch!" Money protested as he trailed up the steps.

Karma's eyebrows raised and her face twisted with ire.

"I got your bitch, you pussy ass nigga!"

"Yeah, whateva! You ain't no different from the rest of these bitches out here!" Money struck back with as he entered his home.

"And neither is ya momma!" Karma hollered over her shoulder as she stormed back to her car. "Fuckin' bitch!"

KARMA

Chapter 15

Sweet vanilla candles flickered and a warm fire burned in the fireplace that centered Soleil's former living room. Karma took little side steps around the grand Christmas tree that was set in the corner by the leather chaise. It was fully decorated with colorful lights, balls, and other holiday ornaments. Karma struggled to decide whether the tree needed more decorations or not. Everyday tasks, like adding or subtracting tree decorations, had become incredibly difficult for her to manage. She hadn't spoken to Money in two weeks. Karma wasn't sure if they were still together or not. She did her best to try not to think about him, but she couldn't help but wonder where he was, who he was with, or what he was doing. Whenever she saw or spoke to Indigo, neither one of the girls ever brought him up in conversation. Karma assumed Money had no desire to pursue her any further since Indigo never mentioned him in her presence.

The doorbell chimed disrupting Karma's thoughts. Karma snapped her head in the direction of the door. She, with a quizzical expression on her face, made her way to the entryway and looked through the peephole in the door. Karma pulled away slowly once she recognized the person standing on the other side of the wooden structure. She began to unlock the door in hesitancy. Karma pried the door open and looked into the eyes of a guilt-stricken Money. Dressed in a gray hooded Sean John sweat-suit and matching house shoes, he stood with his hands in his pockets waiting for Karma to speak. Karma said nothing. She simply walked away leaving the door open for Money to enter.

Money stepped into the warm house closing the front door behind him. He stepped out of his house slippers and placed them in the corner. With that task out of the way, Money pushed his hood off his head allowing his gray du-rag to show and crossed into the dimly lit living room. He admired the way the candles and fireplace created an intimate atmosphere. Money also admired and outlined Karma's powerfully built body through her fitted wife beater and cotton pajama pants. Karma stood before the Christmas tree once again with her arms crossed at her chest trying to find a place for another ornament to go. She hoped Money was there to reconcile. As much as she wanted him to apologize, Karma couldn't turn around to face him. She was just as guilty as he was for disrespecting his mother. They both had horrific tempers and could only hope they would never blow up on each other like that ever again.

Money moved slowly toward his love. He'd missed her throughout the two week period in which they stopped speaking. Money did a lot of soul searching during his time away from Karma and wanted to make things right between them again. He had no right to call her out of her name and compare her to the females who disrespected themselves daily. Karma was above every single last one of them and she deserved the utmost respect. Money pressed his body against Karma. Karma could feel his hardened manhood poking the middle of her back through his sweatpants. She closed her eyes and began to breathe heavily. Money leaned closely down into her neck so she could feel his warm breath on her skin.

"Turn around and look at me," he whispered.

Karma obliged apprehensively. She looked up into Money's

deep brown eyes and bit down nervously on her bottom lip. Neither Money, nor Karma could deny the electricity between them.

"I'm-" Money began.

"Shhhh," Karma instructed as she placed her index and middle finger on Money's thick lips. Without averting her eyes, she leaned into him, placed her hands on the back of his head, and proceeded to contour his lips with her tongue before sliding it completely into his mouth. Money accepted Karma's long moist tongue without hesitation. He wrapped his massive arms around her petite frame, then moved his hands down her back to her muscled behind where he left them to grab and squeeze it. Karma unzipped Money's jacket and pushed it off his toned body. It fell aimlessly to the floor. She ran her hands over his tight crisp wife beater before pulling that over his head and letting it fall to the carpet as well. Money picked Karma up into his arms and made his way down onto the middle of the floor. He removed the tank top from her body and threw it across the room. Money hovered over his love admiring her perfectly round breasts and erect auburn nipples. He bent down and took one breast into his mouth while massaging the other gently with his strong hand. Money wanted to make sure he tended to Karma's upper extremities without fault before making his way down south.

Karma shivered as Money's lips and tongue glided from one breast to the other then down to her stomach. He was mapping out her body creating silk trails of saliva down to the buried treasure between her legs. Money removed Karma's pajama bottoms from her thick legs and tossed them to the side. He was more than pleased to see she was pantiless and her garden was freshly trimmed. Without a wavering thought, Money positioned Karma's legs over his shoulders and buried his face between her thighs. Karma released quiet moans as Money explored her insides with his tongue. God it had been so long since she last received oral pleasure. Karma almost forgot what ecstasy felt like, but was damned glad Money was reminding her. A tingling sensation began to shoot through Karma's body. She grabbed Money's head, held on to it tightly, and began to grind against him. She was ready to climax, but was trying her hardest to keep from releasing the dragon so soon.

Unable to take much more, Karma managed to get a hold of Money's chin and pulled him up towards her. The two embraced in another passionate kiss before Karma parted her lips to speak.

"Put it in, baby. Put it in," she begged breathlessly.

Karma's plea drove Money crazy. He'd never yearned for a woman as much as he was yearning for Karma. The illumination from the fire gave her body such a sensuous glow. He studied her once again before leaning in and kissing her with more force than he had before. Money removed his sweatpants from his legs and threw them behind him. He lifted Karma's left leg and held it in the crook of his arm while he massaged his engorged manhood in an up and down motion along her wet vagina. Karma shivered once again. She was ready to explode from Money's teasing. She could feel the humungous size of his member just by the width of its head. She knew Money's entrance was going to hurt like hell, but swore silently to herself that she was going take it like a pro.

Looking into Karma's lustful eyes, Money knew it was time to make that big move. He carefully bowed forward and slowly slid his throbbing penis inside of Karma's virgin-like tunnel. He let out a loud moan of pleasure as her tightness gripped and suctioned his muscle. Karma gasped and dug her nails into Money's back in response to his oversized penis. She could feel her walls stretching to accommodate his girth and length. Money's face cringed and his eyes closed in sexual bliss as he struggled to keep himself from climaxing early. Karma's "sugar" was, by far, the best he'd ever had…hands down. Karma's hands trailed up Money's back and wrapped around his neck. She lifted her free leg and wrapped that around his waist. She wanted to move beneath him. The two needed to find a rhythm and they did.

Their lovemaking seemed to have gone on forever. Money's slow steady strokes soon transformed into hard vehement thrusts. Karma prepared herself for what was to come. Money was on the verge of blowing any moment now and she was willing and ready to receive everything he had. Money braced himself for a mind-blowing explosion. He buried his head into Karma's neck and continued to bang into her with all of his might. Karma, in return, grabbed his head and locked her legs around his waist. Unprepared for her instinctive move, Money lost all control and let out a loud cry as he released himself inside of his love. He squeezed her tightly against his body as he stroked the last remains of his juices inside of her. Karma laid sweat-drenched and motionless beneath him. She slowly turned her head to the side and closed her water-filled eyes. Karma would sleep to dream that evening. Her greatest fears would finally be hushed by her lover's beating heart.

The wind whistled its own melody outside during the twilight hour. Karma and Money laid entangled in each other's arms and legs beneath the heavy covers of her bed. They'd made love once more beneath the Christmas tree before retreating to the bedroom for a much needed slumber. *"I Love Yous"* were exchanged between kisses and moans sending the two into an inestimable high.

Karma's cell phone lit up and vibrated. The rhythmic pulsing against the wooden nightstand top beside the bed awakened her. She exhaustively turned over and reached for the phone with shut eyes. Karma flipped the phone open and placed it to her ear.

"Hello?" she answered in a hoarse voice.

"Karma?" Stuff replied unaware if he dialed the correct number or not.

"Yeah?" she asked sleepily.

"Oh, my bad, sis. I didn't know you was sleepin'," Stuff disclosed.

"Mm-Hmm," Karma mustered.

"You by yaself?" he asked in concern.

"No." Karma sighed and tried to rewet her dry mouth with some saliva.

"Aiight, den just listen close to what I'm about to tell you," Stuff instructed.

"K," Karma whispered.

"I just got word from Hawk. He told me to tell you dat Owl's gonna put you on to dat nigga, Pimp, from Philly."

Karma's eyes flew open. She didn't know much about this Pimp character except that he was the biggest heroine distributor in Philadelphia, he was the youngest the city had ever bred, and he was Owl's arch enemy. Karma had no idea why Owl and Hawk would assign her to Pimp. Hawk never said anything about dealing with major players in the game the night she'd met with him about her mother. She thought she would do a few drug runs for the duo or something along those lines. She never thought she would be used as bait to take Owl's main adversary out.

"When?" she asked, nervously looking over her shoulder at Money. Thankfully his back was facing her and he appeared to be in a deep slumber.

"New Year's Eve," Stuff responded matter-of-factly.

"That's two weeks away," she said alarmingly.

"It doesn't matter. Shit has to be established now," Stuff verified firmly.

"K. Where?" Karma sighed as she thought about the depth of trouble she'd gotten herself into.

"Da Robert Treat. Nigga's gonna be up in da Mint dat night. So while you in Norf Cackalack visitin' ya pops dis weekend, go shoppin' and pick somethin' sexy out to wear for dat nigga. Indigo's gonna go wit'chu to da club dat night so nuttin'll look suspect, ya dig?" Stuff asked.

"Yeah," Karma replied glumly.

"You went ova what you supposed to do dat night wit' Hawk, right?" Stuff probed.

"No." Karma closed her eyes and rubbed her lids. She was way beyond being ill-informed and ill-prepared for the upcoming drug operation. How was she going to pull this off in two weeks? How was she going to get past Money? She wasn't one to keep secrets from anyone, especially him. How could she? Money was her constant reminder that she wasn't walking alone in life. He was a gift to her from her mother. Soleil. Karma would have to sacrifice her relationship with Money for the pursuit of her mother's need to rest in peace. There was no way she could tell Money.

"Aiight, den, look, since you can't really talk right now or whateva, I'mma hit you up later on in da day and go ova da plan wit'chu. Make sure you answer ya phone, aiight?" Stuff said interrupting Karma's weary thoughts.

"Okay," she yawned.

"Aiight, sis. Peace," Stuff ended.

Karma clammed her phone shut, plugged it back onto its charger, and set it atop the nightstand. She turned back over and pressed her nude body up against Money's for warmth. Karma closed her eyes and tried to ease her mind of its wary thoughts.

"You goin' to let me in on your little secret?" Money asked groggily.

Karma's eyes flew open once again. She became unnerved by Money's sudden outburst. She thought he had been asleep the entire time. In truth, Money had been wide awake from the moment Karma turned over to answer the phone. He hadn't heard the phone vibrate, but he did hear Karma speaking to someone on it. Someone, possibly another man, calling her after midnight didn't sit well with Money. He trusted Karma, but he didn't trust the unknown voice on the other end of the phone. Money decided asking Karma about the call in jest would either get him a yes or a no.

"Love?" Money continued, looking back at Karma over his shoulder.

Karma regained her composure before she spoke. She couldn't let Money sense the panic in her voice.

"Yes?" she responded calmly.

"Did you hear what I asked you?" Money countered.

"Yes," Karma replied in a hesitant whisper.

"Well?" Money asked with raised brows.

"Soon, baby. Soon," she managed to say calmly. Karma slid her arm between Money's arm and his side and rested it there for the remainder of the early morning. Money lied awake partially accepting the 'soon' response Karma felt he was worthy of having. He'd leave the 'midnight call' issue alone for now, but if Karma didn't clue him in on her little secret in the days to come, he'd be forced to take drastic measures. Money would have to call the number of the person she'd spoken to that night. Karma was his woman...no ifs, ands, or buts about it.

KARMA

Chapter 16

Karma and Indigo walked around Wilson's: The Leather Experts store in search of a Christmas present for Lorenzo. They sorted through the diverse styles of leather coats and jackets that were hanging on the racks and walls. Indigo noticed her cousin wasn't talking much. She was lost in her own little world. Karma was worried about something, Indigo was sure of it. Although, she couldn't imagine what was troubling her. Karma's relationship with Money was back on track, the family's restaurant was making more money than ever, and the condominiums her aunt used to own were in tip top shape. The three most important things that took up most of Karma's time were all under control because of her impeccable managerial skills. Indigo paused and thought a little harder about what could possibly be troubling Karma. She couldn't think of anything, so she decided to break the silence between them.

"I'm glad you two finally made up," she said, looking over at her cousin while filing through a rack of leather jackets.

"Huh?" Karma asked, snapping out of her trance. "Oh, yeah. Me, too," she confessed absent-mindedly.

"For real? I can't tell," Indigo replied sarcastically.

"No, I am. It's just-" Karma began.

"It's just what?" Indigo asked, awaiting the real reason behind her irregular behavior.

Karma parted her lips to tell her cousin what was on her mind, but her pride was holding her back.

"Nothin'," she replied dismissively.

Indigo studied her cousin for a moment. She was going to get the truth out of her one way or another. Karma couldn't keep anything from her long.

"You want to tell me what's on your mind, *mamita*?" she asked.

"What makes you think there's somethin' wrong?" Karma countered avoiding eye contact.

"I didn't ask you if there was anything wrong. I asked..." Indigo paused and looked over at her cousin suspiciously. She decided to find the underlying cause of Karma's problem. "Wait a minute. I know there's something really wrong now or else you would have just came out and told me what was on your mind."

Karma bit down on her bottom lip and continued to pick over a table of leather belts.

"It's nothin'."

Indigo leaned up against a clothing rack and placed one hand on her hip.

"Yes, it is. I know you, K."

"For real. It's nothin'. I'm just trippin' a little," Karma admitted with a forced grin.

Indigo crossed her arms at her chest.

"I'm not moving until you tell me."

Karma looked up at her cousin and acknowledged she was having one of her stubborn mule moments.

"Come on, Indigo. Stop playin'," she pleaded.

Indigo began to study the designs on her freshly manicured nails. She would stand there in that store until it closed if she had to. She wasn't going to move until Karma told her what was wrong.

"Can you come on, please?" Karma sighed.

Indigo held her hand away from her face and admired the art

work on it.

"Kathy sure did a bomb job on my nails," she mocked dramatically.

"Oh, you gonna ignore me now?" Karma asked in annoyance. "Fine," she said, throwing her hands up in submission. "You wanna know? I'll tell you. My period's late."

Indigo sucked her teeth and placed her hand back in the crook of her arm. She expected to hear Karma say she was moving away or Money asked her to marry her; something juicy.

"Is that all?" she asked in disbelief.

"What do you mean *'is that all'?"* Karma replied with an attitude.

"Karma, you just started having sex again after going without it for two years, *mamita*. What do you expect? Your body is just adjusting to Money's man-meat is all," Indigo stated decisively.

"No, Indigo." Karma shook her head in dejection. "My period's late because Money and I didn't use protection."

Indigo thought about what her cousin just admitted and tried to look on the positive side of things. Okay, they didn't use protection, no big deal. She and Stuff hardly ever used protection and they were both fine, mentally, physically, and emotionally.

"Okaaay, so one time. I mean, I know it only takes one time, but you know," Indigo said sincerely.

"No, Indi." Karma sighed regretfully. "It was none of the times."

A mischievous smile grew across Indigo's face. She knew how her cousin used to get down back in the day with Joaquin, but she didn't know Karma was going to go all out with Money. Indigo was proud of her cousin for taking such a big step.

"Damn, is it that good?" she teased with her gap-toothed smile. Karma's face grew grim. Indigo immediately changed gears. "Nix that. Did you tell him?"

"No. I'm not gonna say anything until I take a test and I'm sure." Karma scratched the back of her freshly trimmed hair.

"Well, what are you going to do if the test comes back positive?" Indigo probed a little deeper. She didn't really want to ask, but she had to know. Knowing Karma, she wouldn't think rationally after learning the test results. Aborting the child would be the first thing that would cross her mind and she'd surely follow through with it.

"I don't know." Karma shook her head in dismay.

Indigo looked to the ceiling in search of a decent inoffensive reply.

"It's alright not to know, K. It is," she reassured her cousin. "But if the test comes back positive and you tell Money, you know he's not going to let you out of his sight, right?"

Karma rolled her eyes.

"Yes, he will."

"No, he won't. You know Money doesn't play when it comes to Mimi and you can trust and believe that if you *are* pregnant with his baby, that negro's going to make sure he has your bad ass on lock. He is *not* going to let you get into anything that's going to bring harm to his unborn child." Indigo emphasized the silence following her last statement with the raise of her brows. "That means New Year's Eve is out."

"Oh, no, it's still on," Karma stated seriously. "Don't get me wrong. I love Money and everything, but he has no say in this. I gotta job to do. So not goin' through with it is not an option."

"But Karma-" Indigo interjected.

"It's my mother, Indigo," Karma countered with pain-filled eyes. A deafening silence ensued. "Besides, we don't even know anything yet," Karma continued.

"I'm just saying," Indigo said with a shrug.

"Well, if I am, I am. Fuck it." Karma looked around the room with shifting eyes. "I'll just tell 'im after we come back from the job."

Indigo shifted her weight in distrust.

"Does he know you're not staying for Mimi's birthday party?"

"Yeah," Karma replied casting her eyes to the floor. "I told 'im Uncle Miguel was throwin' a party at the restaurant the same night and I would need to step out for a little while to oversee it."

Indigo rubbed her forehead in uncertainty.

"If Money ever found ouuut-" she sang.

"Well, he's not goin' to," Karma snapped. "Unless you plannin' on tellin' 'im, Indigo. 'Cause if you are, you might as well tell 'im that you're in on the shit, too. I'm sayin', are you or are you not goin' wit' me?" Karma asked crossly.

"No, I am," Indigo guaranteed her. "I'm just saying; to spare you anymore grief, maybe you should at least make an attempt to tell him. Keeping something like this from him is not a good idea, K. You know what happened the first time when he didn't tell you about Mimi and her mother," she reminded her.

"You're right," Karma surrendered.

"He's suspicious as it is. Just tell him," Indigo stressed with a warm grin.

"I will," Karma nodded. As she glanced away from her cousin's tender eyes, she noticed a B-3 sheepskin aviator bomber jacket that was hanging on a distant wall. Even though her father wasn't a pilot, she knew he'd look just as good in the jacket as any official aviator would. Karma pointed to the coat. "That's it. That's the one."

Indigo followed her cousin's eyes.

"Ooo, I like that! It's sharp, K."

"Yeah?" Karma asked indecisively.

"Yeah!" Indigo nodded. "Uncle L's going to love it! And you know what?"

"What?" Karma dug into her pocketbook for her wallet.

"You should give it to him *after* you tell him you're knocked up. That way, if he freaks out and starts to beat your *culo*, you can use the coat as a shield!" Indigo teased.

Karma looked over at her cousin and playfully shoved her out of her way. Indigo made her worst days worth living. And even though she had no idea what the outcome of the test would be, she and Indigo were going to laugh or cry *together*. She found comfort in knowing that.

Money sat on the midnight blue carpeted floor of his mother's day room wrapping Christmas gifts with Mimi. Mimi, the color of a chocolate chip and doll-like features, sat between her father's long legs. She assisted him by holding the scotch tape in one hand and picking out the colored ribbons that he should put on certain presents with the other. Elmo sang gleefully on the wide screen television set a few feet away from them.

A cinnamon-colored woman with keen African and Native American features entered the room and sat down on the edge of the large plush couch. Evelyn Parks was a young and attractive forty-seven-year old. Many men who came across her path could not believe she had a thirty-year old son at home. Evelyn made the mistake of falling victim to the sexual and financial advances of New Jersey's infamous drug lord, Owl, back in 1977. He'd swept her off her feet the day they met at Newark's Penn Station.

Evelyn was standing in the middle of the train station lobby looking up at the electronic schedule that was suspended above the crowded room. She was there to pick up her older brother who was coming in from Virginia. Evelyn watched the board flip and sighed at the 'Delay' notice that was printed in boxed white letters beside her brother's train number. Too busy losing her patience, Evelyn didn't realize the black man standing in line at one of the concession stands was watching her.

As she turned to take a seat in one of the wooden pews, Owl jumped out of line and grabbed the opportunity to speak to her. He reached out and gently touched her arm to get her attention. Evelyn glanced his way and almost lost her breath. He was the most beautiful black man she had ever seen in her young teenaged life. The man was decked out in a fine, tailored lavender suit, Stacy Adams and a trench coat to match. She stood in awe at the sight of his flawless dark skin and a huge sheened afro. If that man was a pimp, he was the cleanest pimp she'd ever laid eyes on. He definitely wasn't a Jersey native. The color of his outfit screamed 'deep south,' but Evelyn didn't care. She wanted him. From the moment Owl introduced himself and told her she was the most striking woman he had ever seen, Evelyn was hooked.

Owl introduced Evelyn to the fast lane. They were both, married and divorced, a year after they met. Drugs and sex were the story of Evelyn's life that year. Although she didn't indulge in the narcotic aspect of the game, she did coddle in Owl's excessive sex habit. She became his personal whore the moment she agreed to be his woman. Owl's sexual appetite was more than Evelyn could stand at times. The worst times were the nights he snorted cocaine, because it gave him stone-like erections that would stand until the next day. Owl would climax more than enough times during the couple's love making, but it wouldn't stop him from pounding into Evelyn like a madman or forcing her to perform oral sex on him until she choked. Evelyn's body eventually shut down. And things only got worse after she became pregnant with Money. Instead of pounding into her with his manhood, Owl reverted to using his fist. Evelyn swore every man in his camp hit their girlfriends or wives. She was never one to be disobedient, so she could not understand why he abused her the way he did. Owl never justified his actions; he felt he didn't have to. She thought he would change after learning the sex of the baby, but he didn't. Owl wanted no parts of her or the baby's life. The only thing he asked of her was to name their son after the single thing he truly believed was greater than God-Money. When she asked him what she was supposed to say to their son when he asked her about whom and where his father was, Owl simply told her to tell him he was dead. And she did just that.

Evelyn left the 'man with the lavender suit' the day she stepped out of Beth Israel Hospital holding her 9 lb. 12 oz. baby boy. Owl hadn't showed up for his birth, nor did he call or visit to see how either one of them was doing. Seventeen-years-old, black, and female, Evelyn walked back into the world with her head held high. She didn't have a penny to her name, but her baby boy, Money, was more than enough incentive to go on living.

Evelyn stretched her aching legs out before her. Dressed casually in her scarlet red Rutgers University sweatshirt and denim jeans, the young grandmother reclined on the couch and threw an arm over the back of it. She removed a strand of her frosted, asymmetrically bobbed-cut hair out her face as she smiled down on her only grandchild. By the perfection and whiteness of her teeth, many would conclude that Evelyn was the reason behind her only son's mesmerizing smile.

"Look at my baby down there. Wrapping gifts! Ha! Ha!" she laughed loudly with her husky voice.

Mimi smiled at her grandmother's adulation. She held up a meticulously tied ribbon for her grandmother.

"Wooo! Isn't that pretty?! Is that for me?" she asked touching her chest with her fingertips.

"Yes," Mimi replied in a delicate voice.

"Are you going to come over here and give it to me?" Evelyn asked excitedly.

Mimi shook her head up and down. She stood up and carefully stepped over her father's leg. As she approached Evelyn, she extended her little arm and gave the ribbon to her. Evelyn received the ribbon graciously.

"This is the prettiest ribbon I've ever had," she expressed, looking into her grandbaby's slanted eyes. "It's the prettiest ribbon in the whole world," Evelyn professed. "Can Nanny have a kiss?"

Mimi nodded once again and leaned in to kiss her grandmother on the lips. Evelyn picked Mimi up into her arms and squeezed her tightly. She kissed the child repeatedly on her tiny cheek causing her to giggle. Mimi melted under her grandmother's touch. She was the only woman in her life. She didn't know who her mother was and honestly didn't know she had one. Mimi decided to stay in her grandmother's lap and watch her father finish wrapping a slender gift box.

"You see that gift Daddy's wrapping, precious lamb?" Evelyn whispered in Mimi's ear.

Mimi nodded.

"Do you know who it's for?" Evelyn continued.

Mimi nodded again.

"Yes."

"Who?" she asked playfully.

"Karma," Mimi replied softly.

Money looked over at his mother and daughter smiling from

ear to ear. He'd talked about Karma so much to his mother and little girl; he couldn't help but blush at Mimi's assertive reply.

"Oh, my," Evelyn mocked. "Well, she must be something special for Daddy to have brought her such an expensive gift. That box looks like it's only big enough to hold a piece of jewelry. What do you think, Mimi? Do you think Daddy got Karma jewelry?" She looked down at Mimi with raised eyebrows.

"Yes," Mimi answered with her hands covering her mouth. She giggled at the notion.

"Mama?" Money blushed.

"Mama, what? You're my son. I know you," she smirked. "And I know, in all these years, I've never seen you buy anything more than bath beads, lotion, or underwear for those other little girls you used to date."

Money laughed at his mother's spoken truth. The women he dated before Karma were only worth a couple of dollars. Karma was in a whole other league. She deserved the best.

"True story," he confessed.

"Mm-Hmm. Look at you. You're just as simple," Evelyn teased.

"Come on, Mama. No, I'm not. I'm just happy." Money taped the last side of the box down.

"I know you are," she gloated. "My baby boy. I can't wait to meet this Karma who's got my son so open."

"She's beautiful, Mama." Money's eyes glazed over at the thought of his love.

"I know. You told me. And to tell you the truth, I like any woman who'll stay with a man regardless of him having a child and drama with the mother. It says a lot about her character," Evelyn stated indisputably.

"You're right." Distress suddenly washed over Money's face as he thought about the late night phone call Karma received a week ago. She still hadn't said anything about it.

Evelyn noticed the concern in her son's eyes.

"So what's with the face?"

Money hesitated as he fiddled with the completed wrapped box.

"She's keeping something from me, Mama."

Evelyn looked down and noticed Mimi had fallen asleep.

"Like what?" she asked as she rocked from side-to-side with the little girl still in her arms.

"I don't know," Money shrugged.

"Do you think she's involved with someone else?" she asked.

"No, it's nothing like that," he said as he met his mother's eyes. "See, she talks to Indigo's boyfriend a lot on the phone. He's a dealer or whatever-"

"In the name of God," Evelyn cut Money off. "Please tell me this girl doesn't have a drug problem too."

"No, Mama. She doesn't," he reassured her. "Trust me. It's just that they talk to each other a lot and usually Karma says just enough on her end to keep me guessing. He called her past midnight a couple of weeks ago and I didn't know what to think."

"May I ask how you knew it was him?" Evelyn questioned warily.

"I checked her phone when she got into the shower that morning," Money confessed shamefully. "I mean, Indigo knows what's going on, but she won't tell me."

Evelyn shook her head and held her hand up to stop Money from going any further. She'd heard enough.

"Before you start jumping to conclusions, have you asked Karma about the matter?" Evelyn asked as she placed Mimi gently down on the couch.

"Yeah, I have. I asked the second she got off the phone with him." Money cast his eyes towards the floor. He knew he had been wrong for going behind Karma's back and checking her phone. Deep down inside he knew she was being faithful to him, but the suspicious after-hour telephone calls from Stuff and her nonchalant demeanor towards the whole situation was causing Money to become insecure.

"And what did she say?" Evelyn inquired.

"She said she'd tell me soon," Money said defeated.

"Alright, well, if the child said she'd tell you soon, then, she will. Give her some time, Money. You have to be patient. If Karma is as in love with you as you are with her, then you have nothing to

worry about, son. Trust me. A mother knows," Evelyn confirmed
with the wink of her eye. She wouldn't admit it to Money, but
Evelyn hated to see him so dazed and confused. Whoever Karma
was, she had her son questioning his place in her life and she didn't
appreciate it, not one bit. Evelyn would put an end to Money's suffering the moment she came face to face with Karma. If she rubbed
her the wrong way, she would surely let her know. Mimi's birthday,
New Year's Eve, was only a few days away. Evelyn would sit and
wait until she read into the eyes of the woman who'd stolen her
son's heart. One's eyes were the windows to their soul. Evelyn
hoped Karma's wouldn't deceive her like Owl's had.

KARMA

Chapter 17

Karma drove down the snow-covered winding road of the gated community her father called home in Fort Bragg, North Carolina. The houses on the block were massive in size and black owned. It was nice to drive through an area where African-American achievement was evident. There weren't many black people who owned homes of such magnitude back in Essex County. Karma loved visiting her father down south. The south had a slower, unrushed pace about it. The air was fresher and the people were kinder. Karma thought about moving down to North Carolina to keep her father company over the years, but knew it wouldn't have worked out because of his unstable military lifestyle.

Karma drove to the end of the cul-de-sac and cruised down an inclined driveway. She parked her car behind a newly washed and waxed silver Ford Expedition. She pressed the 'open' button on the garage door's remote control that she'd clipped on her sunvisor. Karma removed her keys from the ignition and placed them in her pocketbook. She decided to leave her coat, luggage, and father's present in the car until later. Karma set the pocketbook on her right shoulder and exited the car. She carefully shuffled into the garage, walked up two wooden steps, and inserted her key into the white door leading to the kitchen.

Karma wiped the bottom of her wet rubber boots on the placemat at the door before continuing down a short hallway connected to the unlit kitchen. The den, set across from the room, shared the same space as the eatery. The lights were turned off in the den as well. Karma struggled to adjust her eyes to the darkness. She needed to see if her father was near. Ironically, she caught sight of him lounging in his cushioned ottoman with a bottle of beer in his hand. She noticed his eyes were intensely entranced on the simply lit Christmas tree in the corner. He was drunk. Karma could tell. Her father had ears like a deer and he never flinched or called out to her when she entered the house. Karma knew he was deep into his misery. Even in the dark, she could see the loss on his face. He was missing her mother.

Karma flipped on the lights before placing her pocketbook down on the island and making her way over to him. The light tapping sound of her boots against the wooden floors broke Lorenzo's trance. He turned his head to see who was approaching him. His bloodshot eyes watered as soon as they set on his concerned daughter. She looked so much like her mother; it was almost too much to bear.

"Baby Doll," Lorenzo rose with outstretched arms.

"Hey, Daddy," Karma replied as she embraced him with a hug and a kiss on the cheek.

"How was the ride down?" he asked as he sat back down in the ottoman.

"Smooth. I was surprised," Karma admitted while taking a seat on the plush foot rest by the ottoman. She studied the redness of her father's eyes long and hard. "There was hardly any traffic on 95."

"I can't believe that myself," Lorenzo chuckled.

Karma looked around the room. It lacked life. The only thing that gave it any vivacity was the tree. Karma figured her father put the tree up for therapeutic purposes. Father and daughter knew it was Soleil's favorite holiday. Lorenzo was never one to celebrate

Christmas, but had always made it worthwhile for his wife and daughter. He would have given them the world if he could.

"The tree looks beautiful," she cooed.

Lorenzo followed Karma's eyes and smiled proudly at the tree he'd put up all by himself.

"Thank you." He closed his eyes and took a big gulp out of his alcoholic beverage.

Karma watched her father drown himself in his bottle. Since her mother's death, she'd made a point to speak to him after she awakened in the morning and just before she went to lay her head at night. Although, he would sound down and out, his tone never took on that of a drunken soldier. But looking at him now, Karma knew the truth. He was just that-a drunken solider. And his lack of self-control was making her uncomfortable. Her father had always been in control. To her knowledge, he'd kept his control when her mother threatened to divorce him years ago and he'd held onto it when she was diagnosed with cancer. She needed him to be strong for her right now and he was failing.

"Daddy, how many beers have you had?" she asked him as she pulled the bottle away from his lips.

Lorenzo glanced at the tree for a brief moment, then reset them on Karma. Her eyes were a deep olive green. He didn't recall them ever having the ability to change colors. His mind had to be playing tricks on him.

"Six," he answered with a slow nod. "Now, I know what you're thinkin' and I'm not drunk."

"Oh, no?" Karma asked in shock.

"No." Lorenzo closed his eyes and laid his head back on the headrest. "I just needed somethin' to calm my nerves."

"Well, then, you should have made yourself some hot cocoa or somethin'," Karma said disgustingly. "You know you're not supposed to be drinkin' liquor, Daddy."

"I know, I know," Lorenzo whispered.

Karma placed the empty bottle at her feet and watched her father's eyes gloss over. She felt so helpless.

"How's that boyfriend of yours?" Lorenzo continued.

"He's fine," Karma said with her head in her hand.

"Good, good. He treatin' you alright?" he asked sternly.

"Yes, Daddy. He is," Karma sulked. She wasn't in the mood to be put on the spot by this man. He was the topic of discussion here, not her.

Lorenzo acknowledged the irritability in Karma's voice. He knew he was wrong for drinking, but he didn't want to own up to it. It was easier to wallow in his tears and in his bottle than to have to accept Soleil's absence that Christmas. The beer numbed his pain. It was the medicine he needed to patch the open wound in his heart.

"Alright, now. I'm just makin' sure, 'cause I don't wanna have to hurt the boy," he teased seriously.

"Daddy, please," Karma sucked her teeth dismissively.

"I'm serious," he replied with a grin.

"I know you are," Karma shook her head in disbelief.

A deafening silence fell between the two. Karma turned her head and scoured the room once again. She noticed the many pictures of her mother and herself around the room. It was funny how they weren't the first things to capture her attention the moment she turned the lights on. Karma sighed heavily as sadness washed over her. She admired a photograph she'd taken of her mother after her final treatment of chemotherapy. Soleil was asleep with her face rested on praying hands. Her bald head was covered with a silk scarf. Karma had never seen her mother so at peace and found it fit to capture on film.

"I see you got the picture I took of Mommy sleepin' up," Karma pointed out sadly.

Lorenzo smiled at the thought of it.

"Yeah. It looks good, doesn't it?"

"Yeah, it does," Karma nodded. The day Soleil received her final treatment of chemotherapy; Karma went out and cut her golden locks off. She saved the hair the beautician excised from her head and had it made into a wig for her mother. Soleil cried at the sight of her daughter's new short hairdo and cried even harder once Karma told her why she'd cut it. Karma didn't feel comfortable with the thought of her mother wearing store-bought hair. After all, she was her mother's child. They shared one body for nine months. Giving her mother her hair was the least Karma could do to show her how much she loved her.

Karma grunted at the memory.

"I still can't believe she's gone," she murmured, shaking her head.

"Me either, baby doll." Lorenzo raised his hand and placed it on the back of Karma's head. He stroked his veined fingers along her slick widow's peak for comfort.

"Thanksgivin' was hard, you know?" she continued. "I didn't feel like there was anything to be thankful for. And then I thought about you and Indigo, Money, Uncle Vic and Uncle Miguel…Aunt Maggie. And I wasn't so angry anymore. But, I don't know how I'm gonna get through Christmas, Daddy. It's Mommy's favorite holiday and she's not here to celebrate it. He took that from her."

Lorenzo removed his hand from Karma's neck and placed it on his lined forehead.

"If I could get my hands on that muthafucka for what he did to your mother, I would. I would snap his fuckin' neck in two! But I try not to think about 'im, because if I do, I won't be able to go on. Nigga's hidin' like a little bitch. But like I told Victor, he's got to come out eventually." Lorenzo sighed. "If I wasn't goin' back in, I swear I would-"

Karma snapped her head around in her father's direction. She hoped she hadn't heard him correctly. She just knew he'd made a big mistake. It was the beer that was talking.

"Goin' back in? Goin' back in where? Not in to the army?"

Lorenzo averted his eyes. He parted his lips to speak, but nothing came out. His words were lost in the depths of his throat.

Karma laughed repulsively.

"Unbelievable. Un-fuckin'-believable!"

Karma jumped up from the footrest and stormed into the kitchen with Lorenzo close behind.

He grabbed her arm, spinning her back around to face him.

"Karma, listen to me," Lorenzo implored.

"No! Get off me!" she screamed. Just when Karma thought her life was getting back to normal, her father found a way to throw her another curveball.

"No! Just listen to me for a minute!" he yelled back.

"You're a liar! You told me you retired! You told my mother!" Karma screeched. She hated the strained relationship she had with her father. For ten years the two had been going at each other's throats; both struggling with their minds to forgive and their hearts to forget. Even so, Karma loved her father and he loved her just the same. But she hated the lies, *his lies*, which caused rifts between them. The next one always bigger than the last. Those lies were the same lies that made her mother cry herself to sleep at night.

"I did retire, baby!" Lorenzo stressed.

Karma tried to pull away from her father, but he pulled her back into him.

"Just listen to me!" he begged. "They called me back to active duty a couple of weeks ago. I leave for Iraq on the first."

"No," Karma shook her head in refusal.

"Come on, baby doll. Look at me. I won't be gone any longer than six months," Lorenzo informed her.

Karma looked up at her father and grimaced.

"That's funny. You know, Joaquin said the same exact thing to me before he left for Afghanistan. And where is he now, Daddy? Huh?! He's dead! What the fuck am I supposed to do if somethin' happens to you, too?! Huh?! What am I supposed to do, then?!"

Lorenzo held his little girl's face in his masculine hands. This argument was far worse than the one they had in Soleil's hospital room ten years ago. Like that dispute, Lorenzo was the cause of this one. He'd disowned his daughter, verbally, in the midst of rage. In actuality, he'd renounced her long before then; Karma and Soleil, both.

"Nothin's gonna happen to me, baby. Nothin'. You hear me? I'll be back."

"No, you won't," Karma said pulling her head away.

"Karma-" Lorenzo started.

"Wasn't losin' my mother enough for you?! It was for me!

You're askin' for a death wish and you don't even care!" Karma cried.

"I have a job to do," Lorenzo uttered remorsefully.

"No! No! This is your job! This right here," she pointed to herself. "Me! I'm your job! I need you here with me, Daddy! Why can't you see that?!" Karma wiped the flood of tears that were streaming down her pale face. "I refuse to bury another parent. I refuse to. I'm not doin' it. I'm not."

"I'll be back home before you know it, baby doll," Lorenzo said trying to convince her.

"If you go...you can forget about ever speakin' to me again. I mean it, Daddy. I'm cuttin' you the fuck off." Karma turned and walked away from Lorenzo leaving him at loss for words.

"Karma!" he yelled to her back. "Karma!"

Karma continued to walk down the dimly lit hallway without looking back.

She turned the corner, disappearing behind a curved wall. The slamming of her bedroom door echoed in the distance. Lorenzo remained in the middle of his kitchen floor looking towards the heavens in search of divine intervention. He needed to hear his wife's voice. He needed Soleil to appear before him, take him into her arms and tell him he'd made the right decision. He stood and watched. He stood and waited. He stood until his knees gave in and he collapsed to the floor. Then he cried. Lorenzo cried for his daughter and for his wife. He cried for the soldiers who were losing their lives everyday in the Middle East. He cried for the children who were falling victim to the child welfare system. He cried for his ancestors-the men and women who'd been beaten, whipped, burned, raped, lynched, spat upon, and stripped of their dignity and identities because they were the *true* people of God. He cried for the homeless. He cried for the young single black mothers who were left to raise their sons by themselves. He cried for the young black men who'd been shunned by society and sent away to rot in prison. He cried for not being the man his wife and daughter needed him to be. He cried because he couldn't run from himself anymore.

KARMA

Chapter 18

C hristmas came and went. The time spent with her father in North Carolina was short, but served its purpose of filling the void of her mother's absence. Karma and Lorenzo spoke later that evening about his spur of the moment decision to offer his much needed services over in Iraq. The two talked until the wee hours of the next morning with Lorenzo telling Karma he would reconsider reconsidering.

Soleil's former lavatory was fit for a queen. The champagne and chocolate marbled flooring and countertops complimented the dark cherry wood cabinets in the space. The spacious shower, with its glassed door, was set next to the massive Jacuzzi tub. Set beside the Jacuzzi tub rested a small compartment that held the toilet. The door to the subdivision was closed.

Karma sat on the edge of the step to the Jacuzzi tub with her head hung. Her arms rested on each thigh while her fingers were intertwined with each other. She bit down on her bottom lip in wariness. Indigo leaned up against the broad toiletry-filled sink with her arms folded at her chest. She looked over at the two pregnancy tests set atop the counter. They were absent of any results.

"I can't believe you threatened him like that," she giggled.

Karma looked up at her cousin and sighed.

"I can't believe it either. The words just came out. I don't know what happened."

"You blacked out is what happened!" Indigo exclaimed. She laughed again, while looking over at the test results once more.

"I guess. I just didn't expect to hear 'im say he was goin' back in." Karma rubbed her throbbing temples at the horrific memory.

"I didn't even see that one coming," Indigo confessed. "Humph. I would have blacked on his behind, too. It was a stupid decision. I mean...really. Uncle L knows he is too old for all of that army mess," Indigo huffed. She looked over at her troubled cousin and let out a soft sigh. "Don't feel bad, okay? You apologized, right?"

"Yeah," Karma twiddled her thumbs.

"Alright, then. You apologized, he apologized. He's not going anymore, he's moving to DC to work on special assignments at the Pentagon instead. It's a done deal," Indigo reassured her cousin. She glanced over at the pregnancy tests one final time and looked back at her cousin with a simple grin. "The results are in."

Karma looked up at Indigo with worried eyes. She tried to read her face, but it was no use. Indigo's smirk could have meant anything.

"Well?" she asked with wild eyes.

"Hi, Mommy," Indigo replied excitedly.

Karma's face drained of color. She closed her eyes tightly and shook her head from side-to-side.

"Oh, no. No," she repeated to herself.

Confused by her cousin's response, Indigo walked over to her and sat down beside her on the step. She threw her arm around Karma's neck and laid her head against hers.

"Come on, *mamita*. It's alright. We were prepared for this. We knew there was a strong possibility you were pregnant. It's not a bad thing," she sang.

"It's not necessarily a good thing either, Indi," Karma said as she ran her fingers through her untamed hair.

"Why do you say that?" Indigo asked in bewilderment. The girls had been raised to believe babies were blessings from God. She couldn't understand why Karma wasn't happy about the news. It wasn't like she was underage or anything. She was twenty-seven years old with *more* than enough money to secure her and the baby for fifty million lifetimes. Karma even had a man who loved her more than anything else in the world. As far as Indigo was concerned, her cousin was set for the rest of the life.

Karma thought otherwise.

"'Cause I don't know what I'm doin'. I don't know how to be a mother." Karma was truly sincere in her conviction. She'd never thought about having children. She knew better than to bring a child into such a cruel world. Indigo did too…at one time. But with time comes change and people were everchanging. Who was going to teach her how to be a mother? She, herself, was motherless. That handicap alone was a setup for failure.

"Then you'll learn," Indigo confirmed sweetly. "I'll help you. My mom will help you. I mean, she obviously knows what to do and you *know* she'll be more than happy to help you," Indigo laughed. "Look how great I turned out!"

Karma smiled and shook her head in response to her cousin's silliness.

"You're not alone is what I'm trying to say, *mamita*," Indigo proceeded. "You know we're all going to be here for you…especially Money."

The smile faded from Karma's face. *How was she going to tell Money?* She was still trying to figure out how she was going to tell him the truth about where she was really going later that evening. *How was she possibly going to tell him she was pregnant with his child?*

"I don't even wanna tell 'im," Karma confessed.

Indigo cut her eyes at her cousin.

"It doesn't matter if you want to or not. You *have* to tell him. It's only right, Karma. No more secrets, remember?"

"I know," Karma submitted hesitantly.

Indigo brushed her hand over her cousin's fine hair and smiled widely.

"You're going to be a mommy," she gloated. "Yay."

Indigo wrapped her other arm around her cousin's neck and hugged her tightly. Karma, in return, let her head fall upon her shoulder. There was nothing she couldn't do without Indigo.

Friends of Evelyn, Money, and Mimi gathered at the posh abode for the toddler's fourth birthday celebration. Evelyn entertained her guests in the kitchen while Money sat in the den among his comrades from the police force. The men, engulfed in an ESPN program, argued over the outcome of a football game that aired earlier in the year. Mimi, along with her little friends, ran through the house laughing and screaming with glee. The mothers of the children stood around talking amongst themselves as they sipped on non-alcoholic beverages. Most of their conversations were loosely based on how good looking Money was.

The doorbell sounded overhead. Money rose from the couch with his eyes still fixed on the television set. He walked through the archway leading to the foyer, unlocked the heavy wooden door, and smiled at the sight of his girlfriend. She did the same.

"Hey, you," he said, pulling the door a little wider for Karma to enter.

"Hey," she said, stepping into the house as Money closed the door behind her. Karma wrapped her arms around Money's neck, hugging him tightly.

Money picked her up and squeezed her with all of his might before setting her back down onto the floor. He kissed her gently on the lips.

"Glad you could make it," he confessed, rocking Karma in his arms.

"I told you I was comin', silly," she said as she gently pulled away and held up the wrapped present she'd purchased for Mimi. "For the birthday girl."

Money smiled and kissed Karma on the lips again.

"True story." Money grabbed Karma's hand. "Come on and let me introduce you to my mother."

Karma took a deep breath in, then released it as she allowed Money to lead her to the kitchen where his mother was waiting. Curious male and envious female gazes followed the couple as they approached Evelyn. Evelyn, in a state of hysterical laughter, tried to regain some composure once her son and his significant other came into view. Evelyn's friends followed her eyes. Eyebrows raised and nods of approval followed. Evelyn patted her heavy chest as her eyes settled on Karma. She was absolutely taken aback by the young woman's beauty. Money told her the girl was gorgeous, but she hadn't been prepared for the sight before her. She had no idea such beauty even existed until she saw Karma. In that moment, she understood why Money was so deeply in love with her. She hoped the young lady's heart was as golden as her hair.

"Pardon me, ladies," Money spoke, interrupting his mother's thoughts. "I don't mean to interpose."

"That's alright, son," Evelyn smiled.

"Mama, everyone..." he began with an outstretched hand. "...this is Karma."

Karma smiled and waved at the group of distinguished black women.

"Hello," she said coyly.

"Well, isn't this a pleasant surprise?" Evelyn asked, looking back and forth from Money to Karma. "How are you doing this evening, Karma?" Evelyn extended her arms to welcome the nervous young woman into a heartfelt hug. Karma received her willingly and relaxed under her motherly touch. She missed her mother's hugs.

"I'm fine, Ms. Parks. And yourself?" Karma asked politely.

"Oh, no, honey. Please, call me Evelyn," she insisted.

"Yes, ma'am," Karma grinned, showing off her deep dimples.

Evelyn's girlfriends nodded in approval of Karma's apparent demure upbringing. Evelyn winked at Money as an offering of her blessing to wed Karma in the future. Her son hit the jackpot with Karma. Evelyn's eyes were warm and her kind spirit shone through them. She wanted nothing more than to have the beautiful young lady as her future daughter-in-law. Evelyn kept her strong arm wrapped around Karma's small waist.

"Money's told me so much about you," she beamed. Evelyn turned to her friends and smiled a little harder. "Isn't she beautiful?" she asked them while rubbing Karma's chin with her thumb. The group verbally agreed without hesitation. "I remember when I was this size," Evelyn jested while bumping Karma playfully with her full hips. She belted out a resonant laugh. "Are you hungry, sugar?"

"Yes, ma'am," Karma rubbed her growling stomach. There were pans and pans full of food set around the kitchen. The aroma of the hot dishes invaded Karma's nose.

"Alright, now. Don't be shy, baby. We all like to eat around here, okay?" she teased. "Fix her a plate, son," she instructed Money.

"Alright, Mama," Money accepted proudly. He took Karma by the hand once again and walked over to the counter across the room where the platters of food were waiting for them.

Karma sat at the edge of Mimi's princess bed watching Money tie the laces on his daughter's sneakers. The miniature chandelier that hung above illuminated the tastefully painted mint green room. Although the room was not filled with much, the white toy chest, matching dresser, nightstand, and rocking chair set accommodated the bed which was centered in the room. Several toys were scattered around the wall-to-wall carpet.

Money completed his task and straightened out Mimi's denim pant leg cuffs. The little girl smiled at Karma as she held onto the top of her father's head for balance. The stuffed black Bratz doll Karma bought her was tucked under one of her chubby arms. Karma was absolutely in love with Mimi. She was the cutest little girl she'd ever seen in her life. Mimi was not only very smart, but she was extremely well-mannered for a child of four. She loved watching Money in action with Mimi. It gave her a glimpse of how he would be with their child in the near future.

"There you go, chunky butt," Money said, patting Mimi on her backside. "Can I have a kiss?"

Mimi leaned in and kissed her father on the lips.

"Thank you," Money stated sweetly.

"You're welcome," Mimi replied angelically.

"Can Karma get a kiss, too?" he asked hopefully.

Mimi shook her head up and down as she walked over to Karma, tilted her head back, and puckered her lips. Karma leaned down, placed her hands on each of Mimi's cheeks, and gave quick pecks on her chubby cheeks.

"Thank you, Mimi," Karma sang with a smile.

"You're welcome," she giggled. "Karma?" Mimi chimed as she shifted her weight from one leg to the other.

"Yes, ma'am?" Karma placed a loose strand of Mimi's hair back into place.

"I gotta mommy," Mimi whispered with her tiny hand cupped on one side of her mouth.

Karma looked up at Money unsure of what to say in response to Mimi's random statement. Money shrugged his shoulders and shook his head in uncertainty. Kids were known to say the darndest things. *What was he supposed to say to Mimi?* She was proud to know she had a mother and wanted to tell anyone who would listen. Money was an advocate for the first amendment and his daughter was entitled to speak her mind. Karma rolled her eyes at Money and turned her attention back to Mimi.

"You do?" she asked with great interest.

"Yes," she nodded rapidly. "You gotta mommy?"

Karma lost herself in Mimi's dark brown questioning eyes. Mimi caught her off guard with that question. She was as unpredictable as her father when it came to conversation. Karma felt her eyes well with tears. She blinked them back as the little girl watched her closely.

"I used to," Karma said choking up. "But she had to go away."

"Where is she?" Mimi asked with furrowed eyebrows.

"She's in Heaven," Karma responded in an almost inaudible

tone.

"Up there?" Mimi inquired pointing to the ceiling.

"Mm-hmm, up there," Karma sniffled.

Mimi, shaken by the sudden negative shift in Karma's behavior, became sad as well.

"Don't cry, Karma. You can have my mommy," she offered with a small voice.

Karma smiled at the child's sincere proposal. Unexpectedly, Mimi raised her arms and wrapped them around Karma's neck. Karma, in awe, wrapped her arms around Mimi's plump little body and picked her up as she stood to her feet. The two embraced for a long time. Money, unable to speak, teared up at the sight. Mimi and Karma exchanged another kiss before she set her back down on the floor. Mimi turned on her heels and ran out of the room with her doll in hand.

Money walked over to his visibly upset love and pulled her close to him. He admired the roundness of Karma's eyes and rubbed his thumbs along her eyelids.

"Thank you for being so kind to her. She loves that Bratz doll."

"You don't have to thank me, baby. She's a beautiful little girl. She's so sweet," Karma pinched her running nose.

"I know someone else who's just as sweet," Money professed, licking his full lips seductively.

"Oh, yeah? Who?" Karma countered.

"You," he stressed. Money bent down and applied a heartfelt kiss on Karma's glossed lips. The exchange was a sensual one. As their lips parted and eyes met once again, Money asked, "You sure you can't stay for the rest of the party? We're going to be bringing in the New Year right."

"I know you are, but I can't. I can't stay," Karma expressed. Time was winding down to the hour. She had to remove herself from the party soon to get back home and get ready for the Mint. Stuff was sure to start blowing up her phone soon. Karma still hadn't told Money what that late night phone call from Stuff was about. Three weeks came and went, and she never uttered a word about it. Keeping Money in the dark was getting to her in the worst way.

"Aww, come on, Karma. Your family won't mind. Step in and step out. Come back here and stay with us for the night after you've checked on them. You going to make me beg, huh?" Money mocked.

Karma outlined her boyfriend's innocent face with her eyes and sighed deeply.

She ran her hands over his strong chest and chewed on her bottom lip in apprehension.

"Let's sit down, baby." Karma took Money's hand into hers and led him over to the bed. The lovebirds sat down beside one another and marinated in each other's presence. Karma folded her hands in her lap as she studied the floor. Money admired her profile as he waited for her to spill the news. Karma inhaled and exhaled deeply. *It's now or never,* she thought to herself.

"I'm not leavin' the party to go check on my family. I'm leavin' to go to the Mint," she confessed, looking over at Money with troubled eyes.

"The Mint?" Money asked in confusion.

"Mm-Hmm," Karma nodded slowly.

Money crossed his muscular arms at his chest and stretched his legs out before him.

"Alright. I'm listening."

Karma scratched her scalp nervously.

"Well, I'm goin' to the Mint to handle some business. As you already know, Indigo's boyfriend, Stuff, is a dealer…who just happens to work for one of New Jersey's biggest kingpins."

"Which one?" Money asked.

"Owl," Karma replied, avoiding eye contact.

Money rubbed his mouth, trying to maintain his composure. He didn't like where this conversation was going. Karma wasn't giving him any eye contact and her uneasiness wasn't sitting very well with him.

"Go on."

Karma hesitated. She was treading unsteady waters and she knew it. Money's tone was dark and terse. She could feel the heat rising in his body.

"Well, Owl goes way back with Jimmy. So I went to Stuff and asked him if he could arrange a meetin' with me and Owl so we could discuss my mother's murder. But he told me Owl didn't meet with outsiders until they dealt with Hawk, his right hand man. So I met with Hawk and he agreed to help me out. But the thing is, he and Owl won't do their part until I do mine. And that's where the Mint comes in. I have to go there tonight to meet a guy named Pimp. He's a big time dealer from Philly. I'm supposed to seduce 'im, get 'im drunk, then take 'im back to the Robert Treat Hotel for Stuff and his boy to..." her voice trailed off. "If everything goes as planned, I'll get to meet with Owl and find out where Jimmy is."

Money's jaw locked. Rage and disbelief consumed him. He stared at a distant wall. He tried to focus on it to subdue the urge of wanting to ring Karma's neck. He didn't know if he was more upset that she'd kept all this information from him for so many weeks, that she'd resorted to seeking assistance from a drug lord and not the police, or the reality that she was actually going through with the whole operation.

"Money?" Karma touched his muscular arm and bit down on her bottom lip in despair.

Money's jaw clenched and unclenched.

"Baby, say somethin'. Please?" Karma continued.

Money slowly looked over at Karma with flared nostrils.

"You're not going," he said simply.

"Money, I have to. This is the only way I-"

Money unexpectedly jumped up from the bed and towered over Karma.

"YOU'RE NOT GOING!" he blared, pacing the floor.

Karma jerked back startled by Money's sudden outburst.

"This is why I didn't wanna tell you. I knew you wouldn't understand."

"What the fuck don't I understand, Karma?! Huh?! What don't I understand?! That you made a deal with the muthafuckin' devil or that you're gonna be fuckin' some other nigga tonight?!" Money screamed.

Karma's eyes grew heavy with regret.

"I'm not gonna be fuckin' anybody. Baby, I'm just goin' to the club to get 'im drunk and take 'im back to the room. That's it," she tried to reassure him. Karma felt awful. She could tell Money she wasn't going to touch Pimp with a ten foot pole and he still wouldn't believe her.

"I don't fuckin' believe you!" Money's voice boomed throughout the closed space. His body swelled within seconds. Karma remained sitting on the bed watching him pace the floor. Money looked like he was ready to hit something and she was surely not trying to be his target.

"I wouldn't do that to you, baby. You know that," Karma stressed

"No, I don't! No, I don't! I don't know shit! I don't even know who the fuck I'm talkin' to right now!" he admitted pitifully.

Karma rose from the bed and approached him with caution. She gently grabbed his wrist, but hc violently snatched it away.

"Don't fuckin' touch me!" he threatened with wide eyes.

"Money?!" Karma pleadcd desperately.

"No! Money nothin'! Fuck all that!" he snorted. "You askin' for it, Karma."

"I had no other choicc, Money! Why can't you see that?!" Karma cried.

Money stopped short and smiled at her. Karma shivered at the sight of it. The smile was inappropriate and wicked.

"No, I'll tell you what I see. I see why bitches get their asses beat. That's what the fuck I see. Ya'll muthafuckas ask for it," he retorted.

Karma's green eyes widened before her eyebrows furrowed. She grimaced at the indirect remark made towards her mother. Without warning, she brutally punched Money dead in the face. Wild slaps and punches followed as he tried to hold his busted nose. A flood of tears fell from Karma's eyes as she cursed him in tongues. Money tried to grab Karma's untamed arms with his free hand, but failed in his many attempts. Karma was a human windmill.

"Fuck you, muthafucka! Fuck you! My mother didn't deserve to die!" Karma continued her hysterical fit while Money finally managed to grab hold of her arms. He could care less, his nose was bleeding and flowing like a river. Money just wanted Karma to calm down.

"I didn't mean that! Look! Look! I'm sorry, baby! I didn't mean what I said!"

Karma struggled with Money. Her unyielding sobs contorted her body. Trying to stand up straight was a battle within itself.

"I hate you! I hate you! Let me go, Money!"

"No, baby. Listen to me," he begged, holding on to her ever so tightly. "Listen, listen, I'm sorry. I'm sorry. I didn't mean it," he whispered in her ear.

"No!" Karma shouted. "My mother didn't deserve it. She didn't. How could you say that to me?" she hiccupped.

"Baby, please," Money strained.

"I'm not gonna have this baby. I'm not," Karma confessed.

Money's face flushed with puzzlement.

"Wait, what? What baby? Karma, what baby?" he asked, turning her around to face him.

"Your baby! I'm pregnant with your fuckin' baby!" she cried, turning to walk away. Money caught her by the arm before she could reach the door and pulled her back into him. He buried his face in her neck.

"Come on, baby. Please. Don't walk out on me. I need you," Money professed. "We need to talk about this. You can't leave here angry. I won't let you."

Karma, unmoved by Money's plea, balled her right hand into a fist and swung it back hitting Money savagely in his loins. Money released Karma's waist and doubled over in pain. He grabbed his manhood as he fell to his knees trying to catch his breath. Karma snatched her purse off the bed, stepped over her Money, and stormed out of the room without looking back. She didn't need someone like that in her life. Karma didn't need a person like Money to disrespect her mother's memory every time they got into a disagreement. She couldn't understand how he could say such hurtful things and then turn right around and try to apologize in the same breath.

Karma was fed up and there was nothing Money could do about it. She wanted no parts of him-no memories, no baby. Aborting their child would not only teach that negro a lesson, but it would spare the little one of a life full of suffering. It didn't need to know its mother and grandmother's misery. And it surely didn't need to be misery's company.

KARMA

Chapter 19

S candalously dressed women and sex hungered men stood under the hazed colored lights hanging above them. The disc jockey worked his magic behind his computer and turntables in the DJ booth while alcohol, profanity, money, and marijuana encircled the fixed space. He hyped up the crowd with his catchy phrases and shout outs to the female admirers hovering around his station.

A tall, slender, light-skinned man dressed to perfection sat in the back of the lounge engaged in conversation with a handful of men sitting around him. Even with a lightening bolt shaped scar beneath his left eye, Pimp was a very attractive man. The waves in his freshly cut Caesar made anyone who laid their eyes on them seasick. Pimp nodded and grinned coolly in response to the bets his friends were making amongst themselves. All of them planned on taking the baddest female in the club back to the hotel with them. To Pimp, none of the women in the club that night were worth taking anywhere. In his eyes, the baddest woman had yet to be seen. Fortunately, his opinion didn't sway the fellas. The night was still young.

Karma and Indigo walked into the club prepared for the evening's events. Karma was dressed in a short black mini dress accentuated by a large red belt. A flowing black feathered wig donned her head. The four-inch stiletto heels upon her feet enhanced the firmness of her oiled calves. She stepped to the side and opened her matching clothed purse to place her wallet back inside of it. Karma tucked the wallet beneath her make-up case and newly bought lingerie. Indigo stood beside her cousin dressed in a red form-fitting sweater dress complimented by a leopard print belt and red high heeled pumps. Karma snapped her bag shut and looked over at her cousin with determination in her eyes. The memory of the fight between her and Money just hours ago was now a distant memory.

"You ready?" Indigo asked.

"Yup. Let's go to the bar," Karma suggested.

"Alright," Indigo agreed. The girls politely excused themselves through the thick crowd as they approached the bar.

"What do you want to drink?" Indigo inquired.

"An Amaretto sour." Karma readjusted her bag on her shoulder.

"K." Indigo turned her attention back to the bar and the bartender to order her and Karma's drinks. All the while, Karma rested her back against the counter's edge and sized up the men in the room. She made eye contact with a few of them and smiled gallantly. She didn't notice the young man who was undressing her with his eyes from across the club.

Pimp leaned over to his friend beside him scratching the scar under his eye.

"Ay, yo, Smurf? Look at that shorty ova dere by da bar."

The overweight, bald-headed man traced his eyes in the direction of the woman his boss was speaking of.

"Which one?"

"Da one wit' da black dress on. Da one dat looks like one-a dem Charlie's Angels." Pimp couldn't take his eyes off Karma. The way that black dress was hugging her tight frame was sending all the blood in his body to his penis. Pimp grabbed and held onto it while he kept his gaze on Karma.

"Yooo, she look good as hell, P," Smurf nodded in approval.

"Sho'nuff," Pimp smacked.

"You want me to go scoop her for you?" Smurf asked, pulling at his overgrown beard.

Pimp looked over at his right-hand man with a smirk of disgust. "What'chu think, nigga?"

Smurf smiled as he rose from the booth.

Indigo and Karma bopped their heads to the booming music while sipping on their light beverages. A handsome gentleman, old enough to be the girls' fathers, approached Indigo. She turned in his direction and entertained him with polite conversation while Karma focused in on the short heavy-set guy walking in her direction. The first thing that captured her attention was the mass of hair on his face and then the wool skully his head was covered with. He reminded her of a cartoon character. Karma thought about it for a moment and smirked at her realization.

Smurf stepped up to the wary young woman and invaded her space.

"How you doin' tonight, beautiful?"

Karma took a sip of her drink and shrugged.

"Aiight. I can't complain."

"Dat's what's hood," Smurf said, cracking his knuckles. "You here by yaself?"

"No, I'm here wit' my cousin," Karma pointed with her thumb.

"Oh, word? She lookin' a lil' occupied right about now. She wouldn't mind you goin' to da back and kickin' it wit' my mans for a minute, would she?"

Karma didn't exactly know what "mans" Papa Smurf was referring to and could care less at that moment. He'd appeared out of nowhere and she didn't need him messing up her game. She needed to be noticed by Pimp, wherever he was. This short sawed-off bastard would have to be dismissed immediately. But then a sudden thought came to mind. Papa Smurf said something about his man being located in the back of the club. Karma knew only the big wigs sat in the back of clubs. The back of the Mint was the VIP section.

If Karma's intuition was right, Papa Smurf was probably in Pimp's camp. She decided to play along with his little game.

Karma wrapped her wet lips around the tiny red straw and took another sip of her drink.

"It depends," she said nonchalantly.

"Depends on what?" Smurf asked.

"Depends on who ya mans is," Karma said, cutting her eyes at Smurf seductively.

Smurf smiled back at Karma's flirtatious advance. If he didn't have so much respect for Pimp, he would have hollered at Karma himself. Pimp wouldn't know what to do with a woman as fine as her. Smurf didn't even know what to do with a woman as good-looking as she was, but he would figure it out somehow. Pimp had women in almost every state on the Eastern Shoreline, but none of them were as fine as Karma. She was way out of his league and Smurf knew it.

"A nigga you need to know and wants to know you."

Karma raised an eyebrow and smiled slyly.

"Is that right?"

"Fa'sho. His name is Pimp," Smurf replied proudly.

Indigo's head snapped in the couple's direction. She looked over at Karma, then to the tubby man standing by her. Her cousin seemed unfazed by what the man just said to her. She never flinched and the mischievous smile on her face remained.

Karma had to keep it cool.

"Oh, really? And why do they call him Pimp?"

"You gonna have to ask him dat yaself, beautiful." Karma's eyes were killing Smurf. He swore they changed to gray the moment he mentioned Pimp's name. A woman's eyes were Smurf's weakness and the fact that Karma's changed colors made him want to say, *"Fuck, Pimp. I got dibs on this one."*

"Aiight." Karma turned to place her empty plastic cup on the bar. She and Indigo locked eyes as she turned back to face Smurf. Karma gave her cousin a nod before walking away with the cartoon look-a-like.

Pimp's eyes brightened at the sight of Karma and Smurf

approaching the table. He instructed his men to remove themselves from the table and they did so without hesitation. Karma and Smurf walked up to the booth. She couldn't help but try to ignore the grunts and swears of approval by Pimp's comrades as they walked past eyeing her down. Pimp definitely won the bet. Pimp became even more aroused by the up close and personal sight of Karma. She was a diamond in the rough. He flapped his legs like bird wings to fight off the rock hard erection in his pants. Pimp wanted Karma and he was going to have her by the end of the night. He and Smurf nodded at one another.

"I'll let ya'll talk." Smurf walked away, hoping Pimp would let him get a crack at Karma once he was done with her at the end of the night.

"Have a seat, gorgeous," Pimp insisted.

Karma walked around the table and sat down in the booth beside Pimp. She made herself comfortable, crossing her legs slowly and whisking pieces of her store-bought hair out of her face.

Pimp shook his head as sweat beads gathered on his forehead.

"Damn, baby. You got a nigga sweatin' over here. What's ya name?"

"Doll," Karma said with a smirk.

"Word? I like dat." Pimp took a strand of Karma's wig and twirled it around his finger.

"Thank you." she grinned.

"Tell me somethin'. What's somebody as bad as you doin' in a place like dis?" Pimp continued to twirl her hair around his finger.

"It's New Year's Eve. I heard this was where the party was at, so me and my cousin decided to come through," Karma lied.

"You and your cousin?" Pimp asked, letting her hair dangle from his finger. *Where was her man? And why would he let some-one as sexy as her out of his sight?* If Doll had been his woman, the world would have never seen her alone. Pimp would have made sure she was *always* seen with him. She was a trophy. He figured she and her cousin must have been doing one of those "girl's night out" bits. Whatever the case, he wanted to know where her man was.

"Yeah," Karma replied.

"You ain't come here wit' ya man?" Pimp asked eagerly.

"No," she said confidently. "I ain't gotta man." Karma eyed Pimp with her dimpled grin. As much as it killed her to admit her relationship with Money was, indeed, officially over, there was nothing more she could say or do except get the night over with—soberly.

Pimp leaned into Karma's neck and took a whiff of her sweet smelling perfume. He allowed his nose to brush up against her earlobe. Pimp must have died and gone to Heaven, because the angel sitting beside him had him wide open. Doll was nothing but class. And if she knew who he was, she was doing a hell of a good job of not letting him know it. He needed to make her his that night.

"I ain't got nothin' to worry about den, huh?"

Karma squirmed under the tickle of Pimp's warm breath against her neck. Falling under the spell of this man was not in the plan. She wasn't usually attracted to light-skinned men. Pimp was the first and he needed to be the last. Karma had to recover and quick. The lust that was building up inside of her was throwing off her concentration. It was all Money's fault. If he'd just tried to understand her point of view on the situation, she wouldn't have been actually considering bedding this Philly nigga at the end of the night. Karma wasn't one to fill her empty voids with sex, drugs, or alcohol, but tonight would be an exception if she didn't get it together. Misery loved company. And out of her and Pimp, Karma was definitely the miserable one.

Karma turned her face toward Pimp's and brushed her lips along his freckled cheek.

"Mm-mm." She slowly pulled away from him and stuck her tongue out just enough for him to watch her rewet her lips.

"Daaamn. I wonder what dat tongue tastes like," Pimp said as he cringed at the thought.

"It tastes just like my kitty…sweet and juicy," Karma teased with a smirk.

Pimp grimaced with more pleasurable pain.

"Aww, shit. I bet it does."

Karma ran her thumb over Pimp's lips.

"You wanna taste it?" she asked with a serious face.

"No doubt," Pimp replied eagerly.

"Good. Let's have a drink then," Karma suggested.

Pimp lay sprawled out on his back across the full-sized bed. He closed his eyes as he took a deep pull from his blunt. A small cloud of smoke escaped his mouth as he exhaled. Pimp massaged his hardened love muscle through his unbuckled trousers to the sounds of Jodeci's *Freakin' You* playing on the room's stereo system. He opened his red slanted eyes and scoured the room in search of the woman he planned to make his better half that evening. Karma disappeared into the bathroom once they reached the room and he hadn't heard a peep out of her since.

Karma sat on the bathroom toilet draining the alcohol from her full bladder. She hadn't planned on getting drunk, but Pimp insisted they should drink until their hearts were content. Karma ordered herself a bottle of Verdi Spumante, took it to the head, and drowned her sorrows. Releasing the excess water from her body was refreshing. She wiped herself, flushed the toilet, and rose pulling up the red laced panties she'd bought to entice Pimp. Karma shuffled to the sink barefoot and stood before the mirror that was hanging above it. Dressed in a red laced bra and panty set beneath a thigh-high red satin robe, Karma contemplated whether she should leave the robe open or closed. She decided to tie it closed. It would tempt Pimp more. As she tied the belt loosely around the wrap, panic set in. Karma hoped Stuff was on his way because the remaining wine in her system was making her extremely horny. Pimp was a fine man waiting to blow her back out. And after the fight with Money; Karma was in a position to make all kinds of unwise decisions.

Pimp called to her from the bedroom. His voice was low and seductive. The yearning for her to be intertwined with him was heavy in his conviction. Karma wished Money was in the other room waiting for her instead of Pimp. She felt the tears well up in her eyes and slowly blinked them back. It was time to handle business. She would deal with her broken heart later.

Pimp took another pull from the blunt. The heat was rising in his body and "Doll" was the only woman he wanted to have cool it down.

"Doll! Bring ya fine ass out here, girl!" he beckoned. *"I'm ready to get sucked,"* he said to himself.

The door of the bathroom creaked open. Karma walked into the room and crossed to the foot of the bed. Pimp peeped her strong legs through the slits of his eyes and nodded. He was going to be riding a bull tonight.

"A nigga's ready to taste dat tongue right about now, ya dig?"

Karma smiled naughtily. She moved slowly towards the bed and placed one knee down on the mattress. She crawled onto the bed and hovered over Pimp.

Pimp, entranced by Karma's eyes, grabbed her waist and forced her hips down to a straddled position.

"You feel dat?" he asked, flexing his manhood beneath her.

"Mm-Hmm," Karma replied with a nod. Her buzz was officially blown. Pimp was working with absolutely nothing! If she considered sleeping with him before, the thought was completely gone now. She could hardly feel whatever it was he was referring to. Her pinky finger was bigger than what he had in his pants.

"I want you to suck da shit out of it," Pimp said, rubbing Karma's muscled backside.

Karma smiled, sitting up. She untied the robe's belt from around her waist and let it unwrap. She pulled it from its loops and proceeded to play with it. Her full laced breasts came into view. Pimp licked his lips as he moved his hands from Karma's behind to her chest. Her nipples grew hard under his touch. Karma gently grabbed his hands and placed them over his head. Pimp noticed she still had the belt in her hand and asked, "What'chu gonna do wit' dat?"

"I'mma tie your hands up wit' it," she grinned.

"Ohhh shit. You into dat kinky shit, huh?" Pimp laughed.

"Maybe," Karma replied, tying his hands together tightly.

Pimp tried to look over his head at his bounded hands. He

struggled to free them, but failed.

"Damn, baby. Dis shit is too tight."

"Shhhh," Karma requested, placing her index finger over Pimp's lips.

Light knocking on the door sounded.

"Now who da fuck is dat?" Pimp asked to no one in particular.

Relieved that Stuff arrived just in time, Karma smiled on the inside and continued to play the rest of her part out.

"Your boys?" she shrugged.

"Hell nah. Dem niggas knew what was up when dey saw me wit'chu," Pimp informed her.

The knocking sounded again.

"What da fuck!" Pimp yelled in frustration.

Karma climbed off Pimp and made her way to the door.

"Don't answer it, ma. Fuck dem niggas," he suggested.

"Shhhh." Karma closed her robe with her hand, peeped through the peephole, and opened the door. Stuff and Karma's eyes met. He and his colleague strolled into the room and set their attention on a heavily sedated Pimp. Pimp lifted his head and looked at the men in confusion. He'd never seen them before and didn't like the mean mugs they were throwing his way.

"What da fuck is dis?" he asked, trying to get his hands free.

Stuff's partner gradually walked over to the wall where the stereo system was built inside of it. He pressed the volume button and kept his finger on it until Jodeci's harmonious voices resounded throughout the room. Stuff gave Karma a nod of approval as she redressed and gathered her belongings. Pimp caught Karma's eye while she struggled to put her other heel on.

"Fuckin' bitch. You set me up," he sneered.

No sooner than he began his rant, Stuff's partner ended it with one solid punch to Pimp's mouth. His mouth swelled up immediately from the first strike. Karma jumped at the sound of the hitman's brass knuckles each time they connected with Pimp's teeth. She felt sorry for him. But her pity only lasted for a moment. She didn't know what Pimp's story was, but he had probably become a victim of circumstance just like she had. All children of the ghetto become products of their environment one way or another. Pimp and Karma were no exceptions.

Karma got herself together, looked back at Pimp's semi-conscious body and turned away, walking out of the room. As she closed the door behind her and started down the hall, echoes of a lust-filled song and snapping bones latched onto her soul.

Chapter 20

K arma sat in one of the cushioned chairs set in the corner of the family's coffee house. With her legs tucked under her chin and her head resting against the picture framed window, she reminisced about the previous evening's events. Her weary eyes danced across the floor as she slipped deeper into meditation. All she could think about was that she'd been an accessory to a murder. In all her life, Karma never thought she'd stoop as low as setting up a drug dealer for his last night on Earth. She didn't quite understand the power of the "P" when her father cheated on her mother years ago. She couldn't comprehend how he could slip the way he did when her mother gave him what he wanted, when he wanted it, and how he wanted it during their late night love making sessions. Karma was subjected to her parents' moans and groans of passion many a night. No, she didn't understand the power of the "P" then, but she did now. A woman's "P" brought the most powerful men to their knees, and Karma was both a witness and the facilitator to such an act last night.

Her stomach was hurting. Everything was getting to be too

much for her to handle. She still hadn't heard from Money since their break-up. She was pregnant with his child and had yet to decide if she was going to keep it or not. It was times like these Karma wished her mother was alive. Soleil had the answers to all of her problems. She cringed at the thought of her mother. Karma rubbed her wet eyes with her hand and placed it back against her head.

Victor watched his niece from behind the main counter. Karma was quieter than usual and it worried him. He guessed she was thinking about her mother. His sister had been in the ground for three months now and the police still had no leads on Jimmy. Like he predicted, Soleil had become another statistic. She was one of thousands of domestic abuse victims who died in vain. He was as much to blame for her demise as anyone else…probably more. How Karma could continue to love and respect him in spite of all he'd refused to do for her mother was beyond anyone's guess.

Victor shook the awful thought out of his mind and retrieved a china cup and saucer from beneath the Espresso machine, filled it, and traveled over to Karma. He carefully placed the cup of hot tea on the small table beside the lounge chair. The sight of her uncle's long arm snapped Karma out of her trance.

"Drink this," he insisted with a warm smile. "It should help settle your stomach."

Karma looked up at her uncle with appreciative eyes.

"Thank you."

Victor placed his large hand gently on his niece's cheek and winked before walking away.

Karma took the hot cup into her hands, brought it to her lips and blew on it before taking a sip. She closed her eyes as she allowed the hot liquid to slide down her throat. Karma placed the tea back on its coaster set atop the table and turned her attention to the world outside the window. She sat up briefly at the sight of Money entering the quarter. Panic set in. She was looking a hot mess and hadn't cared that she was dressed in baggy sweatpants and a hoodie until Money came into view. She didn't expect to see or hear from him until…well, Karma wasn't sure when they'd meet again, but today was absolutely unacceptable. Her hair wasn't even done. Karma closed her eyes and wished silently to herself that she could just crawl under a rock and die. She reopened her eyes and noticed she was still very much alive and sitting in her chair.

Money searched the room for Karma and found her sitting in the corner. He was a little taken aback by her appearance. Not because she was dressed down for the day, but because she looked like she hadn't slept. Money could dig it. He hadn't slept either. He felt horrible for the way he'd spoken to her the night before. His temper had gotten the best of him and he'd said things to her he had no business saying; especially about her mother. Money understood if Karma didn't want to see or speak to him ever again, but he just wanted her to think about the life they created, the life that was inside of her womb at that moment. He wanted nothing more than for her to keep their child. If things couldn't be worked out between the two of them now, he prayed they would later.

Money wanted to be Karma's protector. The fact that she'd gone to Stuff and his people for help instead of him broke his heart. He was her man and it was his job *as* her man and as an officer of the law to serve and protect his own. Money took a step back night before and thought about the predicament Karma was in. If his mother had been killed and the police stopped looking for her killer, what would he have done? *What extremes would he have taken to find her killer, especially knowing who it was?* Money sighed in self-disgust for last evening's behavior. He approached Karma with caution. Karma rolled her eyes and sucked her teeth as he made himself comfortable in a seat across from her. He leaned forward, resting his arms in his lap.

"Hey."

Karma ignored him. She continued to look out the window. As much as she honestly loved having Money there, the thoughts of what he'd said and how he acted last night kept her from feeling complete happiness.

"How are you feeling?" he continued.

Karma remained silent.

Money looked Karma over and noticed a single piece of jewelry on her wrist beneath the sleeve of her hooded sweatshirt.

"I see you're still wearing your Christmas present. That's saying something, right? You can't be *that* upset with me if you're still wearing it."

Karma looked down at the 14-karat-gold charm bracelet on her wrist and crossed her arms beneath her chest to hide the discovery. She was so out of it; she hadn't even realized she was still wearing his gift. Karma looked back out of the window and hoped Money wasn't noticing her face flushing with embarrassment.

"I'm not leaving until you talk to me. So you might as well stop giving me the silent treatment."

Karma rolled her eyes again.

"I'll ask you the question again," Money said seriously. "How are you feeling?"

Karma slowly turned her head in Money's direction with a disgusted smirk. How dare he use that tone of voice with her when he was the one in the wrong. *Was he serious?* He had to be, because even though his tone cut through her like a knife, his eyes were just as full of pain as her own. A man's eyes spoke volumes. *Her* man's eyes spoke volumes.

Karma hesitated and replied in a soft voice, "A little nauseous."

Money knew how stubborn Karma could be and wasn't sure how far he was going to have to go to get some type of response out of her. When she uttered those three little words, he sighed in relief. He was getting through to her.

"Is there anything I can do to make you feel better?" he asked genuinely.

"You can leave," Karma said sharply, cutting her eyes at him.

Money knew what Karma was trying to do. As much as she was trying to push him away, he was pushing back even harder to stay. Karma was going to have to deal with him whether she liked it or not. He loved her and he wasn't going anywhere. Money wasn't one to give up so easily.

"Sorry, I can't do that. It's not a good look. You know I gotta preserve my sexy," he teased.

Before Karma could catch it, a smile grew along her face.

Money was so silly, it was pathetic.

"Is that a smile?" Money asked with wide eyes.

"No," Karma lied, fighting the smile.

"I think it is," Money replied. "I'm glad I can still make you smile, baby...even through all of your pain."

The smile disappeared from Karma's face and she grew serious again. Pain...the story of her life. She knew it all too well. *When was it all going to end?*

"Indigo told me what happened last night with what's his name?" Money continued.

"Pimp," Karma said innocently.

"Yeah, him. I almost called him Pimple, Pumpkin, or something," Money chuckled.

Unable to restrain herself, Karma let out a euphoric laugh. Money loved the sound of Karma's laughter. It was music to his ears. She looked and sounded so much like a child when she laughed; so carefree...so innocent. Money wished he had a camera to capture this moment. He laughed along with his love and admired her beauty. *How could he have been so mean to her?*

"You're so stupid," Karma giggled.

"You gotta glow to you, baby," Money admitted. "It's beautiful."

Karma knew what he meant by that. The thought of their child disrupted her laughter.

"Money-" she began.

Money held his hands up and countered with, "Don't say anything, baby. Just let me talk." He ran his hand over his goatee and continued. "I fucked up last night. I blacked out on you and I disrespected your mother all in the same breath. I apologize for that. I was wrong. No, I was downright mean. You didn't deserve any of that last night. I didn't mean to hurt you, baby. I just...I don't want you to kill our baby out of spite for me. It deserves a chance to live. Please, baby love. I love you and I want to be there for you and our baby, like I am for Mimi. I'm a man. I'm that man my father never had the balls to be. I mean, all my life my mother told me he was dead, but I know in my heart he was probably just another sorry ass nigga who didn't want any part of our lives. And that's fine. I've accepted that."

Karma looked deeply into Money's eyes and nodded.

"I know. And I feel sorry for him." She picked her cup of tea up from the table and took a sip out of it. "I feel sorry for Mimi, too."

"Why?" Money asked in puzzlement.

"Because like *her* father, she doesn't know her other parent either." Karma continued to drink her heated beverage.

Money sat back in his chair apprehensive about where their conversation was going. He didn't want to have another argument with her, especially one regarding the choices he made for his daughter.

"Karma, we've already been through this. Mimi doesn't need to know who she is."

"Yes, she does, Money. Every child deserves to know both of their parents, not just one. I know she's out there, but-" Karma admitted.

"Mimi doesn't need to see her like that. She'll be scarred for life," he crossed his arms.

"Baby, believe it or not, Mimi's gonna grow up seein' a lot around here. Junkies, drunks, pimps, hoes...everything. It's real out there and her mother's right in the midst of it all," Karma confirmed.

"What am I supposed to tell her when she asks me what's wrong with her mommy? What am I supposed to say?" Money asked pitifully.

Karma studied the agony in Money's eyes and gradually looked away. She looked for the answers through the eye of the picture window. God created the world outside, right? He was the all knowing. Karma needed a good answer and quick. She'd stopped asking God for favors after He'd taken her mother from her, but today was going to be an exception. Money needed to hear something to calm his heart. Her man was coming to her for answers and she had to deliver one way or another. It finally came to her.

"You tell her...you tell her, her mommy is very sick, but she loves her very much." Karma slowly turned to face Money and looked him dead in the eyes. "You tell her sometimes mommies have to stay away from their babies because they don't want to bring harm to them. Tell her, her mommy's sickness is not her fault and she'll see her again one day. If not down here on Earth, then up in Heaven with God and the angels. Tell her when she goes away, it'll be okay to be sad. It'll be okay to cry. Because everybody cries...mommies, daddies, even God." Karma looked away again and settled her eyes out the window. "That's what you tell her."

Hawk held the door open for Karma.

"Thank you," she uttered with a gracious smile.

Karma stepped into the room while Hawk walked out into the hallway. He kept the door ajar while he spoke to one of his men outside. It took Karma half of the morning to bring herself to his office. She was still exhausted from her all-night make up love session with Money. He had been merciless last night. Karma was tired and her stomach was upset from the morning sickness that hit her unexpectedly on the way over to Hawk's nest. She wished Hawk would have considered arranging their meeting for another day, but he insisted on speaking to her this morning.

Karma walked around the room admiring the African artwork on the walls. As she made her way over to the guest chairs, she noticed two 8x10 framed photographs set atop Hawk's desk. Both were turned away from the eyes of those who would be seated on the other side of the desk. She sat down in one of the chairs and reached for the photograph farthest from her. Karma turned the picture towards her and admired the beautiful woman resting her head against Hawk's shoulder. She guessed it was his wife. The two complimented each other very well. They reminded her of her own parents in a much happier time. Karma placed the photo back on the desk and reached for the other one. When Karma directed the picture her way, all the blood from her face drained. The slanted eyes of the man standing beside Hawk stared back at her. His wicked smile taunted her. Karma's hands began to shake uncontrollably. He was much younger in the picture than he was now; they both were. Karma couldn't breathe.

Hawk walked up behind her and placed his aged hand gently on her back. He saw she was trying her best to fight the flustered look on her face. Hawk had her right where he wanted her.

"Something wrong, Miss Cruz?" he asked.

Karma looked up at Hawk briefly, then turned her attention back to the picture.

"N-n-no," she stuttered. "I was just looking at the man standing beside you in this picture. His face looks familiar," she admitted through teary eyes.

"Well, it should," Hawk replied with raised eyebrows. "It's the face of the same man who killed your mother. Jimmy "Owl" Hayes to be exact."

Karma looked up at Hawk in shock. A single tear fell from her eye. He gently removed the photograph from her trembling hands and settled down in his seat behind his desk.

"But I thought Jimmy and Owl were two...you knew? All this time?" she asked him in a labored breath.

Hawk looked down at the picture and said, "Yes." He placed the picture back in its place on his desk. "Not too long after our meeting, Stuff came to me and expressed his concern for you and your matter. I asked him what was troubling him and he proceeded to tell me the truth about you and your mother. Believe me when I tell you, Miss Walker, that my heart skipped a beat when I heard your mother's name. I knew her very well. She and I met on many occasions. Mostly at my annual Fourth of July barbecues. Jimmy was very much into showing your mother off. Not only was she beautiful, but she was also very kind. My wife and I had nothing but great respect for her. When the boys brought the write-up of her slaying to my attention, I immediately asked Jimmy about it. He admitted to killing her, then fled to Belize until we gave him word to come back."

Karma couldn't believe her ears. Hawk was the "friend" her mother had been referring to over the last four years in regards to a certain someone's famous cookouts.

KARMA

She wasn't sure when Stuff approached Hawk about his concern for her, but she was thankful for such a loyal friend. He'd put his life *and* his job on the line for her…all just to help her seek justice for her mother. Karma would be forever indebted to him.

"Why did you let me go through with the whole Pimp deal if you knew who I was this whole time?" she asked confusingly.

"Because regardless of who you are or *are not*, Miss Walker, our rule applies to everyone," he answered, folding his hands at his stomach. "You paid your dues and Jimmy and I are forever grateful to you. In fact, he has requested to meet with you as soon as you are free," he said matter-of-factly.

Karma cut her eyes at Hawk in distrust.

"And you're not going to stop me from doing so, knowing that I'm going to meet with him for the sole purpose of killing him?"

Hawk reclined in his chair and bounced back and forth.

"No, I'm not. I was very fond of your mother, Miss Walker. She was a beautiful woman who I watched fall victim to Jimmy's insecurities." Hawk reached into his pant pocket and retrieved a small packet of gum. He took out a stick for himself and offered Karma a piece. She politely declined. Hawk placed the pack back into his pocket and continued. "You see, for as long as I've known Jimmy, he's always had a bad temper. Believe it or not, he was very much the lady's man back in the day and abused most, if not all the women he ever courted. Next to your mother, his ex-wife, who is also my sister, also received the worst of his beatings."

Hearing Jimmy's long history of domestic violence turned Karma's stomach. It was no question of how he got his nickname "Owl." Jimmy, much like the nocturnal bird, struck and caught his prey at night. Owls loved mice. Mice represented the meek and helpless. Her mother had been the weakest mouse out of the pack.

All Karma could think about was how her mother hadn't been the first of Jimmy's victims, but was the last to feel his mighty blow. Repulsion grew along her pale face. She looked across at Hawk and tried to understand why he was speaking with such nonchalance about his friend's unacceptable behavior. He spoke about it like it was something he was used to and eventually accepted. *Had Jimmy or had Jimmy not beaten up his sister?* Hawk was too dismissive for her. He should have been raging mad. Karma was.

"And you didn't do anything about it? You just let 'im beat on her? You didn't try to kill 'im?"

"Ohhh, yes," Hawk nodded for a long time. "On many occasions. But my sister asked me to spare his life for that of her son, my nephew…who you know very well," he hinted.

Karma pondered over the unfamiliar person Hawk was speaking of. No particular names or faces came to mind. She couldn't fathom who he could possibly be referring to.

"No, I don't think so, sir."

"Oh, yes, you do, Miss Walker," Hawk smiled widely. "I hear Money's very smitten with you."

Karma's mouth fell open. She didn't know how to feel in that moment. The love of her life was the nephew of one of New Jersey's most powerful crime bosses and the son of his partner, the king of Essex County, and her mother's murderer. Karma had been sleeping with her enemy's son the entire time and had no idea. When Karma thought about Money and his horrific temper, everything started to make sense. His father's worst trait had been passed on to him. The similarity in their complexions and eye shape never crossed her mind until now. Money never even acknowledged his father at her mother's birthday party. Jimmy never uttered a word either. Just then, Karma remembered that Money grew believing his father was dead. As far as Karma was concerned, his so called "death" was going to be official once she got her hands on him. Poor Money. He was born into a burning ring of fire. His parents' knot was not one tied by love, but of hate. *How was she going to break this news to him?* Their relationship would never recover from this.

"Does he…?" she asked.

"No. Money has no idea who his father is or what he used to do to his mother. Nor does he know anything about this part of my life. And I'd like to keep it that way," Hawk confirmed.

"I understand." Karma knew knowing these truths would eventually eat at her. She wasn't one to keep anything from her loved ones, but if not telling Money about his father was going to salvage their relationship, there was no reason to sacrifice their happiness. It was a risk she wasn't going to take.

"So, you see, Miss Walker, I have no cause to interfere with the business you have with Jimmy. I knew it was only a matter of time before he would meet his match." Hawk folded his hands under his chin and began to bounce back and forth in his chair again. "We all have to pay the piper sooner or later. Wouldn't you agree, Miss Walker?" he asked with a sly grin.

"Yes…yes, we do," Karma replied.

KARMA

Chapter 21

Stuff sat behind the wheel of his black Ford Expedition in a vacant lot across the street from a shabby eight-story hotel. He surveyed the long, dark street for any signs of the evening's target. He'd moved up in rank overnight just by going to Hawk and telling him the truth about Karma. Stuff thought he was dead for sure, but Hawk's reaction was that of remorse. Stuff hadn't a clue about his bosses' connections to his long time friend's mother and her mate. He figured Hawk was getting old, because the man who trained him twelve years ago was a cold blooded killer and drug distributing mastermind. The man who'd taken his father's place shed a tear that night he spoke of his best friend's mother's death. Stuff never saw another man cry before. It tore his heart into pieces to see his mentor fall apart before him. Stuff thought about how he'd felt when his own parents died and the night Indigo called him hysterical about Soleil's death. Then Stuff thought about Karma. His sole purpose for sitting in that vacant lot was to case her mother's killer.

He placed a Black & Mild cigar in his mouth and sparked it. A

KARMA

man walking arm-in-arm with a flimsily dressed cinnamon-colored woman captured his attention. The way the woman was dressed gave away her profession and source of income. Stuff remembered how his father used to tell him how the type of woman a man liked told a lot about what kind of man he truly was. He chuckled at the irony of his father's adage and the sight across the street. Jimmy "Owl" Hayes must have been a renaissance man because he went from loving a beautiful successfully intelligent woman to laying up with a grimy crackwhore who looked like she needed more than just a dick fix.

Stuff took a smug pull from his cigar as he confirmed Jimmy's identity with a slow nod. He retrieved his cell phone from his coat pocket, flipped it open, and proceeded to type a text message to his expecting source.

Karma relaxed in her mother's former Jacuzzi tub surrounded by lit scented candles. With her eyes closed and body enveloped with bubbles, Karma submitted her senses to the sounds of Aretha Franklin. Finding out the truth about Jimmy and his past earlier in the day gave her cause to try to unwind and re-evaluate the approach she was going to take in the upcoming meeting with him. She didn't know when and where they were going to meet. Hawk hadn't elaborated on the details. He just told her it would be sooner rather than later. Karma wasn't sure how much longer she could wait. The thought of actually coming face-to-face with Jimmy again after four long months of searching and suffering gave her goosebumps. She didn't know how she was going to act when she saw him, but she *did* know she was going to ask him *"Why?"*

A beeping sound pulled Karma out of her reverie. She opened her eyes and searched for the item that disrupted her thoughts. She looked down and remembered she brought her cell phone into the bathroom with her. Karma reached over the edge of the tub, retrieved her phone, and opened it. She noticed that the beeping was serving as an indicator of the text message she just received. Karma pressed the view button on her phone and read the message:

"BROKER'S MOTEL ON EVERGREEN IN ROOM 46," to herself. Just as she was about to repeat the address out loud, Money appeared in the doorway and made his way over to the tub. Karma casually placed the phone back down on the step and turned her attention towards her suspicious lover. Money, with a towel in his hand, set it at the foot of the tub. Karma winked at him and flashed her million dollar smile.

"What are you up to?" Money asked distrustfully.

Karma batted her eyes and replied, "What makes you think I'm up to somethin'?"

Money looked over the perimeter around the bathtub and pointed to her cell phone.

"I don't know. Your cell's a dead giveaway."

Karma looked down at her phone, then back at Money with innocent eyes. She thought about batting them again, but decided against it. Pouting always redirected her parents' displeasure with her elsewhere, so she decided to throw the pitiful gesture at Money.

"I don't know what you're talkin' about," she lied.

Money tilted his head back slightly, crossed his arms at his broad chest, and stared Karma down. He didn't know what she was up to. And whatever it was, he hoped it had nothing more to do with Hawk, Owl, Stuff, or anyone else he didn't really trust.

"Yeah, you know what I'm talking about. Who else do you know brings their phone into the bathroom with them?"

"I know a lot of people who do that," Karma said with her upper lip turned up.

"Like who?" Money asked.

"Indigo, for one. Who I was just gettin' off the phone with when you walked in. She and Stuff are comin' through tonight, so I'm gonna go out and get some KFC for us to eat." Karma wasn't proud of her lies, but she'd given Hawk her word that she wouldn't tell Money anything. And besides, the little fibs she was feeding him weren't hurting him any. She knew Money wasn't buying her story, but what the hell? She'd come this far, why turn back now?

Money stood unmoved by Karma's tale. He was going to stand there all night if he had to until she told him the truth. *Was lying something that evolved during the post-traumatic stress that came along after a tragic event in a person's life?* Because if it was, Money was going to have to find a cure for it…well, at least for Karma. Her lying had become a habit.

He smirked at her.

"You don't believe me? Check my phone, then," Karma insisted confidently. She picked up the phone and held it in mid-air for Money's retrieval.

Money would really have to believe her now. His eyes shifted from her to the phone, then back to her again. He shook his head in disinterest.

"No, that's alright. I believe you."

Karma nodded triumphantly and placed the phone back down on the step.

"I'm trippin," Money said, rubbing his hand back and forth along his low cut hair.

"That you are," Karma teased. On the inside, she was relieved he gave up on his interrogation, because she didn't know what she was going to tell him had he checked her phone and not seen any incoming calls from Indigo that day.

Money smiled at her coaxing.

"Listen, I'll go get the chicken so you can stay here and enjoy your bath."

Karma leaned forward and smiled seductively.

"No, baby. That's okay. I don't mind. You'll have plenty of time to make trips to KFC and every other fast food joint around here after I blow up."

Money and Karma shared a warm laugh. Money couldn't wait until Karma started showing. He believed women were their most radiant when pregnant. With her already God-given beauty, she was sure to be some vision once her belly grew.

Money would have to control himself for sure. Knowing him, he would be ready to knock Karma up again as soon as she had this baby.

"True story," he replied, rubbing the sides of his mouth with his thumb and index finger. "True story."

She walked up a dark, narrow stairway dressed in a black thermal top, oversized black sweat pants, and black Timberland boots. She was dressed to kill, pun intended. The motherless child was the grim reaper in the flesh that night and she hoped he was ready to die. She didn't know if he was going to fight back or not and didn't care. Honoring her mother *her* way was what was most important to her now. She'd lost her fight against the NPD, but her battle with *him* had just begun.

Pimps berating their prostitutes, drug addicts begging for temporary relief, and screaming babies echoed on the floors below, between, and above her. Desensitized by the evils freed from Pandora's Box, Karma moved methodically up the stairway to her desired floor. The bright lights set along the walls of the fourth floor barely shone through the sooted cobwebbed miniature lamp shades. Karma's nostrils flared as she took in the ungodly mixture of stenches in the dull air. With her eyes focused straight ahead, she slowly moved forward down the hall. As the grimy floral carpet squished quietly beneath her feet, Karma scanned the numbers on the doors with her peripheral vision.

A woman, the same woman who Stuff spotted with Jimmy twenty minutes ago, exited a room located at the end of the hallway. Dressed in a long black trenchcoat, the woman turned away from the door and proceeded in Karma's direction. The two women immediately locked eyes. Karma noticed a small bulge on the woman's waist that was secured by the coat's belt. As the women's paths crossed, the prostitute swung open the side of her coat that was closest to Karma. A methodically executed exchange was made. She passed two items off to Karma, who took them without hesitation. She gave her a quick nod of thanks and moved forward to her destination while the lady of the night proceeded to her own.

An old radiator hissed in a corner of the dark putrid room. Illumination from a street light fell onto the walls and the rested face of Jimmy Hayes. Honking horns and loud chattering from the street below could be heard throughout the cramped room. Barechested, bound at the wrists with a rope, and sprawled beneath a white sheet and tattered blanket, Jimmy stirred. He turned on his side and ran his arms along the vacant space beside him. Taken aback by the absence of his evening's conquest, he turned back over on his back. His head fell to the side as his eyes struggled to open. He felt a presence in the room. Something was hovering over him and breathing heavy. Unable to make out the figure standing over him, Jimmy rubbed his eyes, forcing them into focus. As Karma's tight visage came into view, Jimmy's eyes glazed over with shock and fear. He couldn't take his eyes off hers. They were two dark gray clouds of thunder waiting for the lightening to strike. His calm had been his sexual rendezvous for the evening. The storm was there now, standing over him. And he had nowhere to run to, nowhere to hide.

"Karma."

Without allowing him to say another word, Karma raised the Louisville Slugger baseball bat above her head and brought it down violently on Jimmy's stomach. He clutched his hands and screamed out in wretched pain as he fell aimlessly onto the floor. Karma jumped back to regain leeway for another blow to his body. She stood over the crumpled man with wild eyes and a heavy heart.

"Muthafucka!" She raised the bat again and brought it down on his back. The cracking of his ribs filled the room. A high-pitched wail escaped from Jimmy's mouth. He unsuccessfully reached for his back as he squirmed in a rolling motion.

"Son of a bitch!" she screeched. Karma pulled the bat back and brutally struck Jimmy's legs. An animal-like howl fell from his salivating lips. He weakly reached for all of the spots struck by Karma's wrath.

"I know all about you, you piece of shit! You can thank Hawk for that!" she hollered.

Jimmy looked up at his cold attacker with quizzical eyes. He shook his head in disbelief.

"He wouldn't-" he began breathlessly.

"Oh, yes, he would. And he did," she replied, twirling the bat in her hand. "Did you really think he was gonna let you get away with goin' upside his sister's head and abandonin' your son without consequence? Your son! He needed you!"

Jimmy's mouth fell open in disbelief. *What were the odds of his son, whom he'd stood less than five feet away from that dreadful September night, dating his dead woman's daughter?* He'd been too drunk to even recognize Money that night. Had Hawk not kept him up to date about his son over the years, Jimmy would have never known a thing about him, from what he looked like to what his hopes and dreams were. And even though he'd decided to live the life of a criminal and not that of a father, he was proud of his son nonetheless. All he had of Money were pictures of him throughout the many stages of his life. And that's all he needed.

"Karma, please," Jimmy begged through salted tears.

Karma placed her left hand behind her ear and leaned down towards Jimmy.

"What?! What did you say?! Karma, please?!"

"Please," he begged again.

Karma, unfazed by Jimmy's plea, straightened her stance and smiled.

"Please, what, muthafucka?! What?!"

"Please," he coughed. The pain was getting to be too much for him. Jimmy tried his hardest to keep his eyes open, but it hurt to do so. He was having pains all over his body.

"Fuck ya please!" Karma snapped. "Did you care about my mother's plea when you were beatin' her ass to death?!"

A fresh flood of tears fell from Jimmy's eyes. His mind went back to the night of Soleil's birthday.

They got back to the house, changed into their nightwear, and settled in Soleil's bedroom to talk. He didn't know what she wanted to speak to him about, but by the look on her face, he knew it wasn't good. She sat him down on the bed and told him Lorenzo finally retired from the service and would be taking back his rightful place in her life. She told him she wasn't going to dispute her husband's decision because that was the news she'd been waiting for, for over twenty something years. Soleil told him she still loved Lorenzo. He was the love of her life, always had been, and always would be. He remembered watching her get up from the bed, walking over to her dresser and getting the engagement ring he'd bought her out of a jewelry box. Before she could turn back around and give the ring back to him, he was already up from the bed with his left hand full of her hair and his right hand connecting with her face. Soleil managed to break free from his grasp and run out of the room into Karma's childhood bedroom. She tried to close the door behind her, but he was already storming through the threshold. Soleil tried to find something to throw at him or strike him with, but Karma's room was only furnished by her bedroom set. He lunged at her, grabbed hold of her nightgown, ripping it at its straps and began to beat her unmercifully in the face again. He wouldn't let her fall to her knees. She staggered some, punch-drunk by his blows. He cursed her and laughed as he watched her sway from side-to-side with labored breaths.

The sight of her tickled him. In his mind, she needed him more than she would ever admit. And he made sure she knew it with every strike of his fist. He knew she didn't love him the way he loved her or the way she loved her husband. Soleil never would and that was fine by Jimmy in that moment. He was the last man she was ever going to be with. He'd made his mark and it was time to finish what he started. He told her to look at him and she tried to, but she couldn't hear what he was saying. *What was he saying?* Everything went silent after the first hit. *What was he saying?* There were three Jimmies before her instead of one. *What was he saying?* There was spit flying out of his mouth as he screamed at her. *What was he saying?*

The blow to her chest sent a shock wave throughout her entire body. Her mouth gaped open as she grabbed her chest, digging into it to stop the fire that was burning deep inside of her. As she stumbled backwards, falling over the wooden bedpost and breaking it in half, she saw her mother. It wasn't the same woman who'd made her life a living hell. Her eyes weren't angry. Her face wasn't in a fixed cringe. No, Ava was floating above her with tears in her eyes. She was crying for her baby girl. She'd seen and been through so much because of her. She never gave her a mother's love because she never had it. It was time to make amends. She reached out to her beloved little girl and mouthed "Come, my love. 'Chour father is waiting."

"I'm sorry," Jimmy slurred as he blinked back into his reality. He'd laughed at Soleil to keep from crying as she was fighting for her life. He'd laughed because he was sick in the head and sick in the heart.

"Yeah, you a sorry ass bitch, all right!" Karma screamed.

Jimmy collapsed back onto the floor and searched Karma's eyes for remorse.

There was none.

"Karma, please…help me."

Karma crouched down, leaned in towards Jimmy and without warning, spat in his face. Jimmy's head feebly jerked back and tapped the thinly carpeted floor. Karma etched in close to his ear allowing him to feel her warm breath on his neck and said, "I am my mother's daughter. Tell me…how do I taste?" She backed away from him staring him dead in his squinted eyes. Karma gradually stood back up and slowly shook her head in disdain. "Look at me," she said through clenched teeth. Her eyes fluttered with tears as she looked down at the shell of the man her mother had given herself to night after night. "Look at me!"

Jimmy focused his eyes on the unstrung young women standing above him. He watched her tighten her grip around the wooden bat as the tears strolled down her reddened cheeks. He didn't want to die, not like this. He was a drug lord, a pimp, a wife beater, a murderer…a true gangster. His way out was going to be by the gun. If a man lived by the gun, he died by it as well. But the game had suddenly changed. He'd beaten and killed the wrong woman. And now her daughter was there to give him a taste of his own medicine. He'd taken a woman's life and a woman was going to take his.

"My mother loved you," Karma cried. "I never understood why or how, but she did. And you turned around and killed her. Why? What did she ever do to you to deserve to die? Huh?!" She wanted to know why and he wasn't giving her an answer. She *needed* to know why and he wasn't saying a word. By the look in his eyes, Karma knew he had no reason for killing her mother. He'd done it just because he could.

Jimmy weakly jumped at the sudden outburst. He couldn't tell her how he'd watched his mother love her father, a man who gave her eight sons, hundreds of black eyes, a thousand kisses, and whispered millions of sweet nothings into her ear. He couldn't tell her about his mother's scars...the ones from his father's fists that never showed. Jimmy loved his mother dearly, while despising his father all the same. John Hayes used to sit in the corner of their dark living room with his rifle at his side and a bottle of moonshine in his hand. His glassy brown eyes would scour the room. He'd sit...waiting, lurking in the shadows for his children, his "no-good lil' niggas." He couldn't tell her it was his father's fault for how he and his brothers turned out. His mother died after giving birth to her ninth son, who soon after his mother, proceeded her in death seven days later.

Jimmy and his brothers mourned the loss of their mother and little brother hard, but managed to send them off beautifully. Their father, on the other hand, didn't mourn at all. On the evening of his wife's passing, he set photographs of her, her clothes, and jewelry on fire while in a drunken rage. The sight of his mother's belongings burning in the shed behind their wooden shack of a home stayed with Jimmy until his adulthood. He had nothing to remember his mother by. Fortunately, Jimmy's father drank himself to death a year later. Some said losing his wife had driven him to drink. But Jimmy and his brothers all knew differently. John Hayes buried himself in his liquor way before he met his wife. He was just an unhappy man who had the inability to love others, because he didn't love himself. No, Jimmy couldn't tell Karma any of that.

Karma, frightening herself, began to sob.

"I hate you! She was my world and you took her from me! You took her from me, Jimmy! You took my mommy!" Her body quaked with intensity. "So help me God," she snivelled, shifting from one leg to the other. "Get on your back," she commanded calmly.

Jimmy's eyes widened with fear. He faltered at the request.

"GET THE FUCK ON YOUR BACK!" she bellowed.

Jimmy winced in pain dreading his fate. He wanted to talk Karma out of killing him, but he couldn't find the words to say it. For the first time in his life, Jimmy Hayes was afraid of someone other than his father. His life had to be spared. He would never hit another woman again in life if she would just let him live. He had to live, but he knew she wouldn't have even given him time to die if the circumstances were different.

Jimmy wept heavily as he slowly rolled onto his contorted back. Bones continued to snap out of place as he settled in his crooked position.

"Karma," he whispered with pleading eyes.

"I'll see you in Hell, muthafucka," she countered unremorsefully.

"Kar-" Jimmy began.

With the swiftness of a professional lumberjack, Karma raised the bat above her head and pounded it ferociously into Jimmy's massive chest, cutting off his final call to her. She was losing all control over her senses. And before she knew it, Karma was unmercifully pummelling the wooden bat into Jimmy's skull. She was hitting him for every time he'd struck her mother. She was hitting him for every one of her mother's hospitalizations. She was hitting him for every day she spent in Clinton's Correctional Facility for Women. She was hitting him for every stroke he'd taken inside of Soleil during her rape. She hit him until the bat broke in two. Karma was left holding the handle.

As exhaustion and all five of her senses set back in, Karma took one more look at the mutilated corpse at her feet, stepped over him, and walked out of the room without looking back. She closed the door behind her as she stepped into the hallway and greeted a stone-faced Stuff with a slow nod. He and his partner had been standing guard outside the room the entire time of the brutal attack. Karma and Stuff's eyes locked as she placed the key and broken baseball bat into one of his hands. Stuff noticed the spotting of blood on Karma's face and pulled out a box of baby wipes from the black backpack he had on his right shoulder. He retrieved a wet wipe and applied to her flushed face.

"You aiight?"

She blinked slow and nodded, "Yes."

"It's ova now, aiight? You ain't gotta worry about him no more," he assured her.

"I know," she replied quietly.

Stuff analyzed Karma's face, making sure it was clean. He reassured her with a wink. He threw the used wipe back into his bag and zipped it closed. With the knapsack secured on his back, Stuff took the two plastic bags of boxed KFC meals from his partner and gave them to Karma.

"I already told Indigo what was poppin' tonight so you don't have to worry about her askin' you any questions when you get back to da house. She's got Money unda control too. So act natural, aiight?"

"Okay," she answered.

Stuff's partner gave him a signal that the two needed to proceed to the room and clean up Karma's mess before anyone became suspicious. Stuff returned the signal before turning his attention back to Karma. Shock was setting in. She was numb and wanted to stay that way forever. *An eye for eye, a tooth for a tooth* was a line from the Good Book. If Karma didn't remember anything else from Sunday school, she remembered, studied, and lived by that line. It was her badge of honor and only desired code of justification for her actions that evening. No one would ever be able to tell her anything different. *Turn the other cheek* had not made an impact of any kind on her life. It didn't apply to her past or present state and it wasn't going to apply to her future.

Stuff held her chin in his hand and grinned sweetly.

"You did good, Karm. As fucked up as dat sounds, you really did do good." He pinched her chin and gave her a kiss on her nose. "I'm proud of you."

Stuff winked at his best friend again before moving past her and disappearing behind the grimy wall with his partner in tow.

Karma took a brief look at the door Jimmy's bloody battered body was lying behind, turned her eyes away and concentrated on the lengthy hallway ahead of her. She took a deep breath in and closed her eyes as she welcomed the smells of life, death, love, and hate into her soul. Karma exhaled slowly, opened her eyes and proceeded to walk down the wretched hallway with her head held high.

KARMA

Chapter 22

Indigo and Money sat on the leather sofa playing a game of UNO. The commentary made by a panel of sportscasters on the television across the room added more voices and sounds to the space than there truly were. Indigo sat with her legs crossed Indian style and sorted her cards by colors and numbers, while Money watched patiently. Indigo proposed the two play a couple of games to keep Money's mind off Karma's whereabouts. She'd been gone for almost an hour and Indigo knew Money was getting worried. He'd made two attempts to leave the house and go to KFC to make sure Karma was in one piece, but she'd told him it wasn't necessary. Indigo told Money that Karma would be out a little longer than usual, because she had to pick Stuff up from "work." The two would go on to KFC from there. Being the skeptical man that Money was, he didn't believe her. So Indigo called Stuff and put him on the phone with Money. Stuff explained to him that Karma hadn't reached his place of work yet, but was on her way. She'd made a pit-stop at a gas station to fill up her tank. Luckily, Money fell for the story and calmed himself down long enough to concentrate on the card game.

"Bam!" Money yelled, slapping the cards down on the couch. "How you like me now, Officer Alonso? Draw eight and the color is red."

Indigo shook her head at her partner's mistake and pulled two cards from her hand. She placed them down slowly onto the small pile.

"I don't think so, Officer Parks," she smiled. "Draw sixteen, please."

"Aw, hell no!" Money replied.

"And the color is now yellow." Indigo sat back crossing her arms at her chest.

Money threw his cards down and dismissed them with the wave of his hand.

"I'm out. I'm not playing anymore."

Indigo fell into hysterical laughter.

"Nooo! Nooo! You can't do that! It's continuation, no elimination, Money. Pick your cards up and pluck your sixteen. Come on."

"Man," he sucked his teeth. Money picked his cards back up and proceeded to pluck the other sixteen from the deck.

"Stop being such a baby," she teased.

"Man, be quiet," he sulked.

Indigo laughed at her partner's childlike behaviour again. He and her cousin were made for each other. They were two big babies.

"Sourpuss."

Money waved Indigo away with his hand.

"Whatever, man."

"And just for that, take two more cards for being a sore loser," she said, plucking two more cards from the deck.

"Get outta here with that, Indigo!" Money replied, placing the two cards at the bottom of the deck. "I didn't lose anything. Stop adding your own rules to the game, cheater."

"Oh, I'm a cheater now? Just for that, I hope Karma gives you another little girl to run your black ass ragged," she spat playfully.

"Okay, now see, that's foul, Indi. For real. That's foul. You know I want a son," he said with a straight face.

"It is what it is," Indigo shrugged her shoulders.

"Apologize," Money demanded softly.

"Nope," Indigo grinned devilishly.

The opening of the front door sounded. Karma walked into the house with the bags of KFC meals in hand. She kicked the door shut with the heel of her foot and locked the door behind her. Money jumped up from the couch and met his love in the foyer. Indigo kept her eyes on her cousin as she neatened the deck of cards and watched Money kiss her on the lips.

"Hey, baby," Money cooed, taking the bags of food out of Karma's gloved hands.

"Hey," she replied, forcing a smile. Karma took her coat off and hung it on the coat rack near the door.

Money noticed the distant look in her eyes and wanted to know what was troubling her. He gently grabbed her chin and smiled.

"You alright?"

"Yes," she answered quietly looking up at him.

"You sure?" Money asked again in uncertainty.

"Yes, Money. I'm fine," she huffed. Karma caught sight of Indigo watching her from the living room. She had to keep her cool. If she let her exhaustion get the best of her, it would blow her, Indigo, and Stuff's cover. "I'm fine, baby," she reassured him in a more loving tone.

"Alright, beautiful. I'm just making sure. You're not acting like yourself is all," Money said worriedly.

"I'm not feelin' too well," Karma admitted while rubbing her forehead. "I think the smell of the gas from the station and the chicken got to me on the way back here. I never even got a chance to pick Stuff up because he's out in the field or whateva it is that they call it," she lied.

Indigo rose from the couch and crossed into the hallway. She was concerned. She had to get Karma out of this jam. Money was going to hit her with a gazillion more questions whether he was satisfied with her cousin's story or not.

"How's your stomach, K?"

"A little upset," Karma said, turning towards her cousin.

"Well, why don't you go upstairs and lay down for a little while," Indigo suggested, while taking a bag out of Money's hand. "I'll fix you some tea or something to help settle your stomach."

"Okay," Karma smiled appreciatively.

"Come on, Money," Indigo tugged on his arm. "Stop staring at my cousin like she's stupid or something. You know she takes offense to that mess with her crazy self."

Karma chuckled at her cousin's humorous act as she made her way to the stairs. She raised her hand and rubbed her thumb across Money's inviting lips. He kissed it in return and watched the mother of his second child disappear in the dark.

Karma kneeled at the base of her mother's former personal toilet throwing up her vengeance from that evening. She held her damp, throbbing head while trying to catch her breath. If she didn't slow down, she was going to miscarry. Her stomach was in knots and she didn't know how to untie it. Karma didn't regret killing Jimmy, but she hoped the baby wasn't going to suffer because of her actions. She and Indigo had been taught as children that children would always suffer the consequences of their parents' actions. It didn't matter in what shape or form; the price would always be paid. It was inevitable.

Maybe God would have mercy on her and the baby's soul. After all, He owed her, right? He'd taken her mother's life and she'd taken Jimmy's. Her mother and Jimmy, both, were His children, but God had a world full of kids. Karma only had one mother. If He were to take the seeded blessing that Money had planted inside of her, she would have to accept it and finally forfeit from her war with Him. In Karma's mind, she'd done the right thing. And since He was an all-knowing God, He knew what she was going to do way before she did it. The damage was done. It was time to move on.

Karma flushed the toilet and gradually rose to her feet. She walked over to the sink, looked at her reflection in the mirror, and blinked a couple of times in an effort to find the unfamiliar person she'd been for four months. But she wasn't there.

Her eyes… Karma's eyes no longer held the same dark gray hue as her grandmother's had once before. They weren't cold or lifeless. They weren't heavy with pain or regret. Her eyes were bright and clear. The windows to her soul were two ghetto sunsets, golden with orange and blue speckles hugging her irises. Karma had her mother's eyes. They were smiling and thanking her for what she'd done.

Karma turned on the faucet, cupped her hands under the rushing water, and washed her face until it was clean. She turned the faucet off and patted her face dry with a towel set atop the counter. Karma took one more look at herself in the mirror as she placed the towel back in its rightful place. She lifted her head and exhaled before walking out of the room.

Karma stepped out of her bedroom and into the hallway closing the door quietly behind her. She peered down the dark hall at the closed door to her childhood bedroom. She hadn't stepped foot inside the room since the day the men came and laid the new carpet down. Since then, the door had been closed and the room unused. But now, it was time to face her fear.

Karma began to walk towards her old room in a measured pace. An image of her mother's lifeless battered body flashed before her eyes. Karma shook her head to remove the horrific memory. An image of her trying to awaken her mother flashed before her eyes. Karma closed her eyes and shook her head again to dismiss the recollection. An image of her mother lying in her casket flashed before her eyes. Karma's eyes welled with tears.

She stood before the door, motionless. She looked down at the doorknob and gradually raised her hand to place it on the fixture. Her wrist slowly turned the door's handle unlinking the lock between the door and its setting place. Karma stepped into the dark room and flicked on the light-switch that was near the door. The vacant room's imbrued walls were repainted a soft pastel blue. The pink bloodstained carpet that once adorned her floor was replaced with a midnight blue one. Karma hadn't ordered a blue carpet. The carpet that was originally laid after her mother's slaying had been black. Karma smiled knowing that Money had been in and out of that room making his mark in preparation for the son he wanted so badly.

Karma sighed quietly as the smile left her glowing face. Her eyes fell upon the spot on the floor where her mother laid beaten to death. It didn't matter how many carpets she and Money could ever put down, that spot on the floor would always be her mother's deathbed. Karma took moderate steps forward. And when her feet stopped moving, she crouched down and sat beside it. She traced her hand over the carpeted pinpoint as the tears began to flow from her eyes. Karma slowly slid into a fetal position and laid her head on her bent arm. She continued to run her free hand over the place where her mother was forced to lay down and accept her fate. A desperately sought peace of mind overcame her. And as the young motherless child laid her burdens down submitting her soul for God to keep…He forgave her.

Chapter 23

oney ran out of the delivery room snatching off the mask
he'd worn throughout Karma's caesarean section procedure.
She'd gone into labor one o'clock Saturday morning and
held on for all the fourteen hours that followed into that Sunday
afternoon. Towards the fifteenth hour, Karma and the baby's heartbeat began to decline with every contraction she had. The negative
readings on the monitors and charts had shown that the contractions
were doing more damage to her and the baby than helping them.
And the oxygen mask they'd placed over her nose and mouth to
deliver air to the baby hadn't done either of them any good. So with
the doctor's directives, Karma was rushed to the operating room to
have an emergency c-section.

Money had never been so scared in his life. Not only had his
child's life been put on the line, but that of his fiancé as well. He
watched Karma suffer for fifteen long hours. She'd requested an
epidural after the sixth hour, but the anaesthesiologist never
showed. Money wanted to take Karma's pain away, but had no way
of helping her. He tried to coach her through the pain, fed her ice

chips to cool her mouth, and rubbed her back during the resting periods between her contractions, but his efforts were doing little to soothe her discomfort. He felt so helpless watching her breathe deep through fallen tears.

The breathing techniques they learned in lamas class had only helped her in the early stages of her labor. Once the contractions began to hit her like clockwork, they became unbearable and Karma experienced fainting spells as a result of them. She went in and out of consciousness seven times over before they gave her something to reduce the pain. Money wished Soleil had been there to coach Karma through it all. She needed her in the worst way and cried for her throughout the whole experience. Her humble cries to her mother took him back to that cold September night one year ago. Money could still see the image of Karma begging her mother to wake up before his very eyes. *Damn, that Jimmy*, he'd thought to himself. But, by the grace of God, she and the baby survived. Money knew he could never ask her for any more children. And he didn't want to. Not if it was going to risk her and the baby's life. It wasn't worth it.

Mekhi Sol Parks came into the world at 9lbs. 8oz. that October afternoon. He'd been born at three o'clock on the dot-the Lord's hour. Money stood in awe as he watched the doctor remove his son from his love's womb. He never got the chance to experience that when Mimi was born. Mimi's mother informed him about her birth *after* she was born. Money would forever resent her for that.

Mekhi was pulled out from his mother and placed on her chest where the nurses cleaned him off with towels, cleared his airway through his nose and mouth with a suction tube, and checked his heartbeat and breathing with a stethoscope. When all of his vitals were cleared, Money was asked to cut the remaining piece of the umbilical cord. A river of tears flowed from his eyes as he cut the cord that connected his son to the love of his life for nine months. Money couldn't believe he actually got the son he wanted so badly. Up until that time, he and Karma didn't know the sex of the baby. And she'd adamantly insisted they find out on the day she gave birth. It was the best surprise either one of them could have ever imagined.

Mekhi was absolutely gorgeous, a blend of Money and Karma. He had his mother's initial blue eye coloring while sharing his father's slanted shaped eyes. Thick, silky black hair covered his perfectly round head. Karma's deep dimples and cleft chin had been marked on his little face. Money's milk chocolate complexion was going to be shared by him due to the darkness on the tips of his ears. As would his mouth, nose, and genitalia.

"Big boy," Money managed to say proudly to the nurse who had been cleaning the baby off.

She laughed and shook her head in response to the obvious thing he'd been referring to. And she knew it hadn't been the baby's weight.

"That he is."

After getting the 'OK' from the surgical team to leave the operating room to go tell the family the good news, Money scurried back over to Karma, kissed her sweetly on the lips and thanked her over and over again for his son. She'd almost lost her life bringing his son into the world and he would always be indebted to her for that. Exhausted and overwrought with pain, Karma simply smiled and held Money's face with her trembling hand. She whispered, "I love you" and sent Money on his way to spread the good news.

All the while, Lorenzo, Indigo, Maggie, and Evelyn waited anxiously in the waiting room to hear the outcome of Karma's emergency operation. Lorenzo sat rubbing the back of his hung head. He didn't know what he was going to do if Karma didn't make it out of her surgery. The thought of losing his only child had never crossed his mind until that moment. He knew how much she loved her mother and if the opportunity presented itself for her to slip away during or after the procedure, Karma wouldn't hesitate to go.

They all had either been sitting or standing around that room for more than an hour and no one came to keep them updated on Karma and the baby's status. Maggie rubbed Lorenzo's back as she hummed an old gospel hymn. Evelyn sipped on a cup of hot chocolate while Indigo stood at a nearby window overlooking the city of Livingston. Indigo reflected upon the deathly look in her cousin's eyes before she slipped into each one of her cataleptic spells. Karma had literally been dying in her hospital bed. And Death was trying to make her transition to the other side as slow and painful as possible.

Indigo was convinced that whoever said women weren't on their death beds when bearing another human life had to have been a man. She didn't want her child bearing experience to be anything like Karma's. She was due next month, herself, and she wasn't sure if she would be able to hang on for one hour let alone fifteen hours like Karma had. *Karma, you need to pull through this*, Indigo thought to herself. *Please, pull through this. We need you.*

Money charged into the room out of breath and teary eyed. Lorenzo and Maggie jumped out of their seats as they watched him try to regulate his breathing. Indigo and Evelyn remained where they were, speechless and fearful of the unknown. Evelyn could usually read her son, but not in that space and time. His face was full of strain and fixed in a cringe. He was one big ball of emotion.

"What happened, Money?" Lorenzo asked with panic in his voice. "What happened?"

Money held his index finger up as a signal to the family to give him another moment to regroup. He was so overwhelmed with happiness, the words wouldn't fall from his lips.

"Come on, Money!" Indigo screamed impatiently.

"Indigo!" Maggie countered back at her uneasy daughter. "Respect."

Indigo shook her head in dismay as she kept her eyes on Money. He finally recuperated and allowed his bright wide smile to appear.

"It's a boy," he beamed. "She had a boy. Mekhi Sol Parks."

The family's grim expressions transformed into smiles of joyous relief. Maggie fell back into her chair and sent prayers of thanks to the Saints, while Lorenzo and Evelyn took Money into their arms and held him close. Indigo clapped her hands overjoyed by the birth of her new little cousin-nephew. She waddled over to her mother and hugged her tightly. Money remained in his mother's arms overcome with tears. Lorenzo patted his future son-in-law's back as he continued to cry into his mother's neck.

"It's alright, son," Evelyn cooed. "It's alright. You did good."

Money cried even harder in response to his mother's praise.

"Come on, baby," Evelyn continued. "Look at me, Money. How's Karma?" she asked, lifting his head from her shoulder and holding it before her.

"Fine, Mama," Money said between sniffles. "She's fine. They're stitching her up now."

The family exhaled again in knowing that Karma was doing just as well as the baby.

"I didn't mean to put her through so much pain, Mama. I didn't," Money sobbed.

Before the family knew it, they were all crying with Money. He was so sincere in his conviction. If he had known Karma's life was going to be put in such jeopardy by bringing Mekhi into the world, he would have thought twice about not using protection with her every single time.

"It's okay, baby. It's okay," Evelyn said, rubbing Money's tears away with her thumbs. "Calm down. Everything is alright now."

"He's so beautiful, Mama," Money smiled through his pain.

"I know he is," Evelyn replied sweetly.

"I wanna go see how Karma's doin'. When will we be able to go to the back and see her?" Lorenzo asked Money.

As soon as Money opened his mouth to reply, Karma's OB/GYN entered the waiting area with a smile across his face and his arms outstretched to the family.

"How's my little girl doin', Doc?" Lorenzo asked in concern.

"Mr. Walker, your daughter is doing just fine. Just fine, indeed. She's resting in one of our special recovery suites on the labor and delivery floor of the hospital," the doctor confirmed.

"Special? Why is it special? I don't understand. Is it some kind of-" Lorenzo asked frantically.

"Mr. Walker, please," the doctor asked with his hands up in surrender. "You misunderstood me. My intention was not to alarm you. I only called the room special because we only offer those particular suites to those mothers who've gone through the most rigorous of labor and deliveries."

"Oh, oh, alright," Lorenzo said in relief. "Can we see her now? I mean—"

"Of course you can see her now. Follow me," he insisted.

Lorenzo, Maggie, Indigo, and Evelyn gathered their belongings and filed out of the room behind the doctor. Money remained standing in the middle of the room looking towards the sky and thanking God for His merciful blessings. He washed his hands over his face before focusing on meeting the family in Karma's room. As he gave the room a once over before exiting, he noticed his mother's wallet lying open on the chair she'd occupied during her wait. Money walked over to the seat and scooped the leather case into his hands. He proceeded to close it until a photograph that was set in the first picture slot of her wallet caught his eye. Money studied the photograph of his young bride mother standing in the arms of a familiar looking man in a tuxedo. As Money brought the photograph closer to his face, his eyebrows furrowed in recognition to whom the familiar face belonged to. He snatched the photograph out of its slot and turned it over. On the back of the photograph it read: EVELYN B.K.A. SPARROW AND JIMMY B.K.A. OWL HAYES-MAN AND WIFE/JUNE '77.

Money turned the picture back over to look at the couple again just as his mother walked back into the room. Evelyn stopped in her tracks the moment she saw the photograph in Money's hand. She'd come back to the waiting room to look for the exact thing Money had in his possession-her wallet and all of its contents. Her smile disappeared as fear settled into her heavy heart. Money lifted his wild eyes from the picture and set them on his mother. Evelyn remained. She didn't know what to say or do, but she did know that look. Money had his father's eyes and they were burning into her like the cigar butts he used to put out on her thirty something years ago.

"What are you doing with that picture?" she asked in her hoarse voice.

"I should be asking you the same question," Money replied tersely.

Evelyn took in her son's curt response and swallowed it right along with her pride. He had every right to be upset, but her reasons for keeping the truth from him were for his own protection. She looked away.

"Jimmy?" Money asked his mother through tight lips. "Jimmy, Mama?!" he snarled. Money didn't know how to control his anger. He was the son of his fiancé's mother's killer. He was the son of the most notorious drug lord in the state of New Jersey's history. He'd passed his tainted blood onto his newborn son. Money found himself standing in limbo.

"*Jimmy "Owl" Hayes* is my muthafuckin' father?!" he screamed with flared nostrils and flying spit.

Evelyn looked back to her son, pursed her lips, and nodded slowly.

"Yes…Yes, he is."

TO BE CONTINUED…

Karma Translations Pg.136

Miguel: ¿Cómo somos nosotros hoy? ¿Hemos otorgado nosotros su cada deseo?

How are we today? Have we granted your every wish?

Antonio: Usted ha otorgado la mina.

Yes, you've granted mine.

Manuel: Acabamos del Karma de decir que el alimento es deli cioso, pero probaría mejor si ella lo servía.

We were just telling Karma that the food is delicious, but it would taste much better if she were serving it.

Miguel: Ah, sí. Sí. Eso es chistoso. Muy chistoso. Pero yo me pregunto cómo Lupe y Vera se sentirían acerca de que desea ungranted suyo. ¿No sería una vista bonita si dijimos, ahora lo hace? Ahora si usted dos caballeros nos dispensarian.

Oh, yeah. Yeah. That's funny. Very funny. But I wonder how Lupe and Vera would feel   about that ungranted wish of yours. Wouldn't be a pretty sight if we told, now would it? Now, if you two gentlemen would excuse us.

Reader's Guide Questions

1. Who do you think is responsible for Soleil's death?

2. Why do you think the family turned a blind eye to Soleil and Jimmy's abusive relationship?

3. How do you feel about Soleil and Lorenzo pursuing other relationships while still being legally married?

4. Should Money have told Karma upfront that about having a daughter? About his previous relationship with Lachelle?

5. How do you feel about Lorenzo's history of going in and out of the service? What were his reasons?

6. Why has Hawk decided to sustain a relationship with Owl, after all that Owl has done?

7. How do you feel about Indigo's profession as a police officer versus her relationship with a drug dealer?

8. Do you think Karma's actions were justified in the end?

9. What do you think Money is going to do with the new-found information he has about his father?

10. In what direction do you think Karma and Money's relationship is going to go after the discovery of his father's identity?

COMING SOON

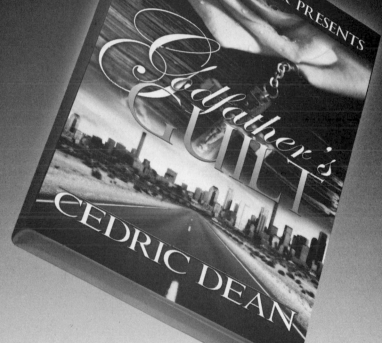

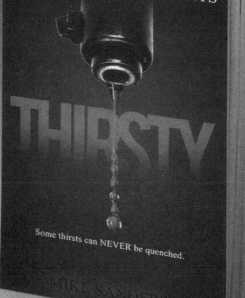